CLUES

17. Deck ____ halls
24. Type of puzzle
22. Morse, e.g.

THE
CROSSWORD
CODE

Herbert Resnicow

Puzzles by Henry Hook

BALLANTINE BOOKS ● NEW YORK

Library of Congress Catalog Card Number: 86-90850

ISBN 0-345-32733-0

Manufactured in the United States of America

First Edition: July 1986

To my beautiful daughter
Eva Resnikova
author, editor and critic,
and ballet maven

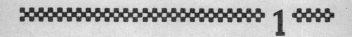 **1**

FROM THE CORNER, LESS THAN ONE HUNDRED FEET away, Tom Burke watched Valentin Zulkov walk down the front steps of his rooming house and head for the bus stop. Today would make it or break it as far as Tom was concerned. There was no way to use binoculars in this part of Washington, and there was no time left to play it safe. If the young Russian noticed him, Tom would just fade into the background; he wouldn't get on the bus and he wouldn't go into the doughnut shop. But there was little chance that Zulkov would notice him or recognize this middle-aged, spare-tired, balding, sloppily dressed passed-over failure as an FBI agent.

Actually, Tom thought, I'm not an FBI agent, not today. I can't even *function* as an agent until tomorrow, when my vacation is over. If I don't get *something* today, something strong, I'll have to drop the whole investigation. I'll also get the horse laugh from my squad supervisor, Clarence Ellerby, the stupid, shortsighted, rule-book-waving, time-serving, supercautious bureaucrat who refused to make Valentin Zulkov a Bureau affair, when anybody who had ever spent one day in the field could see that Zulkov was just too damn impossibly perfectly innocent to be anything but a spy. So I, Tom thought bitterly, have to use my vacation time to follow up my hunch unofficially, privately, without Bureau support or even approval. I may be the oldest agent in this grade, and I sure don't look like the neat, handsome, charcoal-gray this-year's-model FBI agent, but my hunches have paid off in the past and no one can take that away from me. Valentin Zulkov rang bells loud and clear in my head the moment I saw his file, and if Ellerby's brains hadn't settled into his butt . . .

Tom stiffened as Zulkov approached the newsstand. As in the past three weeks, seven days a week, he had the exact change in his left hand and reached for the top copy of *The Capitol Gazette* with his right. At the last second, a dowdy middle-aged woman reached out and grabbed the paper, practically tearing it out of Zulkov's fingers, dropped her coins on the counter, and moved off to the bus stop.

Good old Midge, Tom thought, did it like a real pro, even though she was only a clerk-typist in the Bureau. Thank God for the old-timers; they knew the score. Of course I had to cash in every credit chit I had to get the cooperation I had to have for today; sixteen extra people, this operation needed; no way I could do it myself. Six in the bus, plus Midge; five more in the doughnut shop, and four in front of the Aeroflot office. Thank God Zulkov was an early riser; all my old friends could still punch in on time as though nothing had happened, and if it failed, if I was wrong about Zulkov, Ellerby would never know the details. Of course he'd know that I hadn't turned up anything, at least in these three weeks, but I can live with that, no way I'm going to get a promotion this side of heaven.

Without the slightest sign of annoyance, the slim blond young Russian took the next *Gazette* from the pile, put down his coins, folded the paper under his arm, and took his place patiently on the line at the bus stop.

Well, that proves no information is being passed from the newsstand to Zulkov, Tom thought. I didn't really think it was, but in this business you have to cover all the bases. Tom took his place in the bus line behind Zulkov.

Most of the seats in the bus were filled by the time

Zulkov got on, including the one he usually sat in; that one was occupied by Klein. As Zulkov prepared to sit in the seat behind, Big Al shouldered the slim Russian out of the way, sat down, and folded his arms stubbornly across his chest. Zulkov calmly took a seat farther back, and Tom slipped into the seat directly behind him. Well, that proved that there were no messages on the seat or near it. Just checking. Tom had always figured it was the doughnut shop.

Zulkov, in fact, during the whole three weeks he had been in the States, hadn't shown the slightest sign of receiving or passing information in any way. He never sat in parks, always eating his brown-bag lunch inside the Aeroflot office, where he worked as a bookkeeper. He never went to the movies, or museums, or concerts, or anything. Once he went home to the rooming house, there he stayed. He didn't have a phone and never used the phone in the hall, which Tom had tapped, illegally, of course. Zulkov didn't go to any Russian functions, didn't go near the Russian Embassy, or any of the Russian compounds or apartment houses, didn't even speak to anyone other than at work. None of the people at Zulkov's rooming house did anything the slightest bit sensitive, or had friends who did. And from what Tom had been able to gather, Zulkov didn't even say hello to anyone in the house.

Zulkov didn't even speak in the corner supermarket where he bought his fruit drinks and sandwich fixings. He was so damned unnaturally pure that he had to be *deliberately* avoiding the slightest suspicion that he was a spy. In Burke's book, that made him a spy; one of the worst kind, the most dangerous, aiming for something *really* big. Nobody who was really clean could be *that* clean unless he was hiding something. And when a newly arrived Russian is hiding something, he's a spy, pure and simple. But, Tom wondered, how was he doing it? If I don't find out by today, those bastards will get away with it, whatever *it* was, and I'll have shot my vacation for nothing.

Without hesitation Zulkov folded the paper to the

3

crossword page, took out his pen—a pen, Tom thought, this guy is better in English than most Americans; they train them well at the Moscow Institute of International Relations—and began solving the crossword puzzle. Tom watched over Zulkov's shoulder for a while; there was nothing unusual. Zulkov started at the upper-left-hand corner and began filling in the Across words, occasionally skipping a word, then filling it in with the help of the Down words. Tom took out his diary—in case this turned into something hot he'd make a formal report and try to get that bastard Ellerby to treat these last three weeks as an undercover assignment; God knows Tom had put in enough time for six weeks of work—turned methodically to Tuesday, June 29, and began making notes.

As the bus slowed for Zulkov's usual stop, Tom moved forward so he could be the first into the doughnut shop; less suspicious that way. Once in, a quick glance showed Tom that his five people were already on their stools, filling all the seats. Oakley, at the first seat nearest the door, got up when Tom reached him. Tom took the seat and ordered a regular coffee with a blueberry-filled and a strawberry-filled. The clerk took Tom's doughnuts from the tray in order of position. Zulkov walked past his regular seat without hesitation and took the seat just vacated by Nettie, at the far end of the counter. Zulkov looked at the list displayed behind the counter and, as Tom expected, ordered a regular coffee and a blueberry-filled and a strawberry-filled. Immediately there were four more orders for blueberry-filled and strawberry-filled. The clerks took the doughnuts in rotation from the trays and served them to the nearest customers first. As soon as the clerk picked up the doughnuts intended for Zulkov, Nettie, now at the cashier's position, said, "I'll take those to go." The clerk immediately put the two doughnuts into a bag, put the bag at the cashier's counter, and picked the next two doughnuts, again in rotation, and served them to Zulkov. The young Russian didn't look the least bit put out.

Tom Burke cursed inwardly. He had been sure there was *something* in the doughnut arrangement. Zulkov had gone to the doughnut shop on his first day in Washington and, in apparent wonder at the selection available, had started at the top of the displayed list and was working his way down, sampling one of each of the sixty different varieties at the rate of two a day. Since the list never changed, it would have been easy for anyone who wanted to pass a message to Zulkov to know what he would order that day. But the doughnut shop was clean.

Burke's last shot was outside the Aeroflot office across the avenue, where he had four people, a cannon, a stall, and two shields instead of one, just to make sure; the best pickpocket team in the Washington office. He really owed those guys; if they were caught in an unofficial deal, they'd hang, and Burke with them, so they had better not get caught. Florrie, the stall, had legs that would bring a dead man back to life, a *blind* dead man, so that when she did her tripping act and her skirt flew up, and Zulkov tripped over her—hell, Joey, the cannon, could have taken the gold out of Zulkov's teeth and Zulkov wouldn't have noticed, especially since Zulkov hadn't even *looked* at a woman in three weeks and his folder showed he was straight. The only trouble was, when they finished with the apologies and the brushing off and everything, and Zulkov went inside to work, he'd know he'd been dusted, stripped of his wallet, the newspaper, and any loose papers he had in his pockets. Well, Tom thought, sometimes you got to do what you got to do, and if that didn't do it, there was nothing left.

Zulkov was working on his crossword puzzle as he slowly enjoyed his doughnuts and coffee. He even ate the blueberry-filled first, in the order of the list behind the counter. Suddenly Zulkov stopped, stared at the puzzle, put his pen away, and swallowed quickly. He folded the paper under his arm, put two dollars on the counter— this is *it*, Tom thought: Russians, even spies, are not over-paid, and Zulkov *always* put down the exact price on the check plus ten percent tip—started to leave, then reached back, stuffed the remaining half of the strawberry-filled onto his mouth, and walked out of the doughnut shop fast. He didn't run, but he was moving faster than Tom had ever seen him move before. Tom nodded to his three guys to fall behind, gave Zulkov a twenty-foot lead, and followed.

Oakley, who had been waiting outside the shop, casually got in Zulkov's way. Zulkov darted around him and stopped at the curb, waiting impatiently for the light to change, shifting his weight from foot to foot, like a racer. The moment the light changed, Zulkov darted into the street.

With a scream of tires, a white Cadillac driven by a black teenager jumped the light and made a fast right turn, a racing turn, around the corner, hit Zulkov squarely on his left side, hard, and roared off. Zulkov flew ten feet into the air and landed limply on his head. "Get the paper," Tom yelled to Oakley on his left. "Meet me around the corner. Shield me," he whispered to the others. Tom put the fingers of his right hand on Zulkov's throat and went swiftly through his pockets with his left hand. A civilian ran up. "Call an ambulance," Burke yelled to him, "this man's been hurt. In there." The civilian ran off.

There was no pulse, but Tom knew that; he'd seen too many before. Other than the wallet, Zulkov had nothing on him but some money, a comb, and a handkerchief. Tom took those too; you never knew. Confirmation; an innocent man never walked around with nothing.

"I'm going to Zulkov's place to toss his room, then I'm going home. Without an ID it'll take the cops hours to find out who he is. One of you stick around, call in sick or something, and keep an eye on the Aeroflot office. The rest, scatter." He glanced across the avenue; the pickpocket team had already disappeared; he didn't blame them.

Tom Burke slowly got up and, with his head down, walked rapidly around the corner.

 **2**

"I'M AFRAID, SIR," OLIVER SAID, SHIELDING HIS EYES from the late-morning sun with his black derby, "Miss Isabel will be very put out."

"I have no choice, Oliver," Giles Sullivan said. "Barca doesn't often signal Mayday."

"Knowning Miss Isabel as we do, sir, she will consider that flying to New York instead of driving her surplus jeep here is sufficient of a concession."

"Flying"—Giles looked at his watch for the third time— "is also a good deal faster."

"Miss Isabel would dispute that, sir, with some justice. But I'm pleased that you abandoned your futile arguments based on concern for her safety, since she is under the impression that she is a careful driver. I am highly gratified that you found acceptable my suggestion that you point out to her that flying from and to Vermont would give her an extra two days of your estimable company."

"Yes, and thanks to my listening to you, Oliver, she will be doubly angry with me when she finds that no sooner does she get off her plane than we rush her to the Washington shuttle."

"Who takes the king's shilling, sir, must, perforce, take the king's orders."

"We do not get paid, Oliver, neither in shillings nor in dollars."

7

"I was speaking figuratively, sir. But there is other reward, sir; the exercise of one's skills, the satisfaction of a deed well done, the vanquishing of evil. . . ."

"You are changing the subject, Oliver. The question remains, what do I tell Isabel?"

"As a last resort, sir, shall we try the truth? That when Barca calls, she has no choice? And that she may very well enjoy the Fourth of July celebration this Sunday, if we stay in Washington that long, particularly the President's speech?"

"As you once pointed out, the Scots are very stubborn. And Isabel does not care for this President very much."

"I have great confidence, sir, in your barrister's persuasive skills."

"I have never been able to persuade Isabel of anything she did not want to do. What if more drastic means are required?"

"I am fully prepared, sir. A box of the finest Belgian chocolates."

"That should do the trick, Oliver, if anything can. I hope she will accept Barca's ways. All she knows of him is what I've told her, and I've been putting off giving her a, uh, complete understanding of what to expect."

"If her performance is acceptable, as I am sure it will be, he will speak gently to her."

"And the family?"

"As always, sir, unpredictable and uncontrollable."

"You couldn't, Oliver—?"

"I have even less influence with them than Barca has, sir." Oliver glanced at the Arrivals display. "If Miss Macintosh's plane is late, sir, we can save a half hour by taking a scheduled plane instead of waiting for the next shuttle."

Sullivan stared at his butler coldly. "You know, Oliver, that my cane cannot pass a metal detector."

"I could purchase some gift-wrapping paper, sir, and leave it in the cloakroom until we return from Washington."

Sullivan grasped the gold-headed cane with both hands.

"Where I go, Oliver, my cane goes too. I would feel naked without it."

"If you can maintain that resolute pose for five more minutes, sir," Oliver said, "Miss Macintosh will not dare oppose you. Her plane has just arrived."

3

"GEORGETOWN, SULLIVAN, OF ALL LOUSY PLACES."
Isabel had insisted on driving the rented car from the
airport so she could use the steering wheel as a substitute
for Giles's neck. "That's where they make egg creams
with Perrier, isn't it?"

"Come now, Isabel"—Giles had his feet braced on the
firewall—"that's unfair. Please slow down; the police—"

"Unfair, Sullivan?" She pushed the speed up another
five miles per hour and whipped the car around a curve.
"They don't even know what an egg cream *is* around here.
The last time I had to go to Washington I stayed at a
friend's house. On the way I asked the cabbie to stop at
a florist's so I could bring my friend— Do you know that
at five-thirty there isn't a florist open in all of Washington?
Or a candy store? Or anything?"

"If you're hinting— Would you like another chocolate,
dear? Oliver, please pass Miss Macintosh another chocolate."

"I'm afraid, sir," Oliver said, "the box is empty."

"Empty? The whole box?"

"*One* box, Sullivan? You call that a proper apology?
You committed a monumental crime, Sullivan, a three-
box crime, at the least, and you compound the insult by
running out of chocolates? Belgian chocolates, at that?
Not even Dutch?"

10

"But a whole pound, Isabel?"

"Foreign chocolates, in case you hadn't observed, Sullivan, do not come in pounds. Four hundred grams, Sullivan, is nine tenths of a pound. Not even. If you really loved me, if you were really interested in my welfare, you would have learned that four hundred grams is less than fourteen point eleven ounces, while nine tenths of a pound is fourteen point four ounces, a significant difference to someone who really understands chocolate. Another way you cheated me, Sullivan."

"But a whole box, Isabel? In one hour?"

"One hour and twenty-three minutes since you tried to take my mind off searching for the proper retribution. How many pieces do you think there are in one tiny little box, Sullivan? You don't know, do you? Sloppy, Sullivan, very sloppy; I'd hate to have you defend me against a charge of attempted justifiable homicide. Twenty-four pieces, Sullivan, that's how many. Twenty-four tiny little pieces. At three-minute intervals, which shows my extraordinary forbearance, that makes one hour and nine minutes. Fourteen minutes, fourteen whole minutes, that's how long I've been without chocolate."

"Three times twenty-four is seventy-two minutes, Isabel. One hour and *twelve* minutes."

"Wrong again, Sullivan. The first tiny piece, which Oliver forced down my throat before I could say a word, was at *zero* minutes, which leave twenty-three pieces times three, sixty-nine minutes, or one hour and *nine* minutes. I hope you never have to solve a timetable murder case, Sullivan; your client would fry for sure. Cary Grant would have brought a *case* of chocolate—he *understands* women—and presented it with a graceful compliment. *Two* cases."

"You should have come Friday night, Isabel, then we could have had a whole weekend—"

"So now it's all my fault, is it, Sullivan? You knew that since I became acting president of Windham U. I'd have to spend my weekends at fund-raising functions and entertain the trustees on the traditional Monday nights and attend the Tuesday administrator's dinner. So when I finally tear myself away, what do you do, Sullivan? Abduct me, that's what. To Washington, of all places."

"Turn right at the next— Slowly, Isabel, for God's sake. I'll get you a *case* of chocolates when we get there. Alive."

"Too late," she said between gritted teeth. "And on top of everything"—she zoomed between the big brick columns framing the entry to the estate—"Washington is *hot* in the summer. You're gong to pay for this, Sullivan. You're going to buy me two new outfits, top to bottom. Maybe three. Or four. How long are we going to be stuck here anyway?"

"It depends on the problem," Giles said. "Barca never gets routine work; only communications no other, uh, organization can handle. If I get the right inspiration, we could be back on our way to New York today."

"This is a long driveway," Isabel said. "I still don't see the house. Why are there no guards or TV cameras?"

"Our protection, Miss Isabel," Oliver said, "is in our openness. No one, not even the others in the intelligence community, knows who we are or what we do or even that we exist. The President himself doesn't know." Oliver pointed right. "The house is just beyond those trees."

"Then how does he—the President?"

"Attached to his permanent staff," Giles said, "there is always one person—we don't know who—that passes on the problem to another person by means of a dead drop, checked regularly by a courier. None of them know either of the others. That third person passes on the problem to Barca directly. That same person also handles the special financing and other little details, and has a good reason to come to the Semiotics Institute regularly."

"The old dead-drop cut-out method, eh? So nothing can be traced to Barca? What about sickness, accident, death?"

"There is an automatic succession set up, Isabel, for emergencies. The corporate contributions are made openly, directly, to the Institute, through the corporate public relations managers, none of whom have the slightest idea they are doing anything but supporting scientific studies, and for the most part, they are. Everyone you will meet today in the Institute wing will be an employee of the Institute. Barca is its director. I see from your lingo you've been reading spy novels."

"Not enough whodunits are written today, so, on those cold and lonely nights at Windham, for which you are directly responsible, Sullivan, I take second best. Third best. Was the name Semiotics Institute chosen because the initials are the same as Signals Intelligence?"

"It really is a center of the study of meaning, symbols, and communication, and Barca has published several basic books, truly seminal works, in the field. Under his real name, of course. Ask Norbert Kantor about him next time you're at the Cruciverbal Club."

Isabel pulled the car up in front of the huge Georgian mansion with the discreet bronze plaque at the entrance. "Not here," Giles said. "This is the Institute entrance. Pull around to the family wing, the side entrance. That's where they live."

Isabel swung the car around the big brick building. "So we're at the orders of the President on this problem? You know what I think of him."

"The Group is at the *service* of the presidency," Oliver said, getting the bags from the trunk. "We take no orders from anyone."

"Where are we going to sleep, Giles?" Isabel whispered as they walked up the steps to the columned side porch. "Will we have privacy?"

"I'm sure the family, the girls, have done everything properly. They're very competent, you know, just a little, uh—"

The heavy door swung open.

13

THE FIVE EXTRAORDINARILY BEAUTIFUL WOMEN dragged Giles and Oliver into the vestibule. The shortest one threw her arms around Giles and began kissing him passionately. The second in line, checking her watch carefully, tapped the first one on the shoulder after ten seconds. The first one tore herself away reluctantly and glued herself to Oliver, to repeat the performance, as Number Two clutched Giles to her bosom.

Giles looked at Isabel helplessly, but by Number Five he had his arms around the woman's waist cooperatively. After the kissing stopped, they all lined up opposite Isabel. "We see *so* few men around here," the shortest one explained. "You do understand, don't you?"

Isabel had never seen even one woman like this before, much less five. They were all in their late thirties to midforties, all with long, wavy auburn—deep-copper auburn—hair, big-busted and wide-hipped, with voluptuaries' bodies. And their eyes—Isabel had seen eyes like that only in the zoo; wolf's eyes, bright orange-yellow, with a dark ring around the iris.

The five wore heavy, high-bodiced dark-green velvet gowns, straight from an eighteenth-century English ballroom, very low-cut in front and falling to the tops of their dancing pumps. In opposition to the delicacy implied by

14

their dress, the five, who were enough alike to be quin-
tuplets and were certainly sisters, had strong features,
high brows, firm noses, big jaws, and sensuous purple-
red lips, between which flashed strong white teeth with
exceptionally long canines. *I have fallen into a nest of
vampires*, Isabel thought.

"Let me introduce myself," said the shortest vampire
with a deep curtsy, turned enough toward Giles so he
could look all the way down her décolletage. "I'm Jane,
the most beautiful."

"I'm Elizabeth," said Vampire Number Two, shame-
lessly facing Giles directly as she curtsied even more
deeply, "and *I'm* the most beautiful."

"Wait a minute," Isabel said. "What's—?" She turned
to the youngest vampire. "Don't tell me you're Lydia."

"Not if you don't want me to," Number Five said
politely. "Then I'm really Sir Despard Murgatroyd."
Instead of curtsying she made a deep manly bow, which
was, for her obvious purpose, even more effective than
a curtsy. "In disguise, of course." She put her hands on
her hips, took a deep breath, and turned slightly to show
her bust in profile. "Effective, don't you think? And though
I am the youngest, I'm the tallest."

"She lies in her teeth," said the Fourth Vampire. "*I'm*
Sir Despard Murgatroyd. She's really Mad Margaret;
delusions, you know. And if you look closely, you'll see
that *I'm* the most beautiful. You can call me Catherine.
Or Kitty," she purred, "if you like cats."

"I'm Mary," said the Vampire with glasses. "Though
I read a lot, I don't really *need* glasses; I just wear them
in company so as not to hurt *their* feelings, because
obviously, *I'm* the most beautiful and they have nothing
but looks going for them. I also have the trimmest ankles."
She lifted her long skirt a bit and extended her foot dain-
tily.

"Out of *Pride and Prejudice*?" Isabel asked. "Jane
Austen?"

"Of course I'm proud," Elizabeth said. "I have reason

15

to be, as you can plainly see. But I'm not prejudiced; I love *all* men."

"Jane *Austen*?" Jane looked puzzled. "Is she anyone? I mean, should I feel honored?"

Oliver coughed discreetly, twice. "Of course," Vampire Number Two, Elizabeth, said, "you can't stand around here all day admiring me, much as you would like to. Let me take you to Father." She led them toward the library.

Isabel was now beginning to notice differences between the five vampires other than height and age. Lydia moved confidently, like an athlete. Jane swung her hips exaggeratedly when she walked, and her sisters waited for her to go into the library, as though Jane always had to lead. When Mary turned her head, the light reflected from her glasses evenly, showing that the lenses were, indeed, flat glass. Kitty looked the most playful, with a sweet smile, but her eyes were always moving, checking. Isabel was reminded of the saying that kittens don't play, they practice. And Elizabeth the Outspoken had the sharp tongue, but Isabel felt that she was almost the most removed, observing carefully, critically, from behind her screen of words.

Barca's study was an old-fashioned wood-paneled library in which the books, all the books, looked read. In the far right corner, looking completely out of place, was a mini-computer installation, complete with telecom equipment, far larger and more complex than anything Isabel had ever seen outside the university's central office.

Barca was sitting in a big wing chair, reading a leather-bound book, half glasses on the end of his bulb-tipped nose. His thick, pouting lips were almost hidden between his heavy moustache and a Vandyke beard. His round belly strained the crimson smoking jacket, which was matched by a black-tasseled red Turkish fez tilted on his bald head. He noticed Isabel staring and said, "The blood runs cold when one gets old, and these inconsiderate daughters of mine"—his wave took in all five women—"persist in maintaining sub-Arctic temperatures in this house in complete disregard of the cost of electricity these says." He put his big cigar down carefully, not disturbing the long ash, placed a leather marker in the book to hold his place, and rose heavily to greet Isabel. "I have been looking forward to meeting you, Miss Macintosh," he said in a rich, bass actor's voice. "Permit me to introduce myself. I am Bennet Ackroyd, and I have heard many good things about you from Oliver, whose judgment I trust implicitly." Oliver, two paces back, acknowledged the compliment with a slight inclination of his head.

"And I have been looking forward to meeting you, Mr. Ackroyd," Isabel said, "but with some trepidation. Our welcome was a bit of a surprise."

"My daughters," Barca said, "love to play games. If only I could get them married off." He sighed. "But where would I find . . . ? Whoever would be so obtuse as to even consider, purely as a mental exercise, assuming the burden of the best of them could hardly take responsibility for a guppy, much less support a wife in the manner their doting mother, blinded by love, mistakenly persuaded them was their right. I have something of import to discuss with our guests," Barca said. "All of you have failed to perform the simple task I gave you so many hours ago, a task which, I remind you, was handled easily mentally by a bare-faced youth whose mother tongue contained no Latin, Greek, or Germanic roots." As the women turned to go, Barca pulled a big gold watch out of his vest pocket and said, "We shall dine at precisely eight tonight. And if you do not dispose of those ridiculous fangs at once, I will insist that you eat dinner with them."

Jane led the way to the door. Kitty stopped by the computer, punched in something, studied the screen, then hurried over to Mary with a question. Mary looked off for a second, then began lecturing as they passed out of the room. Lydia slipped smoothly through the door and closed it silently behind them.

"Are they really your daughters, Mr. Ackroyd?" Isabel asked, sitting in the easy chair opposite Barca. "Their names really Jane, Elizabeth, Mary, Kitty, and Lydia?"

"Ah, you have discerned my shame," Barca sighed as he resumed his seat. "Yes, their poor, dear mother"—he gestured toward the fireplace on his right, over which hung a huge portrait of a beautiful young woman with long red hair and the now-familiar wolf's eyes—"loved Jane Austen. Mrs. Ackroyd was an Austen herself; not the direct line, naturally, but a collateral line. When our first child was born, Beverly insisted on naming her Jane. I was but a poor scholar then, and venal as well; it was the Austen wealth that permitted all this"—he waved at the surroundings—"so her wish was my command. And when the second proved to be a girl, she was, naturally, called Elizabeth. And so it went."

"And since your name is Bennet—?" Isabel prodded.

"Beverly thought it amusing to address me as Mr. Bennet. Mrs. Ackroyd and Mr. Bennett. People thought we were living in sin. And now that she is gone, I am alone, at the mercy of the Furies."

Isabel hesitated; it was really none of her affair, and besides, this was so at variance with the respect, the awe, in which Giles and Oliver held Barca that she could not believe . . . Yet the man before her was so clearly, after what must have been many years, so clearly mourning his beloved wife that she could not help herself. "I was once dean of students at Windham University, and situations like this . . . Would it not be better that you sent your daughters away, to live by themselves, in their own homes? If you truly wish them to marry, this is the worst place for them to be, where they reinforce each other's self-sufficiency, their almost tribal exclusiveness."

"I'm afraid that's impossible, Miss Macintosh," he said apologetically. "I am a relict, out of time and out of place here. I live by their sufferance." He shook his head sadly. "Their poor dear mother, not completely blind to her daughters' faults, understood that in order for any of them to marry, one would have to ensnare a fortune-hunter *manqué*, a desperate elderly one at that, preferably deaf, for whom this shrew would represent his last chance to avoid working. Accordingly, and with my misguided cooperation, Mrs. Ackroyd left her entire estate to the girls, equally. I dare not utter a word of complaint."

"They don't socialize at all?" Isabel asked.

"Given the size of their fortunes, there is no shortage of men who dance attendance on them, some of whom I find less objectionable than the average thug one is apt to meet these days in the Senate Office Building, though make no mistake, I would not withhold my consent if even a congressman offered to take one of them off my hands, provided he signed a hold—harmless agreement. Men propose marriage regularly, though by that very act these eager victims show how unfit they are to be at large without a keeper—yet these vixens show no interest in settling down and producing grandchildren for me, out of a—no doubt noble—concern for the welfare of posterity."

"None of them has ever shown any strong interest in any man?"

"Oh, yes. Each of them, several times. But for a short period of time only. When a possible suitor is brought here, as he must eventually be, I am on my best behavior, trying to conceal the perils which lie in wait for the poor soul. But the other girls probe and press and, sooner or later, usually sooner, they find his weakness. Then they tear him apart. Like vultures. Elizabeth is, of course, the worst. The poor gull does not realize she has struck until the poison is already flowing in his veins, until long after he has left. What I fear is needed is a Mr. Darcy. But there are none such in this part of . . . Perhaps at Windham University, Miss Macintosh?"

Isabel shook her head. "Not even in New York. Or Hollywood." She glanced at Giles. "Not even in films. Only in books do such men exist. The old books."

"Yes, I was afraid of that. But I forget myself. You have had a long trip; would you like to visit your suite first? It's right next to the girls' apartments; Oliver can show you the way."

"Yes, thank you," Isabel said. "I'd like to change my

clothes; I wasn't prepared for Washington's heat."

"I'll meet you in the study in half an hour," Barca said, suddenly businesslike. "We have a rather puzzling little mystery to solve."

 **5**

"WHAT IS GOING ON HERE?" ISABEL WHISPERED, SLIP-
ping out of her dress. "Nothing fits; nothing's consistent."
She was trying to put together her lightest, coolest, most
beautiful outfit, but she knew, she absolutely knew, that
she would be the country mouse at dinner tonight.

"No need to whisper," Giles said, pulling on his slacks.
"This house is old-fashioned, solidly built, and Barca would
never tape his guests."

"But Oliver is right next door, and Jane's apartment is
on the bedroom side. Elizabeth is right across the hall."

"Oliver's suite is as large as ours, and Jane's apartment
is even larger; I doubt if either spends much time with an
ear to the wall."

"This is so luxurious." Isabel bounced on the huge
canopied bed. "Are they really that rich?"

"Even richer. This wing is their home, so they've made
it the way they like it. The Institute is more, uh, insti-
tutional. It's also almost self-supporting, although it
requires some outside help. There is a big private endow-
ment as well as annual corporate contributions. It does
some very good work in its field. The work of the Group,
however, our little group, requires very little money."

"From the government? The CIA, FBI, National Security Council?"

"Certainly not. Barca is too smart to take government

21

money; he doesn't want the government to know we exist. How long would we last if some official knew what we do by having to approve a budget for us? Yes, the government may occasionally consult the Institute—for a fee, of course—but they don't know of the Group. They certainly don't suspect that we have access to anything the President has access to."

"Does the President know this?"

"Of course not. All he knows is that sometimes a problem he has, that no one else should know about, suddenly disappears, apparently of its own accord."

"Now, that sounds like the Barca I expected to meet, not the blustering, pompous, whining Bennet Ackroyd I did meet, the one with the five kooky daughters."

"When Barca is Dr. Bennet Ackroyd, the world-renowned epistomologist, he is the man you saw. But when Bennet Ackroyd is Barca, I think even Oliver is afraid of him."

"Oliver? Afraid?"

"Well, maybe not afraid, but certainly very respectful."

"But Barca is pudgy, soft."

"He's stronger than he looks, Isabel, but toughness is not measured by muscle; it's more a matter of attitude. Oliver can be very dangerous, I will attest to that, but he is also a reasonable man. If a mission, as given, is impossible, Oliver will look for an alternate method. If he *must* go ahead as planned, he will do his part and will be prepared to fail, and to die if necessary. Barca is *not* reasonable. If something *must* be accomplished, it *will* be accomplished, no matter what, no matter how. That's Barca."

"Does that mean he will sacrifice *you* if necessary?"

"Unquestionably."

"Are you serious, Giles? Or are you just trying to frighten me?"

"Deadly serious, Isabel."

"And me too, Giles? Sacrifice me? Oh, Giles, I didn't volunteer for that."

22

"You volunteered for everything, Isabel, the moment you discovered I was Hannibal, the mysterious constructor of crosswords." He was silent for a minute. "Let's hope that I—we—can solve Barca's puzzling little mystery."

"And if we can't?"

"Barca will find another way to open the shell. If an oyster knife won't do it, he will use a sledgehammer. Or even a guillotine."

Isabel digested this for a while, then moved away from the danger zone. "How can a man like that have daughters who are so—so—harebrained?"

"Are you really jealous, Isabel?" Giles asked gently. "I feel flattered, but it was all a big joke." Isabel didn't look the slightest bit convinced. "They always pull something like that whenever we come here." Giles saw he wasn't doing very well. "They're not what they—this is a house of mirrors, Isabel. Nothing here is what it seems. Deliberately. We are all playing a role, hiding. Our very lives depend on maintaining our outward innocent appearance. Those women are Dr. Jane Ackroyd, Dr. Elizabeth Ackroyd, Dr. Mary, Dr. Catherine, and Dr. Lydia Ackroyd. Their specialities are, respectively, lexicography, philology, descriptive linguistics, etymology, and semantics. Norbert Kantor, Professor Kantor from the Cruciverbal Club, has been corresponding with Lizzy for years. Ask him about her credentials."

"Does his wife know?" Isabel was instantly sorry. "I'll take that back, Giles; I'm sure it's purely scholarly. But she's—they're all so beautiful, so sexy, so—so unusual that I feel like a skinny little colorless waif next to them. How can you even *look* at me when they're around?"

"Because I love you and I want to marry you," he said tenderly. "Ask them if I ever—no, don't bother. Just marry me, Isabel. I will do my best to make you happy."

"I do love you, Giles, but I don't want to marry. All I want...If you're ever tempted—and I can understand how you would be—if you ever do anything with them, any of them, do me a favor; don't tell me. Let things between us stay as they are."

"But Isabel, I know them—Barca, I mean—since they were babies. Before Kitty and Lydia were born. I wouldn't think—"

"Yes, you would, Giles, and if I were a man, so would I. But it's all right; just don't tell me. Was their mother also . . ."

"Not quite. She was very beautiful, of course—the portrait you saw was quite accurate—but she was, well, more like the Mrs. Bennet of *Pride and Prejudice* than like her daughters. They inherited their father's brains as well as some of his other qualities."

"I think he loved her, still loves her, very much, and her daughters, too, in spite of the way he talks."

"Very much. It almost killed him when . . . We did nothing, the Group, I mean, for a year, almost."

"I think—" Isabel hesitated. "I'm not trying to play psychologist, Giles, but are the girls unmarried because they don't want to leave their father?"

"It's also who would be good enough for any of them? He'd need to have—be made of steel. But yes, that too; they're sure Ackroyd would die without them."

"Barca is very bright, isn't he? Doesn't he know?"

"He knows, but he can't prove it. When he accuses them of not marrying for his sake, they simply deny it."

"A sacrifice like this, against nature, biology, against love, it must tear them apart. The whole family."

"It's a sacrifice *for* love, Isabel, not against. They don't look at it as a sacrifice. It was a rational decision, made by each one individually, no pressure from the others. Besides, none of them has found a man who could interest her for more than a few weeks."

"Not even Jane?" Isabel said casually.

Giles blushed. "When she was a teenager, she thought . . . But I was married, and almost as old as her father."

"You're not married now, Giles."

"In my heart I am, Isabel." He put his arms around her protectively.

Isabel kissed him lightly. "You're forgiven, Sullivan. For Washington, for the heat, for everything. But you still owe me two boxes of chocolates. Dutch."

"It's a deal. As soon as we take care of Barca's little problem."

"How did Barca—? After his wife died, I mean."

"The girls pulled him out of it by taking a very difficult case, an unbreakable code, supposedly, and solving it for him. On their own. In only one month."

"And they were unable to solve this 'puzzling little mystery'?"

"So it seems."

"That's why he sent for you?"

"For us, yes."

"And he's in a big hurry? It's something very important?"

"A very big hurry, Isabel. Whatever we do, we must do fast. And it is—has to be, extremely important. The President's emissary comes to us, to Barca, only with critical problems."

"And if we don't solve the puzzle, or don't solve it in time, Barca may have to use force?"

"If force will help. It doesn't always. Unless Barca can find another way."

"And we'll be the sledgehammer?"

"Or the guillotine, Isabel. Whatever is required."

"I don't think I'd be very good at being a guillotine, Giles. Or even a sledgehammer."

"You will do very well, Isabel, at whatever job you're given, but we, you and I, will almost certainly be the last choice."

"There are others in the Group besides Oliver? There can't be just the four of us."

"There are the girls."

"The girls? Jane, Elizabeth, and the other vampires?"

"Their idea of humor, but yes, the five girls."

"But if they're really scholars? Barca would send his own daughters? They're *girls*!"

"Is this the equal-rights-for-women woman I love?"

Giles smiled sadly. "Yes, Isabel, Barca would send in his own children if it were necessary; he has in the past. I'm sure Abraham wasn't the first father to be prepared to sacrifice his own son for a higher devotion. It was not unknown in Spartan times, or in Roman, for a general to send his own children into battle, or even today. And they are women, Isabel, not girls, quite capable of... They were trained by Oliver, almost from the time they could walk. As for being scholars, Barca is a scholar, and he is very, very dangerous. Half the tyrants of the past and the present were scholars, even clerics. Think of Torquemada, Dr. Josef Goebbels, the Ayatollah Khomeini. Next to any of these Al Capone was a sissy."

"I suppose you're— Would *you* sacrifice me, Giles?" Isabel moved away a little so she could look straight into his eyes. "Would you, Giles?"

"No," he said without hesitation. "No, I would not. But I am not as strong as Barca. If you... I would go ahead of you, protect you with my life. And if you did not want to go, I would challenge Barca."

"You couldn't be completely ruthless, could you, Giles?"

"I am what I am, Isabel," he said. "I cannot change."

She held him tightly. "I don't want you to change, Giles. That's one of the things I love about you," she said, "your weakness. I could not love a merciless man."

"We need such men, though, really need them, to protect us against the truly evil men of this world. After the war I joined the Group. I was ready to die for my country at that time. I still am."

They said nothing for a while, holding each other, protecting each other with love against the world that was. Isabel let go first and started dressing. "Why only nine of us?" she asked. "Security?"

"The fewer who know we exist, the better, and the fewer we are, the easier to hide. The problems that we were designed to solve do not need large numbers, brute force. We need leaps of the imagination, intuition, the ability to analyze and synthesize, more than anything else."

"So, if the whole gang, the Group, is comprised of six imaginative, intuitive, brilliant women, plus three men for the hewing of the wood and the carrying of the water, why does Barca, Ackroyd, speak so disparagingly, insultingly even, of his daughters? It's so overdone, I'm sure he doesn't really mean it, but still I find it offensive. He wouldn't talk that way to sons, would he?"

"You should hear the way he talks to me sometimes, Isabel, but you're right; he doesn't really mean it. It's a carryover from the time he lost his wife, a backhanded way of... He loves his daughters so very much that it's as if he's afraid the gods will become jealous, will take the rest of his family away if he praises them too much. It's a real fear too; we're in a dangerous business, you know."

"Decoding? Deciphering? Come on, Giles."

"There are times when I hope you never... Barca is truly concerned that no harm comes to any of us, and if this ritual, this bombast, makes him feel more secure... Don't worry about the girls, Isabel. They're quite strong, and they often give as good as they take. They read these blusterings as true expressions of the deep love their father has for them; as a way of reducing the pain he feels every time he exposes them to risk. I think he's afraid that if he showed his love openly, he'd be unable to function effectively as Barca."

"It must be hell," Isabel said, "never to be able to say 'I love you.'"

"He does say it, Isabel. Every day. This way."

"Why doesn't he recruit some more people, Giles? Gradually. So that he could ease his daughters, even himself, out of this unbearable situation?"

"Who, Isabel? There are so few."

Isabel thought for a moment. "You know who would have made a perfect addition to the Group, Giles? Humboldt. Professor Fabian Humboldt."

27

"I'm sure he would have," Giles said easily, "but he's no longer available." Giles checked his tie in the mirror, looked approvingly at Isabel, and opened the door. "Barca likes punctuality," he said. "Let's go."

BARCA WAS SITTING BEFORE THE WALL OF BOOKS THAT made up one side of the windowless workroom. He was wearing a brightly flowered Hawaiian shirt and light slacks. "I reduced the cooling," he explained, "and now we can dress in a manner appropriate to the season."

"This looks awfully small for a decoding room," Isabel said. "When Giles told me about MI-8 during the war, he described rooms with dozens of women working on codes."

"There were hundreds of women, actually, at Bletchley," Barca said, "and some men too. The women had the talent, the famous feminine intuition, that was required. And now and then one turned up who was practically telepathic. In Britain they needed large numbers; they had to code and decode hundreds of signals every day, do a tremendous amount of routine work. When we're called in, all the horse work has already been done by some intelligence agency, all the standard methods tried, and all their people and their computers and machines have been found wanting. For all their faults, those daughters of mine have, under repeated application of the rod, developed a certain miniscule level of skill in the solution of simple ciphers and I, in turn, occasionally given them the opportunity to atone for their sins and to earn their daily, unwarrantedly expensive bread. At times one or

29

another manages to find—quite by accident, I assure you—a lapse on the part of the encoder, and brings forth the plaintext, usually full of mistakes, poorly punctuated, misspelled, and badly blotted. To save money, and in the interest of security, I use them instead of hiring a team of really competent men.''

"But don't you have to repeat, or check?"

"We have all the agency results available to us if we want; by hand, or more often by modem and computer printout. That is, over an ordinary telephone connection, scrambled, of course, directly to our own computer in my study. We rarely look at the work of other organizations; we prefer a cold, unbiased approach. And if you're going to work on this project, you should be aware that most of the work done by MI-8, which sounds like its British counterpart but isn't, or for that matter, any black room, is breaking ciphers, not codes."

"I always thought they were the same, Barca."

"Always call me Ackroyd, Isabel; it's safer. Codes are substitutions, usually randomly chosen, of a group of symbols for a word or phrase. Commercial codes are a good example. 'ABCDE,' for instance, may represent 'Buy ten tons of grain at once.' 'AABBC' may represent 'Lease a ten-thousand-ton freighter for a year,' and so on. A code requires a coding book or list, alphabetized for convenience in the order of the plaintext, plus a decoding book or list organized in the order of the code units. The sender must have a coding book and the receiver must have a decoding book. Codes are very hard to break, but if you know the context and have enough messages, it can be done."

"Then the Morse code," Isabel said, "is not a code?"

"Precisely." Barca looked pleased. "It's a cipher, where a symbol, a set of dots and dashes, represents a letter of the alphabet or a number."

"And what you have for us, for me and Giles, to solve, is a cipher?"

"I'm not quite sure. Actually, it's a crossword, which makes it very convenient that you were on your way to

New York when I asked for Giles's help. He tells me you've become quite adept at solving crosswords."

"Not really, Ackroyd, but I'm learning. You said your daughters were unable to solve the puzzle? If they couldn't—"

"No, no, Isabel, they solved the *crossword* puzzle; it was a Tuesday puzzle, and not exceptionally difficult."

"It's true, then, that the Monday crosswords are the easiest and the Saturday ones the hardest?"

"Most newspapers operate that way, yes. The trouble is, I have reason to believe that this crossword contains a message, a very important message, one which involves— But first, here is the solved puzzle, a copy, rather, of the puzzle as solved by the person who, I believe, was to transmit the secret message to unauthorized and unfriendly persons."

"No," Giles said. "Give me the puzzle blank, unsolved, as printed in the paper—you said Tuesday, so I presume it was a daily newspaper—and let me solve it myself, ourselves. Two copies. It may be there is a clue in the *way* the puzzle is solved."

"If your daughters—?" Isabel asked. "Earlier, when we first got here, you said you had given them the task many hours ago. You had to have called Giles before nine this morning to reach him before he left for the airport to pick me up. When did you get the crossword, Ackroyd?"

He squirmed. "Ten. Last night."

"And the five, all geniuses, all students of the word, all experienced decoders—excuse me, decipherers— worked for several hours on this little problem? And couldn't find the secret message? Several hours? Do you mean all night, Ackroyd? When did they quit?"

"Six this morning. The present generation has no stamina. None."

"You didn't let them sleep?"

"Shall I reward incompetence? Failure? They had the opportunity to sleep this morning, but they frittered away the time preparing to welcome you."

"Then they're sleeping now? Until dinner?"

31

ACROSS

1 Nightingale's symbol
5 Spot marked by "X"
10 Philippian P's
14 Peek follower
15 "You___one"
16 Korean War river
17 Choices, of course?
18 Loved not wisely but too well
19 ___-Ude, Russian city
20 Sauvignon or Merlot description
22 Nursery sound effect
23 Emblems
24 Gould's cop
27 Thanksgiving telecasts
30 Pardon
34 Culmination
35 Previous to
36 "Not___bet!"
37 Improved, maybe
38 Section of L.A.?
39 Archaelogical find
41 Nancy's hot time
42 "And___the opposite..."
43 Bitterly glum
44 Accommodations
47 Just as foolish
48 They scratch for food
50 Bride's partner
53 He's got a real case
54 Work units: Abbr.
58 Access road to a highway
59 Actress Cicely
61 10³
62 Great Lake
63 Western Samoan island
64 Cancer's zodiac symbol
65 Drenches
66 Small flycatcher
67 Hardens

DOWN

1 Dear one
2 First to go?
3 Best little madam in Texas
4 Weight
5 Bugger
6 Vacation duration: Abbr.
7 Aged: Latin abbr.
8 Daubing specialists
9 Common contraction
10 Okinawa's cluster
11 Headlight?
12 Buck heroine
13 Catches some rays
21 Oktoberfest quaff
23 Teamsters' watchdog org.
25 Average mark
26 Borden's Exhibit "A"
27 Quiz show group
28 ___man (evolution method?)
29 Obeyed the cox
31 One's performances?
32 Liqueur flavoring
33 He'll punch up the punch
35 Billion years
38 Advertising symbol
39 Muppet pianist
40 Polemic disputations
42 Officeholders
43 Crossword bird
45 Grabs at in the dark
46 ___, you are, he is
47 Name for a Frenchwoman
49 Scatter again
50 Got bigger
51 Hard to find
52 Leave out
55 Knowledge
56 Canoe or sloop
57 Weeps
59 Ram, in Rugby
60 High cloud: French

TUESDAY, JUNE 29

"During working hours? Certainly not. I gave them a minor problem to solve, an even easier one than this puzzle. To build up their confidence, you see. I cannot stand sniveling."

"They gave up at six, Ackroyd?"

"They didn't have enough sense to give up, to realize that this simple little puzzle was beyond their meager abilities. They had begun taking stimulants."

"But you didn't call Giles until nine. You took over yourself, didn't you, Ackroyd? And failed? That's when you called Giles."

"I am a poor, tired old man, Isabel, with diminished faculties, whose main occupation is to avoid—no, no, I cannot *avoid* it—to mitigate the indignities I am subjected to by those harpies."

"And you expect Giles to solve this problem in a few days?"

Barca brightened and stood up, no longer the tired old man. "I think we've made the right choice in you, Isabel," he said brusquely. "Here are the puzzle blanks; I had them ready, naturally, knowing Giles. But not in a few days, Giles, if you please. Twenty-four hours, Giles. Or less. Is that clear? Let me know when you've broken the cipher. At once." He started for the door, then turned. "Oh, you haven't eaten yet. I'll send up some sandwiches; you won't have time for a formal lunch, I'm afraid."

 **7**

I SABEL PUT DOWN HER PENCIL AND LEANED BACK. "I thought you said Tuesday puzzles are easy," she complained. "I never heard of 40 Down or 48 Across."

"You can find them both in any good dictionary," Giles said. He turned to the bookshelves behind him and pulled out a red book. "Here, *Webster's New Collegiate*, check it yourself."

"'Characterized by disputations and often subtle and specious reasoning,'" Isabel quoted. "No wonder a lawyer know about 'eristics.' And 'rasorials'? 'Habitually scratching the ground in search for food.' Like a chicken, evidently. But 'rasorial' is an adjective, Giles; it can't be plural."

"Constructing crossword puzzles is very hard, Isabel. Sometimes you have to bend the rules a little."

"Even so, those words don't belong in a Tuesday puzzle."

"Hannibal wouldn't have used them," Giles agreed. "Whoever the constructor was, he must have had a very good reason to put them in. Such as hiding a message."

"I see plenty of suspicious-looking words here," Isabel said. "Let me pull them out and see if we have a message. 'Stash,' 'Owe me,' 'Yalu,' that's from the Korean War, 'Ulan.' Isn't there a Russian city called Ulan Bator?"

"It's the capitol of Mongolia, but you may have an interesting point. The use of 'Ulan' in the puzzle may be a way of referring to both Ulan-Ude and Ulan Bator. Ulan-Ude is near Lake Baikal, the biggest, deepest body of fresh water on earth, although the Russians have polluted it badly, probably beyond recovery. But more interesting, Ulan-Ude is on the Trans-Siberian Railroad and is the terminus for the line to Ulan Bator, which line is the shortest direct line to Peking."

"That sounds like it, Giles. Now that we know—"

"We *don't* know, Isabel. You'll find, as you get deeper into cryptanalysis, that the obvious is usually not correct. The days of Poe's *The Purloined Letter* are long gone. If it were that easy, the Group would never have been called in. Don't forget, whatever agency this came from didn't solve it in a full day, Barca's daughters didn't solve it in a night of work, and he didn't solve it either, and he's very, very good. You're too young to remember, but the German Cavalry in World War One was called the 'Uhlans,' and if we did some deep research, I'll bet we'd find some more possible connotations for 'Ulan.' In Pearl Buck's *The Good Earth*, wasn't the heroine called 'O-Lan'?"

"All right, I get the point; let's keep going. How about 'Dick Tracy'?"

"It's not a bank robber we're looking for, Isabel; it's a spy." Isabel crossed the name off the list. "No, no," Giles protested, "leave him in. 'Dick Tracy' may be a code name. I just didn't want you to think of crime in general. We must concentrate on spies, military secrets, and the like."

"Here's a good one, 'apogee.' That has to do with ballistic missiles, doesn't it?"

"Yes, it means the highest point the missile reaches in flight. But it also refers to astronomy, that is, the farthest point a satellite, such as the moon, achieves in its orbit."

"Manmade satellites too?"

"Any satellite, so leave it on the list. Keep going."

"Doesn't foot-pounds have to do with missiles, Giles?

And 1000 nearby? One thousand foot-pounds?"

"Foot-pounds is a measure of the thrust of a rocket engine, so it stays."

"Does 'Upolu' have anything to do with rockets or satellites? Or 'Ryukyu'?"

"I don't think so, Isabel, but I doubt that this puzzle would name the subject of its message so directly."

"Well, that's all that I could find, Giles. Doesn't seem like much."

"You have accomplished something, Isabel." Giles smiled. "You've reinvented the Cardano Grille." Isabel looked puzzled. "Some four hundred years ago Girolamo Cardano of Milan invented a means of transmitting secret messages. He had a piece of paper with slots cut in it line-distance apart. You write the message in the slots, then fill in the rest of the letter with an innocuous-sounding message. At the other end, and the receiver places a similarly cut paper over the letter and reads the words exposed in the slots, which is the secret message. It's clumsy and can make for an odd-sounding letter, but it's ideal for crosswords."

"But Barca said, when we first met him, that the spy solved the message easily, mentally."

"It shouldn't be hard to memorize a pattern of box numbers in a crossword to get at the plaintext easily, without a grille. Further, a crossword puzzle permits Down slots for the message, too, not just Across, making it possible to transmit longer messages."

"But isn't it hard enough to construct a crossword as it is without having specific words stuck in just where you don't want them?"

"Harder, yes, but not impossible. Now, let's check what we have."

"Here. 'Los' can stand for 'Los Alamos,' an indication of nuclear devices. 'I on' is obviously 'ion,' a further confirmation. 'Tec' is short for 'technician,' and 'ramp' could be 'launching ramp.'"

"Let's put them all together, Isabel. 'Stash,' 'Yalu,' 'Ulan,' 'Dick Tracy,' 'apogee,' 'ft.-lbs.,' '1000,' 'Los,' 'I on,' 'tec,' and 'ramp.'" Giles studied the list. "We could put together a message of sorts, but nothing very useful, as far as I can see. I think we should attack this as a cipher."

"But haven't—?" Isabel said. "I'm sure the Ackroyds, father and daughters, have already tried. Can't we start from their failures?"

"Barca brought us here because he wants a new viewpoint. If we take their results, we'll be following their line of reasoning and will, very likely, end up where they did. Of course we'll attack the cipher in a formal manner at first, but we'll be looking at it from our own individual viewpoints. Since we're crossword experts, I assume that Barca wants us to try crossword techniques. Let's try a stepquote."

"What's that, Giles?"

"A method of putting a message into a crossword. You start at upper left, go down one box, then across one box, down one box, across one box, making a set of steps. In this puzzle we get 'LABENANDIDEE LON NOALFTIORATS.'"

"That sounds like a message, Giles."

"Well, it may be enciphered, a substitution or a transposition. That is, one letter may be substituted for another, or the letters may be mixed up according to a prearranged pattern. Or both."

"Barca said it was done mentally by a person whose mother tongue had no Latin, Greek, or Germanic roots. Presumably, therefore, a Slav or an Oriental. So it can't be very complicated."

"It can be, Isabel. If the spy had to decode the message mentally, he had to be expert in English. The Russians train spies, some from early childhood, in towns which are as American as Omaha. You may be sure that whoever the spy was, he was an expert at both crosswords and decoding. Certainly expert for their system, whatever that is."

"It still has to be relatively simple, Giles. What other

standard systems are there for hiding messages in cross-words?"

"Stepquotes can have different patterns, two letters at a time, or three, or even whole words at a time, none of which I see here. You can also go around the exterior of the puzzle. That gives us: 'lamp, stash, rhos, suns, lacer, sobs, stes, eewep, stew, werg, lenap, bmal.'"

"How about an inside box, Giles? Starting at 24 Across? 'Dick Tracy, yu, eris, lairosar, g, ega.' Or 'egad.'"

"Egad, indeed, Isabel. It isn't any of these standard patterns. I have constructed hundreds of puzzles, and solved thousands, some with messages, and my eye automatically picks up messages in clear. I don't see any here."

"What about the diagonals? 'LBNNIE O OLTOAS.'"

"Not even if you read it backward."

"The other diagonal? It has no black boxes at all. 'SLLKCXROONAOMRW.'"

"Usually messages are read top to bottom and left to right, but this doesn't work either way. No, I'm convinced it's not a hidden message; it's either a code or a cipher. If it's a code, we're licked before we start. There is an insufficient amount of message here to permit us to break a code, especially since we don't know the context, what it might be about and who is sending it to whom. We must assume it's a cipher."

"I'm not a cryptanalyst," Isabel said. "I wouldn't know where to start."

"I made a frequency count while we were talking." Giles looked at the sheet in front of him. "In the normal order of frequency, there are, in the puzzle, twenty-five E's, nine T's, eighteen A's, twenty-one O's, ten N's, seven I's, fourteen R's, sixteen S's, two H's, and so on. The relatively low count of T's and H's is consistent with crossword puzzles, where two-letter words are illegal, and THE's and AND's rarely appear. So unless the substitution was vowels for vowels and high-frequency consonants for high-frequency consonants, the likelihood is that we're dealing with a transposition cipher."

"Shifting the letters of the message around according to a pattern? A simple pattern?"

"Probably. But not necessarily a simple pattern. It could be a complex pattern, similar to that of a multiple-rotor coding machine, such as the famous Engima from World War Two, in which the letter selected changes the pattern used to select the next letter."

"He did this in his head, Giles? I don't believe it."

"Chess is the Russian national sport. Any player at grand-master level who can plan three or four moves ahead in midgame could easily emulate the action of a two-rotor machine."

"Well, I can't, Giles, and if that's the situation here, I might as well go home right now."

"I was just pointing out the possibilities, Isabel, not the likelihood. I think it more reasonable to assume that there was a substitution that maintained the normal letter frequencies, and then there was a transposition according to some simple pattern that could be handled mentally by any person skilled in both crosswords and cryptanalysis."

"And pray, sir, what brings you to that conclusion, Sullivan?"

"Pure deduction. Barca is far more skilled at cryptanalysis than I am. In fact, any of the Misses Ackroyd are more skilled and more talented at breaking codes than you and I together. Yet Barca sent for us. Why?"

"Because you are Hannibal, Sullivan, the greatest crossword constructor of all time and space."

"Certainly the greatest constructor available to Barca, Isabel; no need to be sarcastic. I am quite skillful at cryptanalysis, too, just not as good as they are. Now, the brute force approach, computer analysis and so forth, has obviously been tried by the agency from which Barca filched the puzzle. The young ladies and Barca have surely tried every technique at their disposal. Therefore, the enciphered message is almost certainly a mixture of crossword and cipher. Since it was solved mentally by a Russian, the pattern must be simple."

"And what is that simple pattern, Sullivan?"

"That, Isabel, is what we're here to find out."

"Then why am I here, Sullivan?"

"A different, a fresh viewpoint. That flash of insight. Clairvoyance. Sensitivity. Feminine intuition. Whatever works."

"If you're depending on me Giles, lots of luck. You'll need it."

 **8**

"Y OU'VE FAILED ME AGAIN, I SEE," BARCA SAID AS HIS daughters filed into the formal dining room. The five women were nowhere near as bouncy as when Isabel had first seen them. They had dark rings under their eyes, and even the beautiful auburn hair hung limp. Now they were wearing light summer dresses, natural linen, each of a different design, and Isabel had no trouble telling one Dr. Ackroyd from another.

Jane, the eldest, was the Leader. When she spoke, no one interrupted; where she led, the others followed. Elizabeth, the observer, was the Lip, facile with words, each word concealing a hidden barb. Mary, with the big black-rimmed glasses, was the Encyclopedia, the one the others turned to for information. Kitty had to be the technician, the Gadgeteer, who kept the machinery running. Lydia, of course, was the Muscle. Isabel studied them carefully. Gone was the vampire look, as was the appearance of the seventeenth-century flirt. The table was silent; even Elizabeth had no answer to her father's reproof.

Out of pity—amazing, Isabel thought, seven hours ago I was jealous of them—Isabel said, "Giles and I failed too, Ackroyd. As you did, didn't you?"

Barca coughed deprecatorily. "I did glance at the problem once or twice, but I didn't put my full attention to it, naturally. One would assume that if a father but breathed a wish, a father who had sacrificed his life for his children, a dutiful daughter would . . . But no," he sighed piteously. "Lear would have understood."

"What problem, Ackroyd?"

"Another crossword. A childishly simple one. On the chance that the message transmitted by the spy might be too long to be fitted into one puzzle, I secretly purchased a copy of today's *Capitol Gazette* and asked these over-educated daughters of mine to find the information within. Did they?" He looked around the table. "Did they? No need to ask. See their faces? No shame. They even came to dinner. A truly repentant child, cognizant of the disgrace, would have fasted or, at the very least, touched no more than bread and water. Moldy bread and brackish water."

"You are so right, Ackroyd," Isabel said. "Let us all, since we all failed, mortify the flesh together. Please tell the cook to throw out whatever she has prepared for tonight and to send out for moldy bread from the nearest greasy spoon."

"See what you have done?" Barca admonished his daughters. "You have disgraced me in the eyes of our honored guests."

A button had been pressed, Isabel decided, because a moment later a plump, gray-haired man wearing a tuxedo appeared at the dining room door. Barca nodded, and the man disappeared.

"You may be right about analyzing today's puzzle too," Isabel said, "but I think the failure lies not in our lack of competence but in our approach."

"You have devised a new technique in cryptanalysis, Miss Macintosh?" Barca's voice was derisive. "One that my daughters, and even Giles and I, are unaware of?"

"Of course not, Ackroyd. I am merely suggesting that cryptanalysis might not work. At least at this stage."

"Cryptanalysis, Miss Macintosh, is, by definition, the decoding of secret writing."

"Yes, but later. You are all so expert, so *centered*, on cryptanalysis, that you attack the problem as a message

43

to be decoded. Why not attack the problem as an exercise in—as a mystery? For instance, why in Washington? And particularly, why a crossword?"

Barca was silent. His daughters sat up straighter. "Keep talking, Isabel," Jane said. "Why Washington, you said?"

"Precisely. And why a crossword? It's part of the same problem. Why use a crossword to transmit a secret message to a spy in Washington?" She turned to Barca. "You are sure you got the crossword from a spy? And that there is a secret message in it?"

"A Russian spy," Barca said, all bombast gone. "And there is a coded message in the crossword. I am as sure of this as one could be of anything in this business."

"Very well, then," Isabel reverted to her professorial style of speech. *In spite of everything*, she thought, *I am still a teacher at heart*. "What is the message? The plans for the latest technical advance in ballistic missiles? A new sub that can operate silently at twice the present depth limit? A low-level radar that operates past the horizon? Of course not. Not only is there no room for this information in a crossword, or even two crosswords, but there is no way to hide a microdot or a similarly reduced blueprint in a newspaper published for sale to the public. No, the message is a *word* message, and the means of transmitting the words is irrelevant to the information. This is a clear case of 'the medium is *not* the message.' Further, the best place to steal technical information, particularly information that is relatively bulky, is at the source, at the manufacturing plant. Not only is Washington the worst possible place to get the plans for the death ray, but the city is crawling with FBI and CIA agents, and security people of all kinds. So what kind of information is being passed? Giles told me that it's important to know the context of the message if you're trying to break a code."

"So you think the secret message is political?" Elizabeth asked.

"Almost certainly. I mean, would the KGB use this means to signal redeployment of their local spies? Or next year's party platform of the U.S. Communist Party?"

"Do you think," Lydia asked, "that they are transmitting information about confidential presidential decisions?"

"Not necessarily the President; it could be the Secretary of State, or Defense, or even the Treasury. Somebody high up whose decisions will affect the U.S.S.R. in the near future, certainly within one year."

"That list could also include the Secretary of Agriculture and the Secretary of Commerce," Mary said. "The Russians will be celebrating their selective seventieth annual drought on their collective farms this year, and with it their centrally planned grain shortage. Advance notice of American farm plans could be very useful. Or manufacturing projections."

Isabel asked Giles, "How far in advance are crossword puzzles selected for newspapers?"

"Anywhere from two weeks to two hours; usually a day or two. It's not a big problem. Since the crossword space is always the same size, the page can be composed in advance, and the crossword set in a very short time before the presses roll."

"That means," Isabel said, "the message is at least one day late. That is, it's transmitted to the spy who is supposed to get it at least one day after the spy who stole the information has it, and more likely two or more days late."

"Agreed," Kitty said. "So to summarize, the message is likely to be political, in the form of a decision by a very high authority, possibly the President himself. It will have great importance to the Russians, and will probably describe decisions concerning events likely to occur in the near future, but possibly as much as a year from now. The message is transmitted by a means that produces a lag of one to seven days. Therefore—no, before I commit myself, I want to hear all the circumstances. How did you get the message, Father?"

"I had hoped," Barca said, now the complete team leader, "to have my two teams decoding the crossword without being influenced by circumstances, but since you have both reached the same conclusion I had, I suppose there is no harm in disclosing the history of this operation."

The plump man in the tuxedo reappeared, wheeling a trolley with a tureen of cold soup. "The weather's been exceptionally warm," Isabel said. "I'll have to get some lighter clothes tomorrow."

"No need to change the subject," Ackroyd said. "All members of the staff have been with the Ackroyd family for a very long time and, though they are not involved in the details or in the field work, they have a fairly clear understanding of our functions." The plump black-suited man seemed to take no notice. "If you require anything, you may ask James, here."

"Can't Oliver—?" Isabel asked.

"Other than for certain personal requirements for which Oliver may be helpful to you," Ackroyd said, "the house staff will handle all duties. I consider Oliver a guest in my house, but for some reason he insists on dining with the staff."

They ate the cold peach soup topped with yogurt as Barca continued. "Tom Burke, an old-time FBI agent, became suspicious of a Russian sent here under a work permit who looked too pure. Valentin Zulkov, twenty-seven years old, assigned as a bookkeeper to the Aeroflot office in Washington, to take the place of a bookkeeper who had gone back to Moscow on vacation. Zulkov, a mild-looking young man, had never been outside the U.S.S.R. before, and was not a member of the KGB or the GRU or any other formal organization, although like every other Russian who comes to the U.S., he was a graduate of the Moscow Institute of International Relations, which is, to a large extent, a spy school."

"So far," Giles said, "nothing unusual."

"Except"—Barca pointed his finger in warning—"the request for Zulkov's visa was delivered to the American Embassy in person, instead of being mailed, as usual."

"But didn't the Russians know this was a mistake?"

Giles asked. "Like waving a red flag? Even an embassy idiot would know that a shortage of bookkeepers in Aeroflot would not warrant breaking a normal pattern."

"I'm sure they knew, Giles, even though their bureaucrats are no smarter than ours. But evidently it was more important to them that Zulkov get here quickly than that they maintain a low profile. Whoever sent him must have figured that even if we became suspicious of Zulkov, we'd never be able to find out what he was doing."

"So Zulkov is a spy who had a single mission to accomplish in a limited period of time. The mission had to start at a particular time not under their control and, after it was done, Zulkov was expendable."

"That's the way Burke saw it. Then the Russians blundered again. To overcompensate for their first mistake, they set him up in a rooming house in Washington instead of in a compound or a secure Russian-owned apartment house. To make matters worse, Zulkov had absolutely no contact with anyone. He never went to a park, a zoo, a movie, never visited a prostitute, never bought jeans or records or did anything a normal Russian did."

Quietly, James removed the soup bowls and served a simple green salad. "A spy," Giles said. "Definitely a spy under very strict orders."

"But a spy who did nothing, Giles. Burke followed him, practically lived with him, for three weeks. Zulkov would leave the house in the morning, buy a paper, *The Capitol Gazette*, at his bus stop, get on the bus, turn immediately to the crossword puzzle page, solve—"

"Isn't *The Capitol Gazette* a pictorial tabloid?" Giles asked. "The one that's always trying to figure out how to get a completely naked girl on the front page without offending the authorities?"

"Exactly, Giles. It calls itself 'the newspaper that entertains you,' but they do have a good crossword page, I understand. Eugene Simon is the editor, and he's said to be one of the best."

"I've never met him," Giles said, "but I've solved some of his puzzles when he was in construction, and he was very good. That was, oh, at least ten or fifteen years ago. He's supposed to be a peculiar duck, works odd hours and never leaves the house. So you think he's involved?"

"I don't know yet, but Burke has some people watching him now around the clock. If there's anything—" Barca returned to his lecturing. "At any rate, Zulkov would turn immediately to the crossword puzzle, half solve it on the bus, in ink, and—"

"Ink?" Giles interrupted. "A Russian expert in American crossword puzzles? Then there's no question he's a spy, Barca, a specialist. And there's no question that the crossword— Are you sure he had no contact of any kind with anyone? The newsstand operator? At the store where he bought food? Anyone?"

"Burke tested all possible contacts, Giles. Negative. Completely negative. At the end of the bus ride Zulkov would go into the doughnut shop opposite the Aeroflot office. There he'd order two doughnuts and a cup of coffee, evidently his breakfast, complete the puzzle as he ate, then go across the avenue to the Aeroflot office."

"How about a message in the doughnuts?" Giles asked. "Or the sugar packet? The check? When he paid the cashier?"

"Fully checked out; Burke is an experienced professional. He is sure the message is in the crossword."

"Did Zulkov try to conceal what he was doing?"

"Not at all. What would be the point? Better to treat it as a hobby. Tens of thousands of people were working on that same puzzle."

"Did Zulkov make any marks on the page? Press more heavily on certain words? Or letters? Do anything unusual?"

"One thing. I'll show you later. I didn't show you before because I wanted you to start cold, without preconceptions. It may be that what Zulkov did, or did not do, was not because he decoded the message mentally but was because he recognized something which caused him to— to want to decode the puzzle in his office, in privacy. Anyway, before he was finished eating his doughnuts, he jumped up, did not wait for his change, stuffed half a doughnut into his mouth, and practically ran into the street. Burke said that Zulkov looked like a man who had won the lottery."

"Burke arrested him and took the paper away? You said you had the original. That wasn't smart."

"Burke was too experienced for that. What could he arrest Zulkov for? Solving a crossword without a license? Burke was interested in the whole chain of spies, not a single link. No. As Zulkov started crossing the avenue, a car ran the light, zoomed around the corner, and killed Zulkov."

"The Chinese?"

"A black teenager with a long record, who couldn't help stealing cars. Some idiot had left a white Cadillac double-parked with the engine running while he bought some cigarettes. The kid couldn't resist the temptation, got into the car, and took off. There is no question it was an accident. Burke liberated Zulkov's wallet and the newspaper, and here we are." Barca turned to Isabel and said gallantly, "Oliver's faith in you, my dear, is clearly well-justified. Welcome."

"If you knew all this, Ackroyd"—Isabel couldn't help feeling exasperated—"why didn't you save us all the effort?"

"Because"—Barca smiled—"while I am never wrong, I may not always be completely right. If I had given you my ideas, even unconsciously, by selecting the format and the order of my relating the background, you might have followed that path and might never have found a better road, if there is one, to the solution. We each have our individual talents, skills, experiences, viewpoints, all of which must be utilized to the fullest. Now, Elizabeth, since you, Isabel, and I agree that there is a message in the crossword, that it involves a political decision by a very high-ranking official, and that it will affect some relationship with the U.S.S.R. in the near to foreseeable future, what shall we do?"

"List all the major problems affecting the Russians,"

she said, "which are now being examined by the President and the major Cabinet secretaries."

"What about those we are not aware of? Shall I find out what I can about problems that are not common knowledge?" Barca looked around the room like a school-master. "Kitty?"

James removed the salad plates and served the roast rack of lamb, fragrant with rosemary. "No, Barca," Kitty said seriously. "Something of that nature can be known only to the President and one or two Cabinet members. Unless we can accept that one of them is a spy, in which case this whole exercise is unnecessary, it is probable that no decision has been made yet, so there is no secret to be transmitted."

"How far back in time do we go, Lydia?"

"A month. Five weeks at most. Zulkov had been here three weeks when the message appeared in the crossword. It took a day or two for the visa to be issued after the Russians made application, and a day more for him to get here. Presumably it had taken the Russians a few days to decide to send Zulkov, and another day or two before that to assess that information about this particular matter was important enough to activate this team of spies and that the information could be stolen within a few weeks."

"Jane, will you list the areas of crisis we should examine?"

"The Iran-Libya threat against the Iraq-Syrian alliance; the anticipated PLO-Syrian attack on Jordan; the increase of major weapons on the Afghanistan-Pakistan border with the threat of invading Pakistan; the International Monetary Fund proposal to extend huge credits to Warsaw Pact nations; the Mass Destruction Weapons Disarmament Conference; the proposed Russian wheat purchase contract; the possibility of the naval blockade of Nicaragua; the increase in the number of Cuban military advisors in Namibia; the new Russian radar installation in Arctica; the Chinese claim to Mongolia; the Russian claim to Sakhalin and the small Japanese islands; the sale of East German visas to West Germany; the Russian rejection of the Human Rights Basket of the Helsinki Agreement; the Russian cheating on the Whaling Agreement; the crushing of Solidarity in Poland; the refusal to allow Jews and Baptists to emigrate; the—"

"Enough." Barca held up his hand.

"It seems that the President of the United States has almost as many problems," Isabel said, "as the acting president of Windham University. Which is why she needs a relaxing vacation now and then." She stared directly at Giles.

"The President," Barca said, "has a few other problems to think about besides those caused by the Russians. Which is why each president develops his own technique for getting the information and advice he needs to make his decisions and to formulate his policies."

"I thought," Isabel said, "condensed analyses, briefing books, specialized advisors, things like that."

"All presidents have these available," Barca said, "but each gets what he needs in a way that suits his own personality best. Eisenhower, for example, liked very short reports, while Kennedy discussed matters in depth with his brother and a very few trusted advisors. Because of his many years as a judge, the President uses what he calls the President's Adversarial Team approach. A small number of experts in the field under discussion—two, three, or four, depending on how many major lines of action are available—present their briefs and argue their viewpoints before the President. After the 'trial,' the President makes his decision and has his people act on it."

"I never heard of that," Isabel said. "Did you, Giles?" Giles nodded.

"It isn't generally known. The 'litigators' are sworn to secrecy and the 'courtroom' is closed."

"And you think that one of these 'adversarial advisors' is our spy?"

"It seems very likely, Isabel. Look at it this way. The crossword spy team did not suddenly spring up overnight; it had to have been established many months ago, possibly years. If the spy who obtains and transmits the secret

51

information is a permanent member of the political establishment, he would have been sending messages all this time."

"How do you know he hasn't been doing just that?"

"Zulkov arrived just three weeks ago. He was rushed here, in fact, which means that it was only about a month ago that the spy was selected for a position where he would have access to very high-level secret information."

"He could have been offered the job of assistant secretary to a major Cabinet officer."

"Then why the rush to get Zulkov here? Such a post would allow the gathering of information for at least a year or two. No, everything points to a sudden appointment of our spy to a position where he would be given highly secret information for a short period of time and then he would leave. This is a perfect job description for a Presidential Adversarial Advisor."

Isabel thought for a moment, then said, "All right, I'll accept that for the while. But why are we starting with Tuesday's puzzle? Couldn't there have been messages in the puzzles last week? Or even two weeks ago?"

"Highly improbable. Burke, the FBI agent, had been watching Zulkov very closely from the day he arrived. The first reaction Burke observed was when Zulkov jumped up in the doughnut shop. Burke was sure this was the first message, and so am I."

"If you are sure of this," Isabel said, "why don't we zero in on the recent appointments to the President's Adversarial Teams? Can't we get enough information together so that you can give us an accurate idea of the context of the message? Giles told me that given enough background and sufficient coded text, any code can be broken."

"Given enough time, yes. But with the number of problems there are involving Russia, at this stage I would only be guessing. And if you multiply these by three, the average number of people involved in each problem, I am not ashamed to admit I don't have the faintest idea which of these could be the spy. So you see, I must have the message in order to cut the field down to which of three is the spy."

"Surely," Isabel said, "some of the problems are more likely choices than others. The Disarmament Conference starts next week; the pressure on Pakistan is supposed to peak in a month; the IMF meeting takes place in two weeks."

"And the attack on Jordan could come any day." Barca continued her line of reasoning. "The Iranians and the Libyans are totally unpredictable; the wheat purchase contract is being negotiated right now, and so on. There is a further complication. We have no reason to believe that the Russians were able to place their spy in exactly the Adversarial Team they wanted. Can you imagine the spy selected for the wheat team refusing to play unless he could be on the Jordan-attack team? What is the more likely scenario is that the Russians had several people as sleepers who were possible adversaries, and waited until one of them was selected for a major team and then activated the crossword-code operation. So, Isabel, we must start by decoding the message; after that, I'll know what to do. I am pleased, very pleased, that you analayzed the problem so well, but cryptanalysis is still the best wedge to open the nut."

"That may be, Barca," Isabel said, "but it's not the only wedge. I'm not persuaded that—why, for instance, was a crossword puzzle chosen? Surely it would have been simpler to pass the information to some spy connected with the Russian Embassy in one of the standard ways."

"Had Zulkov not been killed, the message would have been passed from him to the Russians in a standard way. Every morning some Russian with diplomatic immunity drops in at the Aeroflot office. Once Zulkov handed him the message, it would have been untouchable, and in Moscow's hands a few hours later. Now, this message could have been passed to Zulkov, or to any other spy, in a brush drop in the street or in the bus. It could have been given to Zulkov in his grocery bag, or telephoned to him.

It could have been left in a dead drop, in a book in a library, or under a bench in a park. So you tell me, Isabel, why was this slow, clumsy method, the crossword code, used?"

"Obviously, Ackroyd, because these drops can be detected, observed, in the normal course of counterintelligence operations. The Russians must have felt that this operation was so important, as compared to stealing technical information, say, that they bent over backward not to let us even guess that this information, or information of this kind, was being passed on to them. If Burke hadn't been so suspicious, and Zulkov hadn't been hit by a car, a very unlikely combination of events, no one would have even guessed that the Russians knew what they knew. And we still don't know what it is."

"Unfortunately true. It may interest you to know that Burke's superior, in fact, ordered him *not* to investigate Zulkov, and, given the amount of work the FBI has to do and the number of people they have to do it with, it was not such a foolish order, except by hindsight. What other reason can you think of for using this method?"

Isabel now felt more like the wrong end of a Socratic dialogue than like a teacher. "The only other thing I can think of is to ensure that the identity of the spy is kept secret. Or even the knowledge that there is such a spy who has access to the upper echelons of our government. But isn't there a way to trap such spies? Give them false information and see what gets transmitted?"

They had finished the lamb; dessert was brought in. "This is ice cream," Barca said, "of a sort. It's really very rich chocolate whipped cream, frozen, with shaved Dutch chocolate on top. Made especially for you, Isabel. It melts very quickly, so don't dawdle." Isabel dug in at once. "Yes," Barca said, "we can trap the spy. But first we have to know what information is being sought. Every president has dozens of close advisors, and this President, with his adversarial teams, has many more. He must have a hundred people he uses to analyze specific areas, each of which has a very good idea of what the President intends

54

to do in his own specialized field. Add to that the advisors and assistants the President uses, plus those used by the major Cabinet members and, well, you see the problem."

"I don't understand," Isabel said, "why he has to use the adversarial technique instead of specialist advisors the way other presidents did."

"It's probably an extension," Giles said, "of the time when he was a sitting judge. We lawyers believe that if each of the opposing positions has a strong advocate, one who marshals all the arguments in favor of that position and presents them in the form of a brief, buttressed by reason and fact, that the truth, or, in this case, the best policy, must shine forth."

"Or the cleverest lawyer's ideas are accepted, you mean."

"That may happen in a courtroom, Isabel, but each member of an Adversarial Team is a top-drawer specialist in the field in question. There are, I understand, some fierce rebuttals, and that the discussion sometimes gets heated. The President takes notes of all that is presented, reads the briefs, and makes his decisions. As a lawyer I can understand how this system works, and I do think the President has made good decisions on the whole."

"We're not here," Barca said, "to change the President's way of coming to a decision but to find out who the spy is. We must decode the secret message first, Isabel. After that we can act."

"We can act now, Ackroyd," Isabel said. "The crossword editor, Simon. Get the name of the constructor from him. And if the matter is as important as you think, by force, if necessary."

"I can find the name of the constructor of Tuesday's puzzle easily enough, or today's puzzle. When I'm ready, I'll have his name. But I want the whole crew, Isabel, the king and the queen, not just the pawns. And especially not a pawn who has just bitten into a cyanide capsule. I must have the message first, Isabel; I must know what the Russians want to steal and what they already know."

"But they don't know anything, Ackroyd," Isabel said.

"Zulkov is dead. From the scenario you described, I am sure he was the only one who knew how to decode the signal."

Barca sighed. "The Russians rushed over to the American Embassy in Moscow first thing this morning, that is, the morning of the thirtieth, their time, requesting a visa fast, for another bookkeeper for the Washington Aeroflot office. Most urgent. The books are in disarray. Terrible. No way to run an airline. The new man will be here tomorrow night."

"Zulkov Number Two?" Isabel asked. Barca nodded. "That's why you gave Giles and me twenty-four hours?"

"Sheer generosity on my part. It would be preferable that you decode the messages sooner so that I have time to plan for whatever action will be taken, but I must accept that Giles is not as fast as once he was and that you are a relative neophyte."

Isabel held her tongue. If Giles's earlier analysis was accurate, she was now accepted, even loved, by Barca. But, she decided, she still preferred a simple, straightforward declaration of affection. "I still don't see," Isabel said, "why it's worth all this trouble to the Russians to find out what the President's decisions are on any matter. Won't he have to announce his policies in a short time anyway?"

"All presidents give speeches," Barca said, "outlining their policies in a general way, but this one plays his cards a lot closer to the vest than any of the others. He really likes to surprise his opponents. What is more important is to keep secret the bottom line, the fallback position, in any area of negotiation. If the Russians are trying to buy wheat, for example, isn't it important to them, vital, to know that the lowest price we will accept is two dollars a bushel and that we'll give ten years' credit at three percent? Such knowledge is worth billions and guarantees that the Russians will not pay a penny more than the minimum. In arms negotiations, which is even more important, if the Russians know the minimum position our negotiators will accept, our walkaway price, so to speak, they could plan their strategy so that if these conditions are acceptable to them, they will not offer more, and may even try to squeeze out a few minor concessions from us as well. This is something that could affect the fate of the world. So yes, Isabel, it is worth all this trouble, and more, to have a spy at the top policy-making levels, a spy whose very presence is unsuspected."

"Okay, Barca," Isabel said, "you win again."

"Of course." He nodded, then addressed his daughter Lydia. "I am aware that you have not slept for some time, but set your clock for five-thirty A.M., buy a copy of *The Capitol Gazette*, make copies of the puzzle, and set everything up in the workroom. As soon as you are ready, wake the others. I will arrange breakfast for you as you work."

"Do you really think there will be a message in Thursday's paper too?" Isabel asked. "We're not even sure there was a message in today's paper."

"I don't know if there is one or not, but I must act as though there is. This crew has nothing better to do anyway."

"It seems unfair to burden them. Can't Giles and I do it? Or at least work with them?"

"I'm afraid not, Isabel. I don't want you to follow whatever approach they use, which is likely to be much more rigorously cryptoanalytic than your analysis. I value your intuition highly. Besides, you will be sleeping tomorrow morning."

"Not really; I usually get up at seven anyway."

"Not tomorrow, Isabel, I think. You and Giles will be analyzing today's crossword tonight."

"But—but—" Isabel could hardly get a word out.

"Yes, I know, my dear," Barca said smoothly, not a trace of sympathy in his voice, "but it is required."

Giles quickly stepped in to change the subject. "Can we have seconds on that delicious chocolate ice cream. Ackroyd? And earlier you said there was one thing you didn't show us about the first puzzle."

"Oh, that. Yes. Zulkov didn't finish the puzzle when he jumped up in the doughnut shop. The four-by-four field

ACROSS

1 Cry of the disgusted
4 Rhine feeder
8 "¿Como____usted?"
12 Down Under flock
14 Lonigan or Terkel
16 Tangent from above
17 Meditation method
18 Liza's *The Rink* co-star
19 Tin Man's trouble
20 Hong Kong peninsula
22 Gate or door: German
24 McAuliffe's reply
25 PDQ, memowise
26 Egret's cousin
29 Lilongwe's land
32 Art critic Saarinen
33 Asian goatlike antelope
35 Prepositions
37 Warmonger's foe
38 "...then again, too____
     mention."
39 Swatter's target
40 Parrot
41 Marked by merriment
42 ____coupon
43 Secondary sub
45 Green with lots of green
46 Amerind of Manitoba
47 Secluded setting
49 Pavarotti prototype?
52 They'll drive you mad
55 Skating jump
56 News updates
58 Swag
60 Freshman's due?
61 "Adam and Eve on____"
62 Matador's injury
63 Refused to relinquish
64 Singer Ed
65 See 59 Down

DOWN

1 Ottoman governor
2 Haywire
3 Quasimodo's creator
4 *My Fair Lady* locale
5 Pal of D'Artagnan
6 Archaeologist's find
7 NYC summer initials
8 Zeus carried her off
9 Incite
10 "...going____Ives"
11 Chip in a pot
13 Missed 'em all
15 Hard green skim-milk
     cheese
21 Debussy's *Clair de*____
23 White House pooch
25 Friendship
26 "Mary____little..."
27 Forgo a big ceremony?
28 Ohio or Colorado
30 Took the prize
31 Only when called for
33 Grab
34 Hole-punching gadget
36 Command to Fido
38 "The____nation was riding
     that night"
39 Palindromic Australian
     town
41 Needlefish
42 Ritzy restaurant name, in
     part
44 Chip off the old block?
47 *Grand Canyon Suite*
     composer
48 Makes it
49 Barrel
50 Wheelbase terminus
51 Harvest
52 Happy one?
53 Latitude
54 Wound souvenir
57 Man-mouse link
59 With 65 Across, fast-food
     type

WEDNESDAY, JUNE 30

in each of the lower two corners? He left them blank."

"But that means they were not necessary to the message," Isabel said. "You should have told us that from the first."

"Not necessarily so," Barca said. "Those corners might very well be the most important part of the message. What Zulkov had completed of the puzzle might have been just enough to give him the key word or clue that there was a message in this puzzle, so that he had to take it back to the Aeroflot office to work out completely."

"So it may not have been the simple message you said it was," Giles said, "one that a foreigner could solve mentally."

"It may not," Barca admitted complacently. "Sometimes I find it desirable to say what *may* be accurate in order to spur the troops on to greater effort." He stood up heavily. "Giles, Isabel, you will find the second puzzle in the workroom, and, as a reward for confirming my analysis of the context, you may also have what is left of the ice cream. Good night." He walked to the door of the dining room, then turned. "Of course if you should decode the message, you may wake me at once. If you do not, don't work past five A.M. You will need some rest tomorrow. Clean the tables of all your work before you leave the workroom; the girls must use the study after you go to bed."

 **9**

"**T**HIS IS NOT MY IDEA OF A VACATION, SULLIVAN."
Isabel pushed the completed puzzle away. "I could have
had more fun if I had stayed in Windham, even at a fund-
raising dinner. And certainly more sleep."

"I'm sorry, Isabel," Giles said. "I had hoped it would
be a quick job."

"Bullshit, Sullivan. Has Barca ever called you in for a
quick job?"

"Of course he has. In the beginning—"

"Yeah, before the girls could read. Now he calls you
in only when it's something neither he nor his daughters
can solve. You knew it would be a tough one the moment
the phone rang."

"Well, I— This is *important*, Isabel. The fate of the
world may depend—"

"Sure. That's what they told them in Rome when they
called for Christians to help feed the lions. Only they
didn't go into too much detail then, either, about what
feeding the lions really meant."

"You've eaten almost a pint of ice cream, Isabel, chocolate ice cream. I thought you'd be in a better mood."

"A woman does not live by chocolate alone, Sullivan.
Further, I burn up chocolate very quickly when my sense
of justice is violated." She pulled the puzzle back in front

61

of her. "And there's nothing in this puzzle. 'Kowloon,' 'Malawi,' 'dove,' 'gore,' 'ruin.' Crap. Absolutely useless. Even added to the first puzzle, it's nothing. I'll accept that the Tuesday puzzle has a secret message, the evidence is clear, but this puzzle does *not* have one. We're wasting our time, Giles; let's go to bed."

Giles looked thoughtful. "I'm not so sure. This is a very peculiar puzzle. Look at the arrangement of black squares. I've never seen anything like it in my life. And it's so clumsy, ugly, in fact. I'm surprised Eugene Simon let it go through. And 13 Down, 'saw none'; that's contrived. Look at 31 Down, 'if apt'; that's just as bad. 'Crazers,' at 52 Across; that isn't even a word. No, Isabel, there *is* a message here; no self-respecting constructor would produce such an awkward puzzle unless he was *forced* to do it to conceal a message. Remember what I told you about the Cardano Grille; that the text that was written around the hidden message tended to be very ungainly? Well, this puzzle has the same feel. There *is* a secret message in here; I know it."

"You'd rather beat your brains in on this rotten puzzle, Sullivan, than go to bed with me?"

"I must. We must. Please understand, Isabel."

"I understand, all right. I understand where I fit on your list of priorities. Slightly above having root canal therapy but below sharpening your pencils. And this is while we're *not* married; imagine what it would be like if I ever were drunk enough to say yes." She sighed hugely. "All right, Hannibal, what have you found?"

"Nothing, really, so far. No Stepquote seems to make sense. The open diagonal, 63 to 11, gives 'KLEURTIWIAAOUOA,' which doesn't have the feel of a message at first glance, even reading in the other direction. There is no central square message or any other obvious geometric pattern. The letter distribution looks relatively normal for a crossword. We'll just have to dig in, try all the cryptanalytic approaches."

"You try the cryptanalytic approaches, Sullivan; I don't even know what they are. Barca said he wanted me for my intuition? So I'll intuit for a while. Wake me when you've decided you're licked." She closed her eyes and leaned back in her chair. Giles bent over his pad of yellow legal paper.

After a few minutes Isabel opened her eyes. "Giles, stop what you're doing. Yes, right now. We're going up to see Barca."

"You've decoded the message?" he asked skeptically. "In your head?"

"Of course not," she answered impatiently. "But I'm going to have a talk with Barca. Call him on the house phone; he may still be awake. Hurry."

"But I have to stay here, Isabel. To work on the decoding."

"Okay, you stay. You don't need me for cryptanalysis, Sullivan; you're the big-shot crossword genius around here. And I don't need you for what I have to say to Barca."

"Don't antagonize him, Isabel; he can be very—"

"Now, why would I do a thing like that, Sullivan?" She opened the door. "After I've finished with Barca, I'm going to bed. Don't wake me when you come up. For *anything*." She left, then stuck her head back inside. "Even if I'm awake."

10

Barca LOOKED UP WEARILY FROM THE PUZZLE HE WAS working on as Isabel entered. "I thought," she said, "you let the horses do the horsework. And the mules. Such as Sullivan."

"I let them think that," he replied. "It would not do for a fearless leader to sully his hands with mere crypt-analysis."

"So why?"

"I may get the inspiration; one never knows. This job has the smell of something very important, and my nose is never wrong." He put down his pencil and leaned back against the pillows, his eyes closed. "Giles said you wanted to fight with me. Go ahead."

"I wonder what gave him that idea. Just because I've been bullied, threatened, harassed, and deprived of my sleep and my vacation? Think nothing of it, Ackroyd."

"What will you do if I ask you to risk your life, Isabel?"

"If you *ask*, and if it is for something I feel is worth risking my life for, you wouldn't have to ask."

"That's what Oliver said, but I wanted to hear it from your own lips. Now, my dear, what is on your mind?"

Isabel sat on the chair opposite Barca. "Giles is work-ing on the second puzzle. He won't succeed. If your daughters weren't able to decode the first puzzle, and you couldn't either, nor could Giles, it must be a much more difficult problem than you said it was. And the first puzzle is the only one we're sure has the message."

"It may be harder, Isabel, but I feel it's easy, truly easy. The trick is to find the trick. I was hoping you would do that."

"What I can do, Barca, is attack the problem from a different direction, that's all. We never fully discussed the approach I proposed at dinner. Regardless of what the message says, we can tell a great deal about the spy team just from the fact that a crossword puzzle published in a Washington newspaper was used to transmit the message."

"We've already agreed, Isabel, that the message is political rather than technical, that the spy has access to top-level government information, that a crossword puzzle was used to transmit the information in order to keep the identity of the spy secret, and that were it not for Tom Burke, we would never have even suspected there was such a spy. Further, the information is of such nature that a delay of several days in receiving the information is not critical to the Russians, although their haste in sending a replacement for Zulkov indicates that we should shorten that time to one day, or, at most, two."

"There's much more, Ackroyd. For instance, Zulkov had no contact with anyone, not even the constructor of the puzzle. That means that the constructor must be part of the spy team."

"Not necessarily, Isabel. The constructor could have been given a text that was already encoded, with instructions to distribute the letters in a specific pattern in a crossword. Even more likely, he could have been given a blank puzzle, with a specific pattern of black boxes and some letters filled in, in an apparently random pattern, and required, for a fee, to complete the construction in one day and send it to *The Capitol Gazette* immediately. He was probably told that he could keep the payment he got from the paper for the puzzle."

"That means he would have to be a skilled constructor, a regular contributor to Eugene Simon, to have any chance for that particular puzzle to be published. How many like that can there be in the Washington area?"

"Albert Kosgrow and Frederick Lindenmann are the only two professional crossword constructors in the whole Washington area, and neither of them contributes to *The Capitol Gazette* or to Eugene Simon. They make their livings as freelance crossword magazine editors and as part-time constructors, but they contribute only to the magazines they themselves edit and to the more prestigious publications. There are about thirty constructors in this area who construct crosswords occasionally for the *Gazette*, but only four of these are regulars who are published at least twenty times a year."

"So you've already considered this approach?"

"Naturally," he said tiredly.

"So let's arrest those four and have an intimate little talk with each. With a polygraph attached and a voice analyzer under the table."

"You can't do that in America, Isabel."

She looked at him in amazement. "Are you telling me that you've never . . . ?"

"I have, when necessary, many times. But only when I was sure. Besides, I want the whole team, particularly the spy himself. This whole setup was clearly designed to keep anyone from ever finding out who the top-level spy was, presumably so he could continue his work."

"The constructor had to know who he was."

"Not necessarily. This whole operation, the way it was set up, makes me believe that no one involved, not even the constructor, could, even under torture, reveal who the spy was. The spy must have had a way of getting the coded message, or the blank crossword, to the constructor without revealing who he was."

Isabel thought for a moment. "It's not possible. I don't care how they did it—telephone, mail, homing pigeon—there had to be a contact between them where either the constructor knew the spy or the spy knew the constructor."

"So it seems, Isabel, and on that assumption I spoke

to some of my friends and had Burke assigned in charge of this operation for the FBI. He has had the four semi-professional constructors under twenty-four-hour surveillance since Monday, their phones tapped and their mail read."

"Burke reports to you? Directly?"

"Of course not; neither he nor the FBI knows we exist. But someone would immediately let me know if anything of interest happened. I get copies of all Burke's reports soon after he turns them in. There's been nothing useful so far."

"Maybe the spy is also the constructor?"

"Extremely doubtful. Even if he, or she, were skilled enough to construct a publishable puzzle, and had the time, how could the spy be sure it would be published at all, much less in time? And in order to be published, he'd have to reveal his name, or a traceable pseudonym."

"Giles has kept secret that he's Hannibal for eighteen years."

"Nothing bad would happen to Giles if his little secret came out, but I don't think our spy could afford to take that chance. No, the constructor must be a well-known cruciverbalist with a long record of publication, probably predating the time when this whole scheme was set up."

"It still seems to me a lengthy, clumsy, uncertain way to set up a spy team."

"Only on the surface, Isabel. To me it is a very economical and effective technique; look at the difficulties we're having, even knowing where the message is. Look at the structure. There is a spy, a sleeper or one of a set of sleepers, who was established years ago. One of a group of people who were turned into Communists, possibly in a university. Some time ago, our spy was given the method he was to use for this one big event. If it succeeded, the technique might be used again, but even if it were not, the Russians were willing to make this investment, certain that the information they received would be worth their time and trouble. After that, neither the spy nor the Russians had any contact with each other, nor did they do anything in the least bit suspicious."

"You mean they set this up twenty years ago and just hoped something would work out?"

"It doesn't work that way. They had a group of potential leaders, bright young people whom they recruited. Of these, one or more would be sure to rise in a field that interested them, and some would achieve national importance, possibly be selected as an Assistant Secretary of Defense, a member of the Presidential Adversarial Teams, even though these did not exist at the time, or some position of similar importance, with access to major secrets. When our spy achieved this position, he was given the crossword-code technique along with the activating signal. Some three to five weeks ago this signal was sent, an apparently innocuous signal, and the operation was activated."

"It still sounds difficult to me, and uncertain."

"The Russians invest a lot of time and money in their intelligence operations, a shotgun approach. An occasional failure is more than made up by the high number of their successes. Look at what this method accomplished. No one, not even Zulkov, not the constructor, no Russian agent, in the U.S. at least, knows who the spy is."

"You're guessing, Ackroyd; you couldn't possibly know that."

"It's a lot more than a guess, Isabel; it's inherent in the whole setup. There is no reason for using the crossword code other than to keep any other member of the spy team from knowing the identity of the spy."

"What about a dead drop?"

"What about the pick-up man hanging around the dead drop until he sees who deposits the secret message? No, Isabel, the use of the crossword code proves that the Russians will go to any lengths to protect the identity of the spy, even from their own people. This is why I am sure the spy is very high up and passing on very important information."

"So no one knows who the spy is? That's impossible."

"Other than the man who set it up, no one knows. Realize this: The spy does not know the constructor, or any other Russian agent for that matter, and has no contact with anyone remotely suspicious. The constructor may not even know what the message is, or who he is working for, and he does not know whom the message goes to, or the decoder, Zulkov. Zulkov has no contact with anyone, American or Russian, and does not know who the spy or the constructor is. If Burke hadn't been so suspicious, and had Zulkov not been accidentally killed, we wouldn't even *think* there was a spy, much less that there was a message in the crossword. It's the cell system where, if he is captured, a cell member can betray only the members of his own cell, but here it's carried to its ultimate; there is only one member in each cell. Capture Zulkov, and whom can he betray? Arrest the constructor, and what have you got? What can he tell you?"

"If Zulkov were arrested, he could tell you the decoding method."

"If Zulkov were arrested? For what? By whom? Why should anyone even think of arresting him? Who would suspect him? And even if we kidnapped him, he'd be dead, cyanide, in one minute. Then what?"

"There's a flaw in this scheme, Ackroyd. In order to get the crossword published in the paper, Eugene Simon had to be in on it."

"Not necessarily, Isabel. If the constructor was one of the *Gazette*'s four regulars, the odds are he'd be published in a few days, at most. From our analysis, the information the spy was transmitting was not something that a few days' wait could affect adversely. Evidently, protecting the spy's identity was worth a few days to the Russians."

"But what if the crossword was *never* published? Wouldn't it be almost essential that the editor, Simon, be part of the spy team? To make *sure* the puzzle was published?"

"I have no doubt that if the coded crossword was not published in a reasonably short time, another would be offered, containing the same message, probably worded slightly differently, and encoded slightly differently; repetition is dangerous in secret messages. But yes, though Simon might not have been an essential member of the team, he would certainly have been a very useful one. However, Simon might not have been one of the spy team; he may have been cajoled, or even induced by, say, a few free puzzles—crossword puzzlers don't get rich—to accept the coded puzzle and publish it promptly."

"I'd still like to question him."

"You will, my dear, as soon as we decode the puzzle. Which I hope Giles will do soon."

"But isn't it helpful to know that both puzzles, Tuesday's and today's, and maybe even tomorrow's, contain the same message?"

"Very." Barca smiled ruefully. "If we were sure that was true. But there may be consecutive messages rather than concurrent ones. Or no messages other than in the first."

"You've thought all this out already, haven't you, Ackroyd?" He nodded. "Then why haven't you told Giles? Or the girls?"

"It is possible I may have missed something or that I might be—insufficiently accurate. I want independent thinking. I am confident that they will all come to this conclusion soon, if they haven't already, or to an even better scenario. I mustn't lead them down what might be my primrose path, though I am truly gratified that you concur with my ideas."

"I would like Eugene Simon watched."

"Watched, phone-tapped, mail-checked, and office-bugged. The routine work we do routinely. Or rather, we have it done for us by people skilled in the trade. Leave that to the professionals, my dear."

"Twenty-four-hour surveillance? On Simon as well as the four constructors? Doesn't that take an awful lot of people?"

"The President's office has approved it."

"Without his knowing what's going on?"

"I have some important friends, Isabel, who have faith

in my hunches. I'm rarely wrong, but even if I were, the possible loss to the country, if I'm right, is so great that any cost is justified."

"You don't mean just money, do you, Ackroyd?"

"Any cost," he repeated firmly.

Isabel digested that, then asked, "Should I discuss this, my ideas, with Giles?"

"By all means, Isabel, but don't stop him from working on the puzzles. It's most important."

She got up. "I feel like a fool, running to you with plans you've already put into action."

"Nonsense, my dear, I welcome your views. I am quite pleased, in fact, that you and I think so much alike. One day—I hope it will not be soon, but I *am* growing older and softer—you will outstrip me, and then . . . You have the kind of devious mind, the ability to calculate coldly, the remorselessness, the implacability, that the Group needs."

Isabel was shocked for a moment, then recovered. "What about your daughters? Elizabeth?"

"Ah, you noticed that she's the one who— But the girls are, at heart, scholars. They lack your administrative experience, your easy capacity to give orders, your air of command, your sureness when you know you are right. Elizabeth, strong as she is, dedicated as she is, experienced as she is in this work, could not be the leader."

"Lydia?"

"My second choice, but she could not send a friend to risk his life; that requires a level of courage she is unable to achieve. I tested her once. There was an occasion where it would have been appropriate to send Kitty; technical knowledge and mechanical skill were required, but the mission was quite dangerous. She went herself."

"Evidently she came out of it well."

"Yes, thank God, but it was not the mark of a leader."

Isabel surveyed this strange hard scholar, who had decided his youngest daughter was weak because she risked her own life rather than her sister's. "What about Giles?"

"Too straightforward; too honest."

"You can say this about an ex–criminal lawyer from New York? Come on, Barca, he's strong, brave, brilliant, a natural leader."

"Would he send you, alone, on a dangerous mission?" Isabel was silent. "No, Isabel, you know he would not. He wouldn't even send Oliver. He would go himself, of course, sacrifice himself, thinking it the honorable thing to do. A real leader must be able to sacrifice others, Isabel; that is what is required."

"And you think I could do that?"

"I have no doubt that you could, Isabel." He looked at her with pity. "And that, someday, you will." Barca paused and cleared his throat. "Go to bed now. Rest. One way or another we will have to take decisive action tomorrow, when Zulkov's replacement arrives."

Isabel started to leave Barca's bedroom, then stopped. "Don't tell Giles," she said, "what you—what you think you know about me. I'm not sure you're right."

11

ISABEL SAT DOWN AT THE BREAKFAST TABLE OPPOSITE Giles. "You don't look tired enough, Sullivan," she accused. "You slept, didn't you?"

"When I found myself doing the same thing over and over, I decided— I sense you're angry, Isabel. Why?"

"You *sense*, Sullivan? Very perceptive of you." She stabbed the butter. "Where did you sleep?"

"There's an empty bedroom at the end of the hall."

"By yourself, Sullivan?"

"You told me not to disturb you."

"You didn't have to listen, did you?"

"But I—"

"There've been other times when you didn't listen to me, Sullivan. For less important— Sometimes, Sullivan, you're a lot more cloddish than is permissible in a man. This was supposed to be my vacation, you know. You have an awful lot of catching up to do after you finish your little chore. Did you solve Puzzle Two, or was the whole night completely wasted?"

"Not wasted at all, Isabel. I learned what doesn't work."

"Oh, great, Sullivan. I was afraid you might have accidentally found the key and we'd *never* learn what doesn't work."

"Isabel, you just don't understand. Cryptanalysis is ninety-nine percent perspiration and one percent inspi-

The Crossword Code

ACROSS

1 Shampoo target
4 BLT additive
8 Two-way radio
12 Clean the slate
13 "Lackaday!"
14 Bank for loading cargo
15 Stiff cotton fabric
16 Bar rooms?
18 *The Story___*
19 Hellenic H
21 Shows off
22 Legendary lyrist
24 Temple U. player
26 Deserve
27 Illegal offense
30 Straight-bladed daggers
33 1978 Burt Reynolds film
36 Genetic initials
38 Monterrey moviehouse
39 ___in "Roger"
40 Interceptive rocket: Abbr.
42 RN's sine qua non
44 Just out
45 Xanadu's river
47 Luxury boat: Abbr.
49 Saws
51 Wielded
53 Invalid, maybe
55 Nordic name
57 "Lord, is___?" (disciple's query)
58 Pituitary hormone, for short
62 Turned the other way
65 RSVP write-up
67 Bauxite, e.g.
68 Indoctrinate forcibly
70 Hemingway heroine
72 Bone connectors: Abbr.
73 Raines or Logan
74 Currently ambidextrous?
75 Duel tool
76 Tatum's old man
77 Unquestionably

DOWN

1 Severity
2 ___tree
3 One of the Kellys
4 Nyasaland, now
5 As such-and-such would
6 Squawk
7 Abraham's '85 earning
8 Re H_2O
9 Hit man's work
10 Lot
11 America, U.S.A., or World
12 Former 11 Down?
15 Succeeded
17 Mouthward
20 "A tale___an idiot"
23 Versifier's creation
25 Fraction fig.
28 Kin of Bambi
29 Stick with a kick
31 Baby's perch, at times
32 Bastes
33 Bunker, e.g.
34 Auditorium
35 Undercover work
37 "She's ___From Manhattan"
41 Dais personages, for short
43 CCCXLIX + II
46 Abelard's lady love
48 Weather report abbr.
50 Santa___, Calif.
52 "Phooey!"
54 Sen. Jake Garn, e.g.
56 Not so many
59 Incurable illnesses
60 Farm vehicle, for short
61 LBJ pooch
62 Adjective suffix
63 Clutch
64 *What's My Line?* honcho
66 Render inconceivable?
69 Patty Hearst's captors
71 "Rocks"

THURSDAY, JULY 1

ration. You've got to do the routine—"

"The Lorelei Quintet did the horsework already. Times five. Why do you have to reinvent the wheel?"

"Each analyst sees things a little differently. I might have discovered something they missed."

"You can't even discover where you're supposed to sleep, Sullivan. You're lucky I know the five of them were working all night. What thrilling adventures have you planned for me today?"

"Right after breakfast we're supposed to solve today's crossword puzzle. Assuming the Ackroyd women failed."

"They failed, all right. You don't hear any bells ringing and cymbals clashing, do you?"

"Obviously not, so finish your coffee and—"

"I don't drink caffeine, Sullivan; you know that. Where do they keep the chocolate syrup around here?"

"Chocolate has caffeine in it."

"Much less than coffee or tea; the basic habit-forming drug in chocolate is theobromine, which tastes much better than caffeine. Stop being picky-picky, Giles, and point me at the chocolate syrup."

"It's on the counter over there; the staff knows what you like."

"Better than you do, Sullivan; one of these days I'm going to hire a staff. A big staff." Isabel mixed a tall chocolate milk. "Look, they put out the vanilla extract too. Someone around here, present company excluded, knows how to treat a lady." She gulped down half the glass, and relaxed visibly. "Why are we working on the *third* puzzle, Sullivan? We aren't even sure that the *second* puzzle has a message in it."

"Barca thinks it might. We have to cover all eventualities."

"You would have made a great serf, Sullivan. For your next birthday, if I stick around that long, I'm going to buy you a forelock to tug."

"Save your strength for the puzzle, Isabel; I'm too tired to argue with you."

Isabel put the container of milk, the jar of chocolate

syrup, the bottle of vanilla extract, and her glass on a tray and followed Giles to the workroom. "If I have to be brilliant," she explained, "I'll need a good supply of brain food."

"**A**M I WRONG, GILES," ISABEL SAID, "OR IS THIS THE worst-looking puzzle I've ever seen?"

"It's very unusual," Giles agreed. "I've never seen a crossword with the opening corner squares blacked out."

"And all those short words? Aren't there more than usual?"

"Many more. I counted eighty-four words in this puzzle, ten more than par for a fifteen by fifteen. And look at the large number of abbreviations: 8 Across, 36 Across, 40 Across, 42 Across, 47 Across, 58 Across, 65 Across, 74 Across, 25 Down, 29 Down, 41 Down, 48 Down, and 69 Down. Fourteen together."

"As far as I'm concerned, you can add 18 Across and 39 Across to the list. That's sixteen abbreviations out of eighty-four words, almost twenty percent. Giles, I'm not sure about Puzzle Number Two, but this one has to have a message in it."

"And did you notice that 4 Down is the same word that was used in Puzzle Two at, let me see, at 29 Across? No self-respecting crossword editor would allow that to happen accidentally."

"Are you saying that this proves the editor, Simon, is a member of the gang?"

"Not necessarily a member, but he would have to be involved in some way; I thought you understood that.

There is no way a contributor, a constructor, could be certain that a particular puzzle would be published within the next few days, or even that it would be published at all, without the active cooperation of the editor, Simon."

"So when he sent in—the puzzles are mailed in, aren't they, Giles?"

"Usually, but they can be brought in in person, or sent by facsimile machine or by computer, using a telephone modem, assuming that both parties have the appropriate equipment."

"Okay, but however they arrive, there would have to be an identifying mark on the submission, wouldn't there?"

"The name of the contributor might be enough. Or a variation on the name. If the contributor usually signed his name 'John Smith,' the signal to publish a particular puzzle might be to sign it 'John Q. Smith.'"

"So Simon and the constructor are both spies. Barca said he could easily find the name of the constructor. Why doesn't the FBI arrest them both?"

"Neither Simon nor John Smith may be a spy. Simon might have been told a cock-and-bull story, that this rich amateur would give anything—say, as much as one thousand dollars, to have his puzzle printed within the next few days."

"One thousand? To betray your country? I don't believe this. Forget about spying; if I were an editor, I wouldn't publish a rotten puzzle like this for ten thousand dollars."

"Isabel, you talk from the vantage point of someone who has never been really poor. Even when you were a teacher, you made a living wage. Do you know how much some prestigious papers pay for a fifteen by fifteen, which takes anywhere from two to eight hours to complete and you don't know if it will be accepted after you've finished? Would you believe they pay as little as twenty-five dollars? The average constructor, and the average crossword editor, might find a thousand dollars very tempting. And Simon wouldn't necessarily know what the message was, or even that there was a secret message in the puzzle."

"The constructor would have to know."

"Only that there is a hidden message. He might have been told that his rich patron is sending a secret love message to his wife, to his girlfriend, and be given a string of letters, a coded message, with instructions as to where to place these letters in the puzzle. Add the thousand for the editor, and you have the coded crossword published."

"But wouldn't the constructor and the editor be criticized for—? Wouldn't they be ashamed?"

"Very few readers care enough to write in. For the few who do, you could always explain that you were sick, or your assistant sent the wrong crossword to the paper. You could even tell the truth, that there is a message hidden in the crossword and that you're Cupid's messenger."

"But wouldn't that negate the efforts of the spy gang?"

"Not necessarily. Not many crossword fans are expert cryptanalysts. Even if there were dozens, Barca and the girls are among the best there are, and I am quite competent, too, and *we* haven't the slightest clue as to where to start."

"So let's grab Simon and John Smith and pump them full of scopolamine and sodium amytal."

"There are better truth drugs today than the ones you read about in spy novels, but to what end? If the Russians used the crossword technique to keep the identity of the spy secret, is it likely that they would let the spy himself approach Smith or Simon in person, or through some traceable third party? What will Simon tell us? That he was approached by a blond sexpot named Natasha, or a short bald man named Boris? No, Isabel, if we ever crack this one, we'll find there's at least one more cutout between the spy and the constructor, just as there was one, *The Capitol Gazette*, between the constructor-editor team and Zulkov."

"But Barca said—I heard him—that he could easily trap the spy once we knew what the message was."

"Not necessarily easily, Isabel, but it can usually be done. The point is, we must decode the secret message first." He looked at the solved puzzle. "Come on, Isabel, examine your puzzle. Do you see anything useful?"

Isabel bent over her paper. "Aside from what we discussed before, this one has a few interesting words. 'AM/FM' could stand for radio. It's obvious from the clue, but if you didn't know there was a hidden message, it wouldn't mean anything. 'Quai' refers to shipping. 'Law courts' is a possibility. 'Nero' could be the code name for a spy; after all, you're 'Hannibal' in your secret life. 'Dirks,' of course, a weapon. 'The end' might refer to nuclear war. 'ABM,' no comment needed. 'Olaf' could be code for 'Norway.' 'Brainwash,' another no comment needed. 'Malawi' appeared in two puzzles. 'Aquatic' goes with 'quai.' 'Murdering,' obvious. 'TNT,' equally obvious. 'Trap,' 'espionage,' and 'SLA,' especially if you pronounce it 'slay,' add those. 'A Latin' may be a South American agent. 'CDI'? Is there a Cuban Department of Intelligence? Forget it, Giles; I'm just guessing. Did you check for Stepquotes? Diagonals? Other geometric patterns?"

"Nothing that I can see. Yet it has to be there, Isabel. There has to be some clue that Zulkov recognized; I'm sure of it. I feel it. I know it."

"Maybe it's in Russian, Giles, a code in Russian. Did you ever think of that?"

"I don't know Russian, just a few words. But Mary is fluent in several Slavic languages, and the other girls know one or two each. If they didn't spot anything, I doubt if there's anything to see." He thought for a moment. "It's in English, Isabel; I can sense it. Otherwise, why use Zulkov, a man who is as skilled in English as I am?"

"To solve the puzzle, Giles."

"One day later, Isabel, and the answer would have been published in the paper. No, the message is in English."

"I'm going to ask Mary anyway, just for good luck." She looked solicitously at Giles. "Are you going to spend the next four hours on routine cryptanalysis?" He nodded ruefully. "I can't help you there, Giles. I'm going up to our suite to relax and think. Meet you in the dining room at lunchtime. I'll mix you a good chocolate milk before I go; it's still cold. Maybe if you get enough glycogen and theobromine into your brain . . . It works for me, Giles. And it tastes delicious."

"So you're not angry with me anymore?"

"Don't get any ideas, Giles; you're still in limbo. I'm doing this only for God, Country and Windham."

 **13**

"NOT EATING, ISABEL?" GILES ASKED.

"Twelve o'clock is a bit early for lunch," she answered. "I had breakfast at ten."

"We had breakfast at six," Lydia said, "while we were working. I'm starving."

Although the five Ackroyd women seated around the table must have just risen from at least five hours of sleep, to Isabel they looked even more fatigued than they had at supper the night before. Isabel liked the idea of feeling sorry for them; it reduced somewhat *her* feeling of being the ugly duckling and increased, proportionately, her confidence in Giles's devotion to her. But Isabel had been trained in the jungle groves of academe, had learned that the best time to kick a man was when he was down, the flatter the better. "Cheer up," she told Lydia while dipping a cold shrimp in aioli sauce. "There'll be other messages to decode sooner or later. Easy ones."

The scorpion-tongued Elizabeth responded. "'Providence has hidden a charm in difficult undertakings which is appreciated only by those who dare to grapple with them.'" She smiled sweetly at Isabel. "I quote, of course. Never having been granted the benefits of a literary education, my own version would not have been as felicitous or as euphonious."

"Now, now," Barca chided, "we are all working toward the same goal."

"Of course, Father," Jane said. "'To each according to his needs, from each according to his abilities.' That's a quote too. So we welcome all contributions, no matter how mean."

"To paraphrase Norbert Weiner," Isabel replied, "machines should do machine work, horses do horse work, and humans should do human work."

"Isabel," Giles said firmly to her and the others. "You're taking out on each other the tensions and frustrations of this operation, quarreling over who's the better cryptanalyst and who's working harder."

"Oh, Giles," Isabel said, "don't you understand anything? Do you really think the decoding is the problem? You're such a square. Square? You're a cube. Worse than a cube, you're a hypercube."

"The four-dimensional equivalent of a cube," Mary the Encyclopedia said. "A mathematical construct. If you take four lines of equal length and place them at right angles to each other, you get a square. If you take four squares and fit them together at right angles to each other, you make a cube."

"But a cube has six square sides, Mary," Giles said. "Four sides plus a top and a bottom."

"When you put the four sides together," Mary corrected him, "the top and bottom squares are formed by the array automatically. So four one-dimensional lines make a two-dimensional plane, a square. Four two-dimensional squares make a three-dimensional cube. Extrapolating, four cubes arrayed at right angles to each other should make a hypercube, a four-dimensional object."

Giles closed his eyes. "I can't visualize that."

"Of course not," Mary said, "it's four-dimensional. But sometimes mathematicians use a three-dimensional representation of a hypercube, just as we can draw a cube on paper in two dimensions. Imagine a large cube with a smaller cube inside it, both sets of faces parallel to each other. Draw diagonal lines from the corners of the small cube outward to the corresponding corners of the large cube, and you have a hypercube projected in three dimensions. Four cubes around the smaller inside cube, plus the top and the bottom cubes make six. Add the small and the large cubes, and you have eight cubes, four of which are formed automatically, all at right angles to each other."

Giles shook his head. "That's wrong. The lines from the corners of the small cube to the corners of the large one aren't at right angles to each other; they're diagonals. Each of the shapes surrounding the small cube is more like a pyramid with its top cut off."

"That's because it's a three-dimensional representation. In four dimensions, all the lines, including the diagonals from corner to corner, would be at right angles to each other, and form cubes, eight cubes, and they'd all be the same size."

"That's impossible," Giles said. "The diagonals—" He stopped and stared into space. "Wait. The diagonals. A small cube inside a large cube. A small square inside a large square. Diagonal." He grew excited. "No corners. It's perfect." He looked around. "Get me the first puzzle. Tuesday's puzzle. The original, not the one I solved." He started moving dishes aside. "Isabel, clear the table; we'll eat later." Kitty had slipped out and back, silently and quickly, with a batch of copies of the puzzle and a stack of yellow legal pads.

Giles took out his pencil, using it as a pointer. "Here. Look. Start at the middle of the top row. Box 7. 'A.' Go diagonally down to the right, to 'C.'" He drew the line. "Now go diagonally down to the left, to 'W.' Now go diagonally up to the left to Box 37, 'N,' and then diagonally up to the right back to Box 7. A square, see? A small square inside the large square. On the diagonals."

"That's it, Giles," Barca crowed. "Perfect. That's the message." He checked his watch. "And well within the twenty-four-hour limit. I knew you could do it, Giles, if anyone could."

The five Ackroyd women were all smiles, beautiful again. Isabel was puzzled. "What message? I don't see a message."

"Oh, it's not in clear yet," Jane said, "but that's routine. This is obviously the secret message. Now all we have to do is decode it."

"Obviously?" Isabel asked. "How do you know? It looks like a random batch of letters to me."

"That's because you're not experienced in cryptanalysis," Elizabeth said gently. "Look at the path, the diagonal square. It's a perfectly clear path on the white squares, not a black box in the way; that in itself is very unusual. Then, it's twenty-eight letters, not a lot, but enough for a short message and almost twice as many as on the open diagonal from bottom left to top right. It's a simple pattern that can easily be followed mentally, even by a Russian spy, not like a Cardano Grille. Now look at the text." Elizabeth began reading. "'AMDIYSNCSSSFNLWPTMRDTNPRDCDW.' Only two vowels in twenty-eight letters. That's very improbable. That's the message, all right. It screams 'message.'"

"But if it's a cipher," Isabel argued, "some of the consonants could stand for vowels."

"It's not a substitution cipher," Lydia said. "See the three S's together? With another S two letters away and no other S's? That's very unusual."

"Aren't there ciphers where you change the letters that stand for other letters according to the previous substitution?"

"Sure. Ciphering machines work that way," Kitty said. "But this was solved mentally by a Russian spy who didn't have to write anything down to read the message, or, at least, to recognize that it was a message."

"The lower left and the lower right four-by-four fields are left undone," Jane said. "That fits the geometry of the diagonal square inside the large square perfectly. Zulkov didn't fill them in because he didn't need any letters from those fields. It wasn't because he couldn't solve those corners; other than 'eristics,' those corners are pretty easy."

"He didn't need any letters from the top left and top right corners either, but he filled those in." Isabel pointed out.

"Sure," Mary said, "because he needed those lights to get the letters on his diagonal square."

"Let's look at the message," Giles said. "I'll bet it's a transposition."

"How can it be a clear message with the letters mixed up?" Isabel asked. "Wouldn't there have to be the appropriate number of vowels if it were?"

"Sure," Elizabeth said, "but with only twenty-eight boxes available, the encoder probably just left out the vowels to get more words in and to make my life harder. English is a very redundant language. You could leave out every other letter in most messages and still transmit the information quite accurately."

"But there are two vowels, an 'A' and an 'I.'"

"These were probably necessary," Lydia said, "to make the message intelligible."

"Please remember," Barca said, "that the message almost certainly refers to political matters."

"We'll attack at the vowels," Giles said. "That's the weak point."

"AMDIY," Elizabeth said. "Does that mean anything to anyone? I'm considering 'Y' as a vowel for the moment. Think. It should. In the whole text three vowels in five letters? There must be something there."

"Try six letters," Isabel said. "AMDIYS. Three of the letters, D, I, and S, that's almost what Barca said was one of the Russians' possible areas of interest. SDI, the Strategic Defense Initiative."

"It comes out right," Jane said, "if you interchange the letters in pairs. Transpose each pair so it becomes 'MAIDSI.' Perfect."

"But that's backward," Isabel said.

"No law that it has to read forward," Lydia said. "That's

cute, a simple transposition by pairs. If it works, that explains how Zulkov was able to read the message mentally. Write it out, Giles."

"MAIDSYCNSSFSLNPWMTDRNTRPCDWD," Giles wrote.

"Hey," Kitty said, "look at the last four letters. Reading backward, like 'SDI,' it's almost 'MDWDC,' the Mass Destruction Weapons Disarmament Conference."

"That's it," Mary said. "The message doesn't necessarily start where we started. If we tie the ends together, make a circle, the 'M' from the beginning hooks on to make the end letters, read backward, 'MDWDC,' the Mass Destruction Weapons Disarmament Conference. In fact, we now have 'Strategic Defense Initiative at'—the 'A' has to stand for 'at'—'at Mass Destruction Weapons Disarmament Conference.' Let's reverse the coded text and put what we know first."

"*SDIAMDWDC*PRTNRDTMWPNLSFSSNCY."

Isabel studied the text. "I still don't see a message, and I'm accustomed to reading students' writings."

"Try breaking it in different places," Giles suggested. "'SDIAMDWDC' is surely not the beginning of the message."

They all bent over their pads. There was silence for several minutes. "I can't find the beginning," Jane said. "Every time I think I'm making sense, I hit an impossible combination that makes no sense."

Isabel put down her pencil and studied the puzzle. "Maybe we shouldn't make a continuous string of it," she said. "It might be logical to break it into four parts, the sides of the square."

Giles stared at her, excited. "Yes, Isabel, yes. That's it. That has to be it." He wrote four lines. "Counterclockwise, of course, since we got 'SDIAMDWDC' by reversal from the clockwise path. Starting with 'A.'

"AWDCDRPN
TDRMTPW
LNFSSSC
NSYIDM.

"Now we reverse them in pairs.

   "WACDRDNP
   DTMRPTW
   NLSFSSC
   SNIYMD."

"No, that's no good, we've lost 'SDIAMDWDC.'"

"Why does it have to be in one direction only?" Isabel asked.

"It doesn't," Giles said. "It doesn't. That's our problem. We're so used to going clockwise in a single continuous path that—"

"And we're so used to going from left to right and from top to bottom that—"

"Please remember that the encoded message has to be easy to decode mentally by a Russian."

"We're almost there," Giles said. "I feel it. And if we work the sides of the square right to left, that's no harder than going around in one direction. The reversal by pairs is simple enough."

"But where do we start?" Lydia asked. "The encoder had designed a very simple code hidden in a crossword. So simple it could be decoded mentally by a Russian spy. But the problems he presented us were tremendous. To recognize that there was a code to begin with. Then to find where the message was, the pattern of the text. Then to realize it was a transposition code without vowels, practically. Then to realize it was in reversed pairs. All very simple steps, but virtually impossible to decode. Then he made it read along the sides of the square, diagonally and discontinuously, from right to left; still very simple, but again adding difficulty. Do you think that this genius would start at the 'A' in Box 7? It's not in his character to do anything that straightforward."

They all stared at their copies of the puzzle. "When I was dean of students," Isabel said, "and a student came to me with a problem, I learned to imagine what I would do if I were that student. I could often figure out what she would do next long before she did. You have to think like the encoder. Here is a complex mind forced to hide a message in the plain sight of tens of thousands of people, so that it would be practically impossible to decode even if a cryptanalyst knew there was a message there, yet the message had to be so easy to decode that a Russian spy could recognize it at once. All the spy had to do was solve the crossword puzzle, which for him was easy, start at the beginning, follow along the sides of the square, but only from right to left, reverse the letters in pairs, and there was the message."

"So where do we start," Elizabeth asked, "now that we are simpatico with the Russian encoder? Or should we try each of the twenty-eight boxes? It ain't elegant, but it would work."

"Box 29," Isabel said simply. "And go right to left."

"Why 29?" Giles asked.

"Because the puzzle was published on June twenty-ninth."

"Ohmygod, yes," Giles said. "Kitty, write this down. 'RPN'; go to the bottom and move left and up, 'WPTMRDT'; go to the right side and move down, left, 'CSSSFNL'; stay at the right side and move up, left, 'NSYIDMA'; go to the top and move down, left, 'WDCD.' Put them all together."

"RPNWPTMRDTCSSSFNLNSYIDMAWDCD."

"Now transpose in pairs."

"PRWNTPRMTDSCSSNFNLYSDIAMDWDC."

"Perfect. Our 'SDIAMDWDC' is intact, at the end, which makes sense. Let's get the whole message."

"'PR' is 'PRESIDENT,'" Jane said.

"'WNTPRMT' is 'WILL NOT PERMIT,'" Elizabeth said.

"'DSCSSN' is 'DISCUSSION,'" Mary said.

"'FNLY' is 'OF ONLY,'" Kitty said.

"And 'SDIAMDWDC' is 'STRATEGIC DEFENSE INITIATIVE AT MASS DESTRUCTION WEAPONS DISARMAMENT CONFERENCE," Lydia said. "'(THE) PRESIDENT WILL NOT PERMIT (THE) DISCUSSION OF ONLY (THE) STRATEGIC DEFENSE INI-

TIATIVE AT (THE) MASS DESTRUCTION WEAPONS DISARMAMENT CONFERENCE.'"

"By Jove," Isabel said, "I think we've got it."

"You did it, Isabel," Elizabeth said. "Congratulations."

"I had the advantage of not being a cryptanalyst," Isabel said. "And I can't believe that Zulkov did all this mentally."

"It sounds a lot harder than it is," Giles said. "Don't forget, he didn't have to go through everything we did; he knew exactly where to look and exactly what to do. He just started at Box 29, and went around the square counterclockwise, not continuously, but reading each side of the square from right to left. He didn't have to decode the whole message to know this was the right crossword, the one with the secret message. When he transposed by pairs, the 'SDI' and the 'MDWDC' jumped out. That's why he was rushing to the Aeroflot office, where he could write everything down in privacy."

"Lydia," Barca said, "bring in the other two puzzles. Now."

"**W**EDNESDAY'S PUZZLE," MARY SAID, "EVERY body has a copy? Okay. Starting at Box 30 and going left, we get 'WPFADR.' Continuing left downward, we have 'TCLNRLD.' Dropping to the bottom, there's 'MRFSCRP.' Jumping to the middle of the right side, 'TPTNZSF,' and from the same point up to the left, 'F.' The coded message reads: 'WPFADRTCLNRLDMRFSCRPTPTNZSFF.' Transposing by pairs, the clear message is: 'PWAFRDCT-NLLRMDFRCSPRPTNTSZFF.' Okay?"

"That's what the central square reads, all right," Isabel said, "but if that's the message, it's not clear to me."

"It's not that bad," Jane said. "Assume that this one is political too—the spy can't be in two places at once—and that it's in the same field as the first. So now the encoder can use shorthand. If we let the first 'P' be 'PRESIDENT,' the 'W' is probably 'WILL.' When I take notes, I write 'h/w' for 'he will.'"

"'RMDFRCS' has to be 'ARMED FORCES,'" Lydia said.

"If that's right," Elizabeth said, "then 'PRPTN' isn't 'PRESCRIPTION;' it's more likely to be 'PROPORTION.' If so, then the 'T' that follows is 'TO.'"

"But there's no 'N' before 'PROPORTION,' for 'IN PROPORTION TO,'" Jane said. "Either it's left out, or the 'L' at the end of 'PROPORTIONAL' was left out."

"Either way it means the same thing," Kitty said. "Then 'SZ' must be 'SIZE.'"

"And 'RDCTN' is 'REDUCTION,'" Mary said. "Therefore 'LL' is 'ALL,' and it falls apart. '(THE) PRESIDENT WILL ASK FOR (A) REDUCTION (IN) ALL ARMED FORCES (IN) PROPORTION TO (THE) SIZE OF (THE) FORCES.' Boy, the Russians will *love* that."

"They don't have to love it," Kitty said, "as long as they know it's coming. If they know what the President's position is in advance, they can plan for it, attack it in advance, so that their tame propagandists can whip up public opinion against his policy."

"It's clear that the spy is very close to the President," Giles said. "He must be one of the people on the Presidential Adversarial Team working on the Mass Destruction Weapons Disarmament Conference."

"Let's see what Puzzle Number Three has to offer," Barca said, "before we make our minds up."

"I'm having trouble with today's puzzle," Mary said. "The paper is dated July first, and Box One isn't even on the diagonal square. In fact, there are black boxes blocking the square, too, and the distribution of vowels looks normal."

"It doesn't have to be the middle diagonal square," Isabel said. "Since it's July first, try starting at Box One and go around to the left as before."

"It's a long narrow rectangle," Mary said, lightly tracing the shape, "but it's clear all around, all consonants, not a single vowel, so it must be right." She printed the coded message: "RWWSCPN THCBNDRFRCRCNDLNCWTNP." "Now to transpose by pairs: 'WRSWPCTNCHNBRDRFRCNCLDC NTWPN.'"

"That's easy," Elizabeth said. "'WRSWPCT' is 'WARSAW PACT.'"

"'NCHNBRDR' is 'AND CHINA BORDER,'" Kitty said. "And 'FRC' is 'FORCES.'"

"This one," Jane said, "reads: 'WARSAW PACT AND CHINA BORDER FORCES (TO BE) INCLUDED (IN) COUNT (OF) WEAPONS.' Fits right in with the other two messages."

"Well, now we know who the spy must be," Barca said.

"We do?" Isabel was astounded.

"Not precisely," Barca admitted, "but the rest is routine. He is definitely one of the President's advisors, advocates, adversaries, whatever you want to call them, one of the Adversarial Team that is helping the President decide on his policy for the Mass Destruction Weapons Disarmament Conference."

"Couldn't it be one of the President' secretaries?" Isabel asked.

"No one sits in on the President's adversarial trials," Barca said, "but the 'attorneys,' the three or four people who present their arguments and briefs to the President, who is the final, the only, judge. The judge may ask questions of the advocates, but the main cross-examination is conducted by the proponents of the opposing positions, and, from what my friends tell me, the witness doesn't have any of the Constitutional protections. The advocates are not only expert in their own fields, but they come very well prepared, partly, I am sure, to avoid being torn to pieces by their opponents." Barca turned to Mary. "Who are the members of this particular team?"

"It's a secret," Mary said. "But I called my sources after we decided that the spy might be a member of one of those teams, just in case. Let me check the list. Kitty, would you bring in a printout? The access code is 'adversary.'"

Kitty was back in a moment. "The finalists are," she said with a flourish, "Bishop Anders Maylinger; General Lasswell Connerly, Retired; and Professor Horton Fitzgerald."

"But these are highly respected." Isabel couldn't accept the idea. "One of them a Russian spy? That's ridiculous. Dr. Maylinger is a Nobel Peace Prize Laureate. He's done more for peace than any ten men, risked his life in Lebanon trying to save the hostages, and in Iran. General Connerly? No one in his right mind could even imagine him being pro-Russian; he's the prime advocate of the iron fist in diplomacy. And Professor Fitzgerald hates the Communists, been fighting to get the Sakharovs out of Russia, and Scharansky, for years."

"All of this is true," Barca said, "nevertheless, one of these three is a spy. There is no doubt about it. And I will net him, have no fear." He rose and addressed Giles. "Good work, Giles. As in the past, you've come up with a brilliant solution, though I do wish, in the future, you would not drag things out to the last second. Very dramatic, no doubt, but hard on the nerves. And thank you, Isabel, for your hypercubic epithet. Possibly if others"— he glared at his daughters—"would look outside their narrow little fields occasionally, we might have had less difficulty with what is, in truth, a simple little transpositional cipher. You may all go now. Get some sleep. I will need you tomorrow and you must all be fully rested. As usual, I will be working while you take your ease. Kitty, it's your turn to wake up early to get the *Gazette*. Breakfast at five-thirty, workroom at six."

"Why do we have to bother buying the paper?" Isabel asked. "Can't we get a copy late tonight from the *Gazette* itself? Surely some of your friendly sources have a line to every newspaper in Washington."

"Our not-so-friendly opponents may also have such a line," Barca replied. "I don't want anyone alerted that there is any interest at all in crosswords, or even in the *Gazette*. I did get one bit of information, however, that may be useful. Wesley Warren, the features editor of the *Gazette*, had evidently gotten several complaining calls about the quality of yesterday's puzzle. He was overheard calling Eugene Simon's office, telling him to shape up and directing him not to use that constructor again."

"Constructor X?" Giles asked. "Were any names mentioned?"

"No, but you'll track him down, I'm sure. It shouldn't

be very hard; one out of four."

"If Warren thinks yesterday's puzzle was bad," Isabel said, "wait until he looks at today's. He'll blow his top."

"More than that," Giles said. "He may even get rid of Simon. Warren would have no trouble replacing his cross-word editor; there are two top professionals in this area, Albert Kosgrow and Frederick Lindenmann. Both real pros."

"Which shows," Barca said, "how important it was to Simon to publish these puzzles, no matter how bad they were. This is the final nail in his coffin; he'll never be able to claim a momentary lapse for three clumsy puzzles in a row."

"Couldn't he have edited them?" Isabel asked. "Cleaned them up a little?"

"He was probably under orders," Giles said, "not to touch those puzzles. He must have been given some great inducement to work this way. Even spies have pride in their work."

"Maybe he was threatened," Barca said. "Or maybe he's a sleeper too. Whatever it was, we'll find out tomorrow. Meanwhile, I want you all to relax, rest, get all the sleep you can now. We're all on full alert from this moment on, so have all your equipment, and yourselves, ready to move on a moment's notice. I expect some action tomorrow." Barca walked to the door, opened it, and started walking to the study.

The five Ackroyd girls quickly and quietly rose and left the dining room, not even finishing their glasses of cold lemonade. Giles started following them; then, when he saw Isabel wasn't moving, said, "Come on, Isabel, let's go upstairs."

"Does Barca tell you when you can go to the toilet too?" she asked, her face dark.

"Of course," Giles said, "when we're in the middle of an operation. He knows what's necessary. Besides, I thought you wanted to—"

"I don't," she snapped. "I'm not a robot to be pro-grammed."

"It's not like that at all, Isabel. But if we have to work tomorrow, we really must rest now. I had very little sleep last night and the others had even less. One weak link may jeopardize the mission, or cause great damage. We all depend on each other to be in top shape. I'm sure Barca has informed Oliver of the situation by now."

"You can jump when he says 'frog'; I'm not going."

"Please, Isabel, don't be foolish. Barca knows what he's doing."

"No, he doesn't. He's all wrong. And I'm going to tell him. Right now." She walked quickly toward Barca's study.

"GO AWAY," BARCA SHOUTED IN RESPONSE TO ISABEL'S knock. "I'm busy."

"I have to talk to you," she shouted back through the closed door. "Right now. I'm coming in."

"And I want it done right now," Barca said into the phone, and hung up. He looked up, face flushed, and did not invite her to sit down. "Can't this wait?" he growled. "The MDWDC opens on the morning of the sixth. I have only four days to get everything done and tied up neatly."

"No, it can't wait, Barca," Isabel said, annoyed. "You're going about it all wrong."

"Going about what?" Barca's face took on the wolfish look Isabel had seen in his daughters' eyes.

"Whatever you were about to do. Isn't it clear that— look, in order for the secret message to be decoded, it had to appear on a specific day. The encoder, in order to have his message read, had to start it on the box numbered the same date the paper appeared."

"We proved that. So?"

"Don't you see? Eugene Simon, the crossword puzzle editor, he was the only one who could arrange for the puzzle to appear on the right day. He was the only one who could ensure that any puzzle with a message hidden in it would be accepted in the first place. Without him— Simon is the key. He has to be part of the spy ring."

"That's obvious. What about it?"

"What about it? Why don't you arrest—why don't you tell the FBI to arrest him? He must know who the encoder is."

"Undoubtedly he does. What then?"

"Make him talk. There are ways."

"Those ways, Isabel, will produce the answers the torturer wants to hear; they will not necessarily produce the truth."

"You can question the encoder too. Compare answers. Use what each one tells you against the other."

"Thank you for the advice, Isabel, but I am quite skilled at interrogation. Now go to sleep."

"Aren't you going to do *anything*? You said this case was a critical, a vital case. Are you going to let him get away with it?"

"For the while, yes. It is essential that they not be disturbed." He looked at her fallen face and relented. "Sit down, Isabel. I'm very busy, and must get certain things done quickly, but you won't rest until—" He drew a deep breath. "If I took them, or rather, had Simon and the encoder taken into custody, what would I gain?"

"You'd break up the spy ring, to begin with."

"Indubitably. I'm sure the Russians don't have a second crossword puzzle editor waiting in the wings in case Simon gets hit by a car. They do have another decoder to take Zulkov's place—that we know—and they may even have another encoder and constructor standing by, but it takes years to establish a crossword editor. Let us say we arrest or abduct Simon. Now what?"

"The Russians wouldn't get any more information about the President's fallback positions in the Disarmament Conference."

"I'm sure of that. But they have quite a bit of information already. When Zulkov's substitute gets here tonight, he'll have no trouble obtaining the three back issues of *The Capitol Gazette* and passing the secret messages on to Moscow. There's no way to stop him."

"Another car accident?"

"Why don't we just send a telegram to the KGB saying we know what you're doing, please take all precautions to hide your key people?"

"All right, but at least there wouldn't be any more messages passed on."

"The *spy* will not go out of business if Simon is arrested; he'll find, or be informed of, another way to communicate. And he will likely rise to even greater importance in the government in the near future. The spy may not even know—didn't you understand the import of our discussion yesterday? About why this slow, clumsy method of transmitting stolen information was used by the Russians?"

"Of course I did; it was to protect the identity of the spy."

"Yes, but it also—let me put it in proper order. What sort of message did the spy transmit to the encoder? Was it a message in clear? One that the encoder could understand?"

"No, I don't think so. It would be dangerous in case it was intercepted."

"Correct. The encoder was not necessarily a spy, remember? He did not have to know, and probably did not know, what he was putting into the crossword. What would he have made of, let me see"—he picked up the puzzle from the table—"'RPNWPTMRD' from the first puzzle? Nothing, I am sure, even if he tried to decode it. The encoder received a message that was already encoded; from here on in, we should call him the constructor. So what can he tell us? That someone hired him to make a crossword puzzle with twenty-eight letters in a certain position and then give it, or send it, to Eugene Simon? Maybe write his name a little differently on the sheet, or put a symbol on it for identification? So that Simon might not even know there was a secret message in the puzzle? So what do we gain by arresting either of them? What can they tell us about the spy? Don't you see, Isabel, they don't even know there *is* a spy? Or that a message is being transmitted to the Russians. How many readers does the *Gazette* have?"

"Aren't you going to watch the three adversaries? The ones working on the MDWDC? Tap their phones and everything? If you did it for Simon and the four crossword constructors, why not those three: the professor, the general, and the bishop? Especially the bishop."

Barca motioned to the phone. "I was about to do that when you interrupted me."

Isabel sat, deflated. "All right, Ackroyd, I see. I'm sorry. I'll go now."

"No, Isabel, wait another minute or two. Let me finish the picture. So the spy does not know who the encoder, the constructor, is. The spy does not know that his secret message is inserted, hidden, in a crossword puzzle; he doesn't know Eugene Simon, he doesn't know Zulkov, and, most important, none of them knows him. Zulkov doesn't know Simon or the constructor or the spy. Simon knows who the constructor is, or at least knows his pen name, but he doesn't know what the message is or even that there is a message. If Giles, as Hannibal, the great constructor of crosswords, could keep his secret for eighteen years, so can Constructor X, so maybe Simon doesn't even know the constructor. The constructor knows he sends his puzzles to Simon and that his puzzles contain a message, but he doesn't know even what the message is about. And were it not for a lucky accident, we wouldn't even suspect there was a message to begin with. Our spy is protected against any betrayal by anyone under any conditions or circumstances. So maybe the slow, clumsy technique was not so slow or so clumsy; maybe it was exactly right for its primary task, protecting the spy."

"So all we can do now, Ackroyd, is destroy the transmission line?"

"Precisely. Which I am not about to do just yet. I need Eugene Simon and Constructor X to function freely; there must not be the slightest indication that they are blown."

"The two of them get away scot free?"

"They're being watched very closely and very discreetly, Isabel. When I'm ready, we'll pick them up and interrogate them. Thoroughly." Barca looked like a very fierce wolf now. "We'll turn them inside out, you may be sure. But only after I get my hands on the spy."

"You seem very sure of that, Ackroyd. Are you really?"

"Within twenty-four hours," he said grimly. "Make that twenty-four hours and ten minutes, Isabel. I didn't count on your interruption. And with a little luck, possibly even before this day is out; it's still early." He smiled sweetly, for a wolf. "Now go get some rest, Isabel; we may need you later." His voice was warm, fatherly.

As Isabel reached the door, Barca said, "Don't challenge me again during this operation, Isabel." His voice was no longer warm. "You're not ready yet."

16

THE PRESIDENT GLANCED AT HIS WATCH AND HELD UP his hand almost apologetically. Professor Horton Fitzgerald stopped speaking at once. The bright lights glared at the three men seated opposite the President's desk, highlighting every fleeting emotion that crossed their faces. Fitzgerald looked a bit annoyed at the interruption, but immediately regained his bland look.

"I'm sorry," the President said. "We've run out of time; there are only five minutes left. Would you each take one minute to summarize your recommendations, everything we've discussed these past five days? You first, Anders, please."

Bishop Anders Maylinger took a moment to gather his thoughts. He swept his long gray hair back, took off his wire-rimmed glasses, and began speaking in the soft sweet tones known so well to the TV audiences. "In order to effect a change in a person, you must first understand his needs and his desires. This applies to a nation as well. From its point of view, the U.S.S.R. inherited a poor, disordered land which, after World War One, was attacked by the other major nations, including the United States. A generation later it was attacked by Fascist armies which devastated large areas of the country. The leaders of the U.S.S.R. determined that never again would their country

103

be attacked and invaded, and that the way to ensure this was to build a strong military, second to none, and to make sure that the countries bordering their land could not be the springboard for an attack on them.

"They built the world's strongest military machine, one capable of defeating any probable combination of enemies, even the Chinese and, just before their security arrangements were completed, the United States, under the Reagan administration, began building its military strength to the point where the U.S.S.R. could no longer feel secure. In the Soviet government, as in ours, there is a spectrum of opinion, hawks to doves. The hawks feel that the U.S. is preparing to attack them, that the buildup of U.S. arms, even defensive arms, is in preparation for an offensive strike to destroy the motherland and its political system. They point to the unending vilification of their political system and the attacks on its philosophic base, Marxism. These hawks want to make a preemptive attack now, while the U.S. is not fully prepared. They point to our nonexistent civil defense system, our small armed forces, and the weak will of our allies. They believe that if they attack now, suddenly, with, say, half their missiles, and simultaneously their allies launch a conventional attack on our allies in Europe, Asia, and South America, they will find that under the threat of using the rest of their missiles, neither the U.S. nor its allies will dare to retaliate against the U.S.S.R.

"The concept of a cheap quick victory is very tempting to the government, but the doves in the Politburo are not without support either. They point out that the result of any war is uncertain, that the actions of any head of state are not completely predictable, that one minor miscalculation could leave the U.S.S.R. and the rest of the world a radioactive sheet of glass. As long as the U.S.S.R. is safe, not directly threatened, there is no reason to risk annihilation. Marxism must eventually conquer as a historical imperative, and capitalism contains within itself the seeds of its own destruction.

"But this viewpoint can prevail only if there is no direct

threat to the U.S.S.R. The installation of cruise missiles practically on the border of the Warsaw Pact nations, the increased military spending by the U.S., and, worst of all, the beginning of the implementation of the Strategic Defense Initiative, so aptly called the star wars system, has upset the balance of strength. If we continue to test and to come closer to installing the SDI, I predict the hawks will take control of the Politburo and, in their fear, will lash out with a preemptive attack."

"What is your recommendation, Bishop Maylinger?" the President asked.

"Draw back. Stop all work on SDI. Halt delivery of advanced weapons systems to Europe. Reduce the money allotted to the military in the next budget. Offer to go to Moscow to discuss the permanent institutionalization of detente. At the coming Mass Destruction Weapons Disarmament Conference make it the policy of the United States never, under any conditions, to initiate the use of nuclear weapons. Clamp down on anti-Russian propaganda. Restore confidence in the peaceful intentions of the United States."

The President completed his notes on his ever-present yellow legal pad. "Thank you, bishop," he said. "Let's hear from you now, Lasswell. One minute only, please."

General Lasswell Connerly, Retired, stood up, as straight as when he was on active duty. He stepped behind his chair, put his hands on its back, and leaned forward earnestly. His shaven head gleamed in the glare of the lights, and his heavy thick black-rimmed glasses flashed as he spoke. "As you know, sir, I disagree with what Bishop Maylinger has presented as facts as well as with his interpretation of them. And I emphatically disagree with his conclusions and his recommendations. If the Russians have any fear at all, it is fear of their own people and those of their satellites. They know their system is a failure and they cannot, *because* of the system, ever feed, clothe, and house their people. They have chosen to attack, either directly or through the use of their surrogates, their neighbors as well as weak countries all over the world, not out of fear of military attack by the United States but to give their impoverished and enslaved citizens an outside enemy to take their minds off the great problems inside Russia.

"The Russians are not fomenting trouble in South America, Africa, Asia, and Europe, not to mention the Middle East, because of fear of a U.S. attack; they are not invading Afghanistan or crushing Poland because they're afraid we'll bomb them. This is nothing but old-fashioned colonialism, the imperialism they are constantly accusing us of. When we had the atom bomb and the world was helpless before us, we did not use it, or threaten to use it. Instead, we implemented the Marshall Plan to freely help other countries, just as we helped Russia.

"On the other hand, we do have to face up to the situation as it exists now, a situation that our previous administrations had allowed to come about. The Russians are now stronger than us militarily, they have absolute control of their satellite nations, their government has absolute control of its people. If they launched a preemptive attack that wiped out much of our military establishment, and threatened to use the rest of their missiles on our cities if we retaliated, would you, Mr. President, order that strike? Can you depend, absolutely depend, on our European allies? Suppose the Russians simultaneously attacked Germany, West Germany, twenty thousand tanks rolling across Europe? Would you use nuclear weapons in that theater? The Russians are not afraid of starting a nuclear war; the only thing that prevents them from striking westward is the uncertainty as to your action, reaction. That is why they're constantly probing, testing, starting small fires in every trouble spot around the globe. That is why they are constantly spreading their propaganda through favorable or accommodating media, that there is no difference between us and them. And it works, Mr. President. If you think you have the country solidly behind you, you are wrong. Dead wrong.

"So"—General Connerly took a deep breath—"much as I hate the idea, I recommend accommodation at this time. At every meeting, discussion, conference, give a little, take a little. Make sure you get something, preferably the equivalent, in return for what you give up. Not only because we need all the help we can get, but to show strength, or, rather, to avoid showing weakness. If the Russians ever decide you're afraid of them, they will increase the pressure until you crack, and the world will die. Bend, Mr. President, but don't break. Trade, Mr. President; don't give anything free. Show them that we, that you, our representative, are dealing from strength, not from fear."

"Thank you, General," the President said. "Will you wait a moment, Horton, while I jot down a few notes?"

Professor Horton Fitzgerald did not look like a fire-breathing dragon, as he had so often been portrayed in the editorial page cartoons. Short, plump, and cuddly, he seemed more a Paddington Bear than a Godzilla, but those who came up against him in debate soon felt the sting in his tongue.

"Maylinger and Connerly," Fitzgerald said, his high, shrill voice contrasting oddly with his teddy-bear appearance, "regardless of their intent and, I hope, their loyalty to this country, are treating this problem as though there is a rationality, an accepted medium of discourse, between the United States and Russia. There is not. Our goal is freeing; their goal is conquering. Our method is open competition and free choice; their method is conversion by the sword. Our philosophy is based on the state in the service of the people; their philosophy is that the citizen is owned by the state. There is no compatibility between the two systems possible; no middle ground where the two nations can, albeit with some discomfort for each, exist together. We should name, once and for all, the battle: It is Armageddon, the final struggle between Good and Evil. And we should realize, should understand, for our very lives, what is at stake and what we are dealing with.

"The Russians will not be satisfied if we weaken ourselves, no matter what we call it: exemplar of good will, inducement to follow suit, sign of lack of aggression, no matter. They will recognize the act for what it is, a sign of weakness. No bully has ever been stopped by a show of weakness, no attacker by an accommodation of his claims. Remember Hitler? All he wanted was a little lebensraum? And all the Russians want is freedom from fear? Ha! Nor will the Russians be slowed down by a treaty or any other agreement. Such an agreement, which *we* will honor, will be broken from the first day on by the Russians. Remember the Helsinki Agreements? The Third Basket? The human rights for their own people for which we traded ownership of a third of Europe? Today our soft-headed liberals are urging us not to bring up human rights at the Helsinki Agreement Verification Meetings for fear of offending the torturers and murderers. Why, under such circumstances, should the Russians ever abide by an agreement any longer than is convenient for them? No, any treaty they will sign can serve only to weaken us and to strengthen them. And subsequent treaties will be more and more one-sided until, finally, we are presented with an application to become one more Soviet Socialist Republic."

"Your time is up, Professor," the President said calmly. "What recommendation do you have, consistent with your argument?"

"Go into a crash military buildup. Yes, throw money at the problem. Institute a draft of all citizens between sixteen and fifty-five; there is always work someone can do if he is not bedridden. Four weeks of military service every year for everyone. A massive civil defense program. Tighten all alliances; warn any recalcitrants that if there is not full cooperation with us, we will remove all our defense installations and personnel and announce that if they are attacked, we will not lift a finger to help them. Warn the outlaw nations, the Cubans, the Libyans, the Iranians, the Syrians, that unless they stop all anti-U.S. actions and pull back their Hessians and provocateurs within a stated short time, we will remove them from the face of the earth. Draw a line, in terms of actions as well as geography, that the Russians may not cross, and prepare to make an all-out preemptive attack on them *automatically* if that line is crossed. Strange as it may seem to the nonrational, such actions will prevent a war for the forseeable future."

The President wrote rapidly for a full minute, then said, "Thank you, gentlemen, for your very helpful time and effort, and for allowing me to take you away, on such short notice, from your other affairs."

The three advocates murmured assurances. The President continued. "I want to assure you that the positions, the defendants, in effect, I assigned to you were for the purpose of enabling me to examine the three major positions on this issue, and that I realize that the arguments you presented, though not entirely foreign to your expressed views, do not necessarily represent your personal views fully and accurately any more than a court-assigned criminal lawyer's actions exemplify his personal standards of probity. I admire your flexibility, as shown by your ability to reverse roles when requested, to attack the weak points in your claims as though you were cross-examining yourselves."

The President tapped his papers into an orderly pile and stacked them on top of the briefs. "I have one more request to make of each of you," he said. "As you leave my office, one of my aides will show each of you to a quiet, private room, where I will ask you for one more service, something that will take no more than an hour of your time." He glanced at his watch. "Two o'clock. Couldn't be helped. You will each be served lunch, a late lunch, I'm sorry to say, in your rooms. I'll be in to see you while you're eating."

"Aren't you going to give us your decision on this matter?" General Connerly asked.

"I haven't decided yet," the President said. "I think I know what I will do, but I want to go over my notes of this last meeting for a few minutes first. There is good rationale for each of the three general positions, the lines of action I heard today, and a great deal of risk as well.

I will make the decision shortly. I must; there is a great deal to prepare before next Tuesday."

The President pushed a button on his desk, and as the three advisors rose to leave, he said, "I also want to assure you, each of you, that whether I accept all, part, or none of your recommendations, this series of meetings has helped me make some very important decisions for our country, decisions I alone can, and must, make. I wish it were possible to publicize the service you have done your country over the past three weeks, the patience and grace with which you accepted the challenge, and the skill you showed in your briefs and arguments. I need not remind you of the need for confidentiality. Thank you again; I will see each of you, in turn, in a short time."

17

"THAT'S ALL RIGHT, PROFESSOR FITZGERALD," THE President said, "finish your coffee while I talk; it won't take long. I've finalized my decision. Now I need your help, you and your colleagues. I know it's not completely in accord with your position, nor does it follow your recommendations, but my proposal is, I believe, the one with the minimum risk and the maximum chance of success. Further, it is the one that Congress and the American people will support, and, as President, I must take cognizance of the people I represent."

"You make it sound like something I would not care to support myself, Mr. President." Horton Fitzgerald looked troubled. "In my experience, the majority is usually wrong, and that is particularly true of Congress." He sighed like a tired little teddy bear. "Well, whatever it is, I will do my job. But I will not promise to lend my support to something I believe to be wrong."

"Just don't oppose it publicly, Professor, with anything you may have learned from our little mock trials of the past few weeks."

"I have never done anything dishonorable in my life, Mr. President, and I don't intend to start now. What do you want me to do?"

"Write a speech, or, rather, the first third of a speech,

111

for me. No more than a thousand words. Don't worry about the rhythm of my way of speaking; I will rewrite it myself—this is too important to be left to a speech-writer. Give me the approach, the reasoning, the justification, an orderly presentation of the facts, and I will do the rest. If something strikes you, a powerful phrase or a slogan, by all means include that. I need to have the hearts and minds of the world with me."

"This is the speech you will deliver at the opening of the Mass Destruction Weapons Disarmament Conference?"

"Exactly. I will propose a ten percent unilateral reduction in all United States weapons across the board, and invite the Soviet Union to do the same. If they accept, if they actually join us in this, it will mean the world is well on the way to peace, and we will do our part wholeheartedly to keep the process going."

"And if they do not reciprocate, Mr. President?"

"Then I will know what to do. Can you finish in an hour, Professor?"

"Easily. But why ask me to write this speech, knowing how I feel? Why not use your regular speechwriters?"

"It would take hours to brief them, and even then I could not be sure that every nuance of every argument was fully apprehended, much less understood. You and your colleagues have had three weeks of total immersion in this matter. No one on my staff is better qualified to write this speech. Then, too, security. Right now there are only four of us in the entire nation who know my decision; I don't want to make that five. Or more. This is my custom, as you will know should I require your services again, and it is the way I ensure there will be no leaks. For speeches of this importance I don't even use a secretary; my wife types it out herself."

"Very well, sir, if that's the way you want it. But this decision—with all due respect, Mr. President, you are opening the window of opportunity for a first strike by the Russians."

"I am aware of the risks, Professor Fitzgerald. I have

weighed them against the possible gains, and I believe it will work. Thank you again for your help. I must see your colleagues now."

"Parts two and three?"

"Unless you'd rather write the conclusion?"

"I never did like sad endings, Mr. President."

"I'd like you to write the middle portion, General, the body of the speech."

"That's easy, sir, but the long windup, the hearty thanks—that sounds like you're going to ask me to do something I think is wrong."

"In your military career, General, you sometimes followed orders you disagreed with."

"Many times, sir. Each time it ended badly; good men lost their lives unnecessarily. When I was on active duty, I sometimes gave my opinion of the actions I was ordered to take. I followed orders, but when I could, I presented my ideas. I am no longer on active duty, Mr. President. I will do what you want, but I reserve the right to disagree."

"Of course, as long as you don't oppose me publicly with information you picked up at our meetings."

"I would do nothing to hurt our country, Mr. President. What is your decision?"

"I am going to pull all our cruise missiles out of Europe, General, and invite the Russians to make a reciprocal move."

"The Russians will see this as a sign of weakness, sir. It may well encourage them to apply further pressure on our allies, particularly Germany."

"Then I will take whatever steps are necessary. On the other hand, world opinion may pressure them into removing their intermediate-range missiles to behind the Urals."

"It's not a balanced situation, Mr. President. Even if they do pull back those missiles, it's a lot easier for the Russians to move them back again than for us to get our cruise missiles resited in Europe."

"It's a test of intentions, General. If they meet us half-

ACROSS

1 g + 2g + 3g + ...
4 Be caustic
11 Jackie's second
14 Daisy intro
15 Everlys hit, "___Clown"
16 Heavyweight?
17 "How now?___?":
   Hamlet
18 Phony
20 Ancient folklore
22 Music appreciation
23 Playing area?
24 Soapbox occupant
26 Summer sign
27 Gettin' broader
29 Superlatively atypical
30 *Avis*'s flaps
31 Symbols for lutetium
33 Serenade Diana?
34 Full of tricks
35 Cat's dog
37 "Ferd'nand" cartoonist
40 Backer's favorite sign
43 Freeway motorcyclists,
   maybe
45 November obligation
46 Pick up the phone
49 Erode
51 Do as you're told
52 Feather vanes
53 ___of hay
54 *2001* computer
55 What *immerger* means
58 About 20,000 cps
61 Rigorous chastisement
62 Wet wiggler, old style
63 Thatcher's beau
64 "The___llama/He's a
   beast": Nash
65 June honoree
66 Oscar song from *Nashville*
67 Sexist suffix?

DOWN

1 Agana's land
2 Astairelike
3 National paper
4 ___*Sons*
5 H.S. subj.
6 Accepted Mae's
   invitation?
7 Face value-wise
8 Hammering Scandinavian
9 Gardner and Averback
10 He portrayed a 43-Across
11 Suddenly
12 Some cosmetics
13 Gusset
19 Lascivious
21 Jose or Juan
25 Up to
26 Pen pal?
27 Existed
28 "___be!"
32 Pouch
36 Velocipede stunts
37 Kills
38 Call-day connector
39 Cryptographer's need
40 1984 Derby winner
41 a k a Othello®
42 49ers' find
44 Longstreet's dog
45 Lennon debut album
46 Humiliated
47 Crab, e.g.
48 Used a lathe
50 Bitty bird
52 Chekhov's uncle
54 Singer's rival
56 Pedestal figure
57 John Paul II, e.g.
59 Mismeasuring tailor
60 Johnnie Ray hit

FRIDAY, JULY 2

way, we may have staved off a nuclear war."

"If they read the action wrong, sir, it may bring on a preemptive attack."

"Write the speech so they don't misunderstand, Connerly. I'm depending on you."

"Give the U.S.S.R. most favored nation status?" Bishop Maylinger lost his beatific look. "Is that all, Mr. President? It's an empty gesture that will have no significant effect."

"They've been asking for it since Jackson-Vanik, Bishop."

"But it's so little. It will help our business interests as much as it helps the U.S.S.R."

"If they offer a little something in return, Bishop, I would be willing to carry things a step further."

"What will match our offer, Mr. President? Lowering the price of caviar and sables? We really should do something in terms of unilateral disarmament. Destroy the MX missiles, stop work on the Stealth bomber, mothball five aircraft carriers and ten nuclear submarines. Then see what the U.S.S.R. will do in return."

"I don't dare risk that, Bishop. If we weaken our military significantly, we may strengthen their hawks."

"On the contrary, Mr. President, only if we do something of real significance will their doves gain ascendancy. We will have the opinion of the world behind us; our relations with the Third World will improve tremendously. We will be the leaders of, the champions of, Peace on Earth."

"I will have too much opposition in Congress if I disarm. This compromise is the best I can achieve; if the U.S.S.R. responds at all, we can take the next step with greater confidence."

"It isn't enough; the U.S.S.R. will read it as an insult."

"We shall see. Will you write the close of the speech, Bishop? With a prayer for peace and understanding at the close?"

"Of course, yes, but my heart will not be in it."

"But you will do a good job, won't you?"

"I always do a good job, Mr. President, even under the worst conditions."

18

"**A**NOTHER UGLY CONSTRUCTION," ISABEL SAID. "EVEN if Eugene Simon is part of the spy ring, he must know that he's calling attention to himself by publishing such rotten puzzles."

"It isn't that bad," Giles said. "Some of the clues are good. Look at 16 Across, 33 Across, 35 Across, 64 Across, nothing to be ashamed of there. And there's 8 Down, 26 Down, 50 Down, and 59 Down. Whoever did this is a real pro."

"The pattern is clumsy," Isabel pointed out.

"What would you have him do, Isabel?" Giles asked. "He has to have two lines of consonants next to each other, no way to avoid it, and there are a lot of low-frequency letters. I don't think I could have done any better."

"Why don't you two," Elizabeth said, "fight about whatever you're really fighting about later, in the privacy of your suite? We have to get the message to Barca *asap*. Call it out, Kitty."

"Starting at Box 2," Kitty read, "it's 'SUNWT TXECPLNRTRLCDLTPWSNTSTS.' I've already transposed the pairs. It reads 'USWNTTEXPC NLTRLRDCTLWPNSSTST.' The message is: 'U.S. WILL NOT—' I don't see the next word."

"Something's wrong with that," Jane said. "Let's go

118

to the end. 'WPNS' has to be 'WEAPONS' but 'STST' isn't clear."

"'NLTRL' could be 'UNILATERAL,'" Mary said.

"That's it," Elizabeth said. "Then 'RDCT' must be 'REDUCTION.' There's no 'N' because he didn't have enough letters left. That part of the message reads 'UNILATERAL REDUCTION ALL WEAPONS.' He also dropped one 'L' as redundant."

"'UNILATERAL REDUCTION ALL WEAPONS AS TEST,'" Lydia said. "Now it all falls apart. It's not 'U.S. *WILL NOT*'; it's 'U.S. WILL INITIATE.' 'XPC' is 'TEN PERCENT,' the *ten* is in Roman numerals because it's shorter than 'ten' or 'one zero,' and if he used 'one zero,' it could be misunderstood."

"'UNITED STATES WILL INITIATE (A) TEN PERCENT REDUCTION (OF) ALL WEAPONS AS (A) TEST,'" Isabel said. "No doubt about it. Let's take it to Barca."

"Who'd have thought it?" Barca said, shaking his head. "I would rather have put my money on the President's granddaughter before. . . . " Barca was still in his dressing gown, but his eyes were no longer sleepy.

"But he was the hawk of hawks," Isabel said.

"What better disguise?" Giles said. "The perfect spy."

"But he was always speaking out," Isabel said, "very forcefully, against Russia. I would think he would have *promoted* communism."

"There are plenty of 'useful idiots,' as Lenin called them, in America," Barca said, "working hard to persuade us how terrible we are and how great it would be to serve Big Brother. Professor Fitzgerald's stated views were so extreme that they may have dissuaded some of his students from opposing Marxism."

"Was he a sleeper," Isabel asked, "or turned?"

"My guess would be both," Barca said. "I don't mean he was a Russian cuckoo who was slipped into the eagle's nest forty years ago, but rather that he was enlisted as a student along with dozens of other promising prospects, and was kept as a sleeper until he rose to a position of trust, to be activated only when a sufficiently important operation made it necessary."

"The Mass Destruction Weapons Disarmament Conference," Giles said.

"Precisely. And I'm sure the activation did not involve any personal contact or traceable communication."

"If I were the spy's controller," Isabel said, "for simplicity's sake I would use *The Capitol Gazette*. The same technique that transmitted the secret information."

"A crossword?" Giles asked. "But we agreed—we analyzed that the spy did not know how his messages were transmitted."

"Not that," Isabel said. "And not a news item; too uncontrollable. An ad."

"I do believe you've hit it," Barca said. "Kitty, check the *Gazette* starting from three-and-a-half weeks back to about five weeks back. A Russian ad. Turn on the computer modem to search the newspaper database. Set it for anything Russian being advertised: vodka, caviar, furs, the usual."

"Aeroflot," Isabel said positively. "I'm beginning to understand, feel, how the spymaster thinks. An Aeroflot ad. A half-page ad, at least."

Barca studied her for a moment. "Yes, Kitty," he said, "Aeroflot."

Kitty was already at the computer keyboard. After a few minutes she pressed a button, and the plotter began humming. "It's at a reduced scale," Kitty said, tearing the sheet out of the plotter, "but the graphics are perfectly legible. Five weeks ago. Aeroflot is offering, for one month only, a sixteen-and-two-thirds percent reduction in fares from Washington to Moscow starting July sixth, so that progressive citizens of the United States can have the opportunity to meet the peaceloving Russian people."

"And July sixth," Jane said, "is the opening day of the Mass Destruction Weapons Disarmament Conference. The key has to be sixteen-and-two-thirds percent in an Aeroflot ad."

"I knew it would be like that," Isabel said smugly. "Now, let's get the whole gang."

"Timing, my dear," Barca said, "timing. First we get the spy, then Eugene Simon, then the constructor."

"What about the mastermind?" Isabel said. "The one who set up this whole affair?"

"The spymaster?" Barca said. "Oh, he's in Russia. Untouchable, at least for now. I am sure there is no one in the U.S. who knows anything at all about this little project, much less who the principals are. Possibly no one in Russia either other than the spymaster himself. Not even the head of the KGB. From all the evidence, this was played very close to the vest by a single controller."

"Then let's get started," Isabel said. "I want to get this over with."

"Ah, youth, youth." Barca shook his head. "So impetuous." Isabel's face fell. "Never mind, my dear, we will act very soon. Today, if possible. But first, a bit of preparation, then your assignments. Eat a good breakfast, then report back here."

"Aren't you going to eat breakfast, Father?" Lydia asked.

"Later, Lydia, I want to keep my stomach empty for a while; eating dulls the senses. After breakfast Giles and Isabel will report to me in the study; I will have decided by then."

"Nothing for us, Barca?" Lydia sounded disappointed.

"For what I am presently considering, Lydia, Giles is the one best suited."

"Then why is Isabel going? If there's trouble, she'd be—"

"I don't anticipate that kind of trouble; this is a small, middle-aged academic we're dealing with. Isabel's function is to provide the rationale for the visit and make Giles look harmless. Kitty? A small car, please, fully prepared. Check it yourself. Mary? What is the distance to Fitzgerald's house?"

"Thirty minutes, Barca, if they miss the morning rush hour. Fifty minutes if they start at eight."

"I think it would be best to start early, for insurance, but to be at his front door a bit after nine. Fitzgerald will be more relaxed after breakfast."

"Anything else?" Jane asked.

"For the moment, no; just hold yourselves in readiness from this moment until the end of the operation. Go now." The five women turned and left, Lydia leading this time.

"Will Oliver be going with us?" Isabel asked.

"Most assuredly," Barca said thoughtfully. "He may well be needed."

✖✖✖✖✖✖✖✖✖✖✖✖✖✖✖✖✖✖✖✖ 19 ✖✖✖

AT THE DOOR ISABEL TURNED BACK TO FACE BARCA. "You sounded as though you had the whole operation planned. Why do we have to report back to you after breakfast?"

"I have one of the possible scenarios planned, Isabel. Now I want to think about the others."

"It seems we have no choice but to turn him over to the FBI."

"There are always several choices, Isabel, in any situation. The trick is to find the best one."

She thought for a moment. "You said earlier that you were waiting to find the spy before you went after Simon and Encoder X." Barca nodded agreement. "Well, we've found the spy, and Giles and I are going to visit him this morning. What about Simon? Is that where you're going to send Lydia?"

"Lydia is always straining at the leash to go out into the field, but Simon will be your assignment. After you find Encoder X."

"But there are four crossword constructors," she protested. "We'll be driving around all day. Can't you go to Simon if you don't want to send Lydia? And the other four to the constructors?"

"You may get information from Encoder X that will be useful in your dealings with Simon. None of us can go to

123

any of them safely. It would look very odd, after living in Washington all my life, if I or any member of my family were to decide suddenly to visit any of the crossword constructors, or even Eugene Simon, particularly since I am not known as a crossword puzzle aficionado. No, that has to be you and Giles bringing greetings from the New York Cruciverbal Club."

Mollified, she turned again to go. Barca stopped her. "Let me give you something to put your mind to while you are waiting. A puzzle. Yesterday morning, shortly after we discovered that the spy was transmitting information about the President's decisions regarding the MDWDC, I had all three of the Adversaries involved placed under heavy surveillance: mail, phone, personal contact, the same kind of net I placed around Simon and his four regular constructors. During that twenty-four-hour period of airtight coverage, the President gave three different messages to each of the three Adversaries analyzing the MDWDC for him, and we discovered that Professor Horton Fitzgerald was the spy."

"We're aware of that, Barca. What is the point you're making?"

"Since that time," Barca continued, "Professor Fitzgerald has not left his home nor had any visitors. He did not speak with anyone on the phone nor did he receive or send any mail. Yet shortly after he left the President's office, he transmitted his secret information to Constructor X. As long as you are doing nothing, Giles, Isabel, figure out how he did it."

"You said twenty-four-hour period," Isabel said. "Does that mean Fitzgerald and the others are not under surveillance now?"

"Simon is still being watched, but I don't think it is necessary to watch Fitzgerald and the constructors anymore, and it is rather costly in terms of manpower; I do not have unlimited use of the FBI, you know."

"But I thought you could—"

"Only when there is truly an emergency, my dear. Don't worry; they will not get away, nor will Fitzgerald have

124

any more messages to send. Even if he did, we could not—Fitzgerald clearly has some way to transmit a secret message to Constructor X that our net cannot contain, so we do not need the net. Besides, it would be inconvenient. If any of us decided to visit Fitzgerald or any of the constructors, we would be photographed and identified by the FBI. We can't have that."

"Then how do we visit Simon?"

"When I order you to take Simon, the watchers will have been sent away."

"Then why not take them away now?"

"Are you sure there is only one spy? Possibly there is a second, somewhere high up, using Simon in a similar way. I'm going to keep Simon sewed up for a bit longer." He turned to Giles. "You've been silent. Any ideas on how Fitzgerald transferred the message to Encoder X?"

"Someone on the President's staff?" Giles suggested.

"Other than the President, his secretary, and the chauffeur who took Fitzgerald home, our spy was isolated completely. But please don't think along those lines. The only reason for the crossword code, we agreed, was to keep anyone from knowing that the spy existed and, equally, from knowing that Fitzgerald was the spy. That anyone means even the head of the KGB in Washington. So there is no contact with Fitzgerald allowed, not even a dead drop."

"How about a blinker from an upstairs window in Fitzgerald's house?" Giles offered. "A semaphore? A window-blind code?"

"Not acceptable, Giles, for the same reason. Nothing that could involve Fitzgerald in any way, or even point toward Fitzgerald. The transmission had to be anonymous."

"Homing pigeon?" Isabel asked. "A different animal? A cat or a dog with a message tucked into its collar, going home to Constructor X's house?"

"Not only uncertain, but dangerous. If it was seen being tossed out the window or let out the door, Fitzgerald becomes an object of suspicion. But the reports show *nothing* entered or left his house, even when he wasn't home. That house was blanketed."

"Radio?" Isabel asked.

"There was a continuous sweep of all frequencies by three different receivers out of phase with each other. Nothing was picked up. Besides—"

"A burst transmission," Giles broke in. "That would be possible to miss even with a triple setup."

"What's a burst transmission?" Isabel asked.

"A highly compressed message. You tape it at a very slow tape speed and send it at a very high speed. Twenty-eight letters could be sent in a fraction of a second. It would be very easy to miss as the searching receivers swept across the radio frequency band."

"No," Barca said. "If a radio transmission were feasible, *certain* of never being detected, the crossword code wouldn't have been used. Fitzgerald, or, rather, the spymaster who set all this up some years ago, knew that radio transmission, even bursts, can be intercepted if someone happens to be on the same frequency at the time, as many receivers are at all times. All you have to do is slow down the signal and the message is right there. Also, if and when Fitzgerald got to the position when he would have access to high-level information, a radio transmitter in his house would be highly suspicious."

"Even if it were hidden?"

"Especially if it were hidden. Many spies have been caught because they had radio transmitters that seemed to be hidden well. More important, a burst transmission is a clear signal that the spy exists; the crossword technique conceals the presence of a spy."

Isabel thought for a moment. "Are you saying that all people who—? Their houses searched? Isn't that..."

"It's easier with bachelors like Fitzgerald," Barca said, "but even families have to leave their houses uninhabited, often for hours."

"You—your specialists, break in?"

"Walk in. It's easy to get or to make keys, and looks much less suspicious, if anyone notices at all. A team of experts could go through your house very thoroughly in a surprisingly short time, Isabel, and you'd never know it."

"Could?" Remembering her fancy lingerie, she grew red. "Do you mean 'did'? You picked my lock?"

"Your door was unlocked, not that it matters. The first time in, we do it the hard way, but once in, we make keys for every lock in the house, even desk drawers, so the next time we have no trouble."

"You invaded my house? How many times?"

"Fitzgerald and the others in his position were checked once a week. You were checked only once."

"That's rotten, Barca."

"Prudent, Isabel; our lives depend on being sure. In your case, nothing of a personal nature was noted or reported to anyone. If it will make you feel any better, I've arranged that my house and the Institute be checked regularly too. By people who don't know what we are. For our own protection."

Giles wanted to get the discussion onto another track. "So Fitzgerald didn't have a radio transmitter?"

"Not a single thing that could be used as a transmitter even if he were an electronics wizard."

"But Fitzgerald *did* transmit the secret message," Isabel said. "The one that was in this morning's paper. It's obvious that you arranged for the President to give different information to each of the three Adversaries. When did he do that?"

"About two o'clock yesterday afternoon. But the three Adversaries didn't leave the White House until almost three. They were each taken home directly with no stops, by a limousine driven by a Secret Service chauffeur, who kept an eye on the occupant. And to forestall your next question, the windows were tinted dark and kept closed. No messages were held up to the windows or thrown out of the car."

"What time did Fitzgerald get home?"

"Three-fifteen, exactly."

She turned to Giles. "How long would it take to construct a puzzle like that one? With two lines of low-frequency consonants adjoining each other on the long diagonal?"

"It depends on many factors," Giles said. "The skill of the constructor, the letters which come next to each other on the two diagonals, the pattern of black squares chosen, and the selection of entry words in that area."

"How long, Giles?"

"A good constructor could do it in about four hours. A professional, probably in three."

"Not less than two hours?" Isabel persisted.

"Even Hannibal would have difficulty constructing that one in less than two hours."

"So by the time Fitzgerald settled himself at his desk, composed the message so it would be twenty-eight letters long, transposed the letters in pairs, and put on his magic telepathy helmet, it's three-thirty, at least?"

"Easily. Closer to three forty-five."

"And when does the encoded crossword have to get to *The Capitol Gazette*?"

"I can tell you that," Barca said. "The presses roll at eleven. A reporter might yell 'stop the presses' for the end of the world, but no one would wait for a crossword. They like to have the puzzle in their hands by six, and they won't make a fuss for an hour or two late, but if the puzzle isn't in their hands by ten, and preferably nine, the features editor would just pull a reserve puzzle out of his emergency file and print that one. No panic. After all, the size and position of the daily crossword is fixed, and usually they're a week's puzzles ahead."

"So," Isabel said, "if Fitzgerald's homing pigeon flies fast, Constructor X would start constructing at about four o'clock at the earliest, and possibly a little later, right?"

"That's reasonable," Giles said.

"So Constructor X had to construct the puzzle and get it to Simon, and Simon had to look at it at least once, and get it to the *Gazette*, all in two hours? And *absolutely* not more than six hours, otherwise that puzzle doesn't get printed in the next day's paper?"

"The arithmetic is right, Isabel."

"Do any of those four regular constructors live right next door to Simon's office?"

"Simon's office is in his house," Barca said. "None of his regular constructors lives within ten miles of Simon."

"So," Isabel said, "Constructor X didn't walk the puzzle over to Simon's house."

"No one entered or left Simon's house," Barca said, "other than Mildred Burdock, his secretary."

"My point is—not even Simon?"

"He never leaves the house; he's quite old and in very poor health."

"You checked his mail and phone too?"

"For the past four days, Isabel, yes. Like the others."

"So he has to have a machine like the one I have in my office in Windham. A facsimile machine, to transmit the puzzles to the *Gazette*, the mails being what they are these days."

"It's a lot cheaper than messenger service, Isabel, and it's much faster. We have one too." Barca pointed to the corner where the computer system reigned. "Right there. They give remarkably good copies at the other end, if you have a compatible machine, in a very short time. Even across the country, anywhere there's a telephone."

"So the *Gazette* has one too?"

"At least one that I know of, probably several."

"My point was that there had to be such a machine; the timing proved it. So now you know who Constructor X is," Isabel said triumphantly. "He's the one with the fax machine hidden under the floorboards."

"We haven't been able to search any of the four homes yet, Isabel; there's always been someone home. But you and Giles can look things over when you visit them."

"Give me the list," she said. "Giles and I will find him and his fax machine."

Barca handed her four index cards. "Don't go to any of them directly. Call me as soon as you're done with Fitzgerald, and I'll let you know what the next step is, when and who and in what order."

"I thought you were in a hurry, Barca. I am too. I'd like to salvage at least part of my vacation."

"When you get to be my age, Isabel, you will learn that sometimes slow is fastest." Barca reached for his phone. "I'm pleased you're thinking of these things, Isabel, but while you're driving around, I wish you'd solve the problem I gave you before: How did Fitzgerald transmit the coded message to Constructor X? You and Giles may leave now; I have some things to arrange.".

20

"If we're going to be driving around all day," Isabel said, "why did Barca make us take such a small car?"

"It's less conspicuous, Miss Isabel," Oliver said, steering carefully around a bicyclist, "and easier to park. Washington is quite congested in the morning."

"What do we do if Fitzgerald isn't home, Giles?"

"He's home," Giles said confidently. "A man his age doesn't go jogging before breakfast. Don't be so nervous, Isabel; Barca wouldn't give you a hard job for your first field trial. This is routine, almost."

"I don't think it's all that easy," she said. "I got only an answering machine with one of those creepy robot voices at his university phone."

"That proves only that he isn't at the university," Giles said, "which we know already."

"It doesn't prove that at all, Giles. I'm sure he has call forwarding; everybody has it today. In my office, after I leave, all calls are automatically forwarded to my home phone."

"Even so," Giles said, "a man in his position usually has two phones, one listed and one unlisted. I have two phones, and I keep the answering machine on at all times on my listed phone; saves a lot of trouble answering

131

unwanted calls. Your call to the university must have reached his home answering machine, with a synthesized voice, so if anyone reached him accidentally, they wouldn't know it was Fitzgerald. He has a distinctive voice, and he's been on TV a lot in the past year."

"Then why didn't he answer me? Or call me back? I did say I was acting president of Windham University. That should count for something."

"Maybe he did call you back. At Windham. You didn't leave the Institute's number, did you?"

"Of course not. But if you knew all this, why did I bother calling?"

"I didn't *know*, Isabel, but if there was the slightest chance he'd pick up the phone, it would have made it much easier to get in to see him."

"Barca could have gotten his unlisted number easily."

"A lot more easily than you could have explained to Fitzgerald how the acting president of Windham University got it. If you had called on that number, he would never open the door to us."

"He still won't, Giles. You have no idea what a long shot this is, from the viewpoint of scholarly protocol. The proper way would be for the chairman of Windham's poly sci department to write to Fitzgerald, suggesting an international political science symposium in his honor next summer, theme to be mutually selected. Then Fitzgerald would write back listing his commitments and accepting the honor if the available dates are mutually convenient. What reason can I possibly give for just dropping in?"

"Tell him you're in Washington just for the one day, and you wanted to meet the great man personally."

"And you think he'll believe that?"

"Smile prettily, tell him what an honor it is to meet him, and hold your card up to the peephole. Anything. Just get me into that house."

"You'd better pray his housekeeper answers the door; I might be able to impress her."

"I'm praying. But if prayers don't work, Oliver will

have to get us in." He spoke to Oliver. "Shouldn't we be there by now?"

"In a moment, sir; I think there's a car about to leave just across from Professor Fitzgerald's house."

"No one's home, Giles," Isabel said. "That's the fourth time you've rung the bell."

"If Fitzgerald's gone, the housekeeper should have answered."

"Friday? In the morning? I don't believe it. Something strange . . . I'm going in." He took a small ring holding two shining keys from his pocket.

"From the surveillance team, Giles?"

"Copies of their keys," Giles said. He looked across the street and tilted his head toward the back of the house. Oliver got out of the car and slowly walked toward the rear of the lot. Giles fitted the keys into the upper dead-lock and the lower latch. He turned the upper key completely, waited a second, then turned the lower key. "Stand to one side, Isabel," he said. Using the keys only, he pushed the door open wide, holding himself outside the open doorway. After a moment he peeked in. The hallway was empty.

"Stay behind me," Giles told Isabel, and walked in cautiously, his hand on the handle of his cane.

Oliver hissed at them from the back of the hallway and motioned them to stay where they were. He had a large automatic in his right hand; his eyes searched right and left. Giles and Isabel shrank against the wall as Oliver slowly mounted the stairs to the second floor. Giles carefully maneuvered his body so he was in front of Isabel.

It was a full two minutes before Oliver came down. He shook his head once, his open left palm keeping them in place, and carefully went down the cellar stairs.

Oliver was back a minute later; the gun was nowhere in sight. "It's all right, sir," he said in a normal tone of voice. "No one's in the house. The housekeeper is in the kitchen. Don't bother looking; an ordinary kitchen knife, not matching anything in the house. Entry through the terrace door, professional; glass cut and removed, not smashed in. Within the past hour I would say. I'll find Professor Fitzgerald."

"We'll go with you," Isabel said. "I don't want to stay here alone."

Professor Horton Fitzgerald was sitting in his study in front of his computer terminal. An ordinary kitchen knife was in his chest. "It matches the one in the housekeeper," Oliver said.

"There must have been a sale," Isabel said, suppressing a nervous giggle.

"He has a very elaborate computer installation," Giles said. "Terminal, hard disc drive, printer, telephone modem, and—what's that over there, Isabel?"

"A streaming tape recorder. For storage," she said. "But no fax machine."

"We'll leave at once," Oliver said. "Touch nothing, wipe nothing. Use the keys only, to close and lock the front door."

"Shouldn't we call Barca?" Isabel asked.

"Not from here," Giles said.

21

"WHY DOES BARCA WANT US TO CHECK OUT THE CON-structors?" Isabel asked. "Shouldn't we be going directly to Simon? He's at the center of everything."

"First of all," Giles said, "he's still sleeping; remember his odd hours? Then, he's going to be the hardest nut to crack. The more we learn from the constructors, the more pressure we can apply to Simon."

"And why are we going to the four constructors in order of distance, Giles? Doesn't that show ignorance?"

"Not just Barca's, Isabel; mine and thine too. Do you know anything about any of them that I don't? Something that makes one more likely to be Encoder X than another?"

"Might I suggest, sir," Oliver suggested, "rather than criticizing Barca, we discuss the implications of the Fitzgerald murder, which you and Miss Isabel have so carefully been avoiding for the past ten miles."

"We know so little," Giles said. "We were in Fitzgerald's house for only five minutes."

"Could it have been attempted robbery?" Oliver pressed.

"Of course not," Giles said. "There were some good paintings untouched, and many other things that looked valuable."

"Then, perhaps, a left-wing terrorist group, sir, angered

135

at his outspoken criticism of the Soviet Union?"

"No manifestos stuck to his chest with a knife; no slogans scrawled in blood on the wall. Oliver, are you trying to provoke me?"

"Yes, sir. What about the KGB?"

"Why should they kill him? He made more enemies for the anti-Soviet movement than Stalin did."

"Then who did kill him, sir? And why?"

"Very well, Oliver. I see you will not let me be. Horton Fitzgerald was killed by reason of his connection with the spying he was doing, by someone connected with the crossword-code ring."

"By Mr. Simon? By Encoder X?"

"Neither Simon nor Encoder X knew who Fitzgerald was; that was a major purpose of the crossword code."

"The FBI? The CIA?"

"We learned Fitzgerald was the spy only two hours ago or so, and I'm sure Barca didn't tell anyone else."

"The President, sir, knew yesterday that one of his three Adversarial Advisors on the MDWDC team was a spy. Maybe he ordered all three killed, just to play safe."

"And risk an investigation by his political enemies? When he knew we'd have the spy in a few hours? Killing all three is a sure way to publicize that there was a spy in his administration, right at the top. No one that dumb gets to be president, and this one is famous for his shrewdness."

"Possibly the organizer of this operation? The spymaster?"

"We agreed that he's almost certainly back in Russia, and has been there for years."

"Which leaves—?" There was no answer from Giles. "Sir?" Oliver prompted.

"There was a guardian left behind, Oliver, a watchman. In case anything went wrong. To tidy up the scene; to make sure the operation was untraceable. So, having found Fitzgerald and Simon, we now have to look for another player in the game."

"Well done, sir," Oliver said, not a trace of sarcasm in

his voice. "I knew you could do it. Now, when was Professor Fitzgerald killed? Possibly Miss Macintosh has some idea?"

"All right, Oliver," Isabel said, "drop the phony catechism routine. Giles is now thinking on all three cylinders."

"I do only what is necessary, Miss Macintosh. I am very pleased you are taking over the questioning of why Professor Fitzgerald was murdered."

"I wasn't going to—we've just seen a bloody murder, Oliver. Two, with the housekeeper. My God, can't we take a breather?" Oliver shook his head. "Oh, what the hell, Oliver." She took a deep breath. "Giles, was Fitzgerald killed because his usefulness was ended?"

"No, certainly not, Isabel. He was killed only minutes after we discovered he was the spy. No one but the nine of us knew we had pinpointed Fitzgerald. There was no way anyone could even guess his usefulness was ended. On the contrary, it would be reasonable to assume his usefulness was going to increase."

"Maybe there was a reason, Giles, that had nothing to do with the spy ring. Maybe he was fooling around with someone's wife. Or daughter. Coeds do these things. I know."

"Fitzgerald? Come on, Isabel."

"There's no accounting for taste," Isabel said with a meaningful look at Giles, "when it comes to love."

"Then why kill the housekeeper? No, that is so improbable that—the murder must be connected to the spy ring, and I was thinking of something when Oliver interrupted the thought."

"What?"

"If I knew what it was; if I could remember . . ."

"Here we are," Oliver said, pulling up in front of a modest row house. "Encoder X; probability: twenty-five percent."

22

"**I** WISH YOU HAD CALLED FIRST, MR. SULLIVAN," HELEN Goldstein said, embarrassed. "The house is a mess. But all right, as long as you're here, come in anyway."

Mrs. Goldstein was short, plump, gray, and motherly and, Isabel thought, looked as likely a spy as she did a linebacker. Which is what a spy should look like. On the other hand, as a spy's dupe, Central Casting had done a great job. "Come into the kitchen," Mrs. Goldstein said. "My kitchen is always clean and neat. Sit at the table. You like iced tea with lemon?"

"That would be fine," Giles said. "We've been looking forward to meeting you."

"You came all the way from New York just to see me?" Mrs. Goldstein said. "The famous Giles Sullivan from the New York Cruciverbal Club?"

"Not really. We came here to visit friends and to see how Washington celebrates the Fourth of July weekend." Isabel glared at him. "But I've heard about you and Eugene Simon's other regulars, so I decided to visit you all and discuss the idea of a D.C. chapter of the Club."

"It's a good idea, Mr. Sullivan," she said, dropping ice cubes into the tea pitcher. "Try these chocolate chips, my own recipe. There must be enough fans in the D.C. area to support a club. Not as big as the New York club, of course, but enough. But you really should talk to Al Kos-

grow and Fred Lindenmann; they're the real professionals. If they would serve on the board of directors, we'd
be sure to succeed."

"I'll visit them tomorrow," Giles said. "Today it's just
Simon and you four."

"Forget about Simon," Mrs. Goldstein said. "He'll
never join. He's an old crab, won't do anything that doesn't
bring in money. You might get Mildred Burdock; she's his
secretary. She's crazy about crosswords, and she's very
efficient. She'd make a terrific club manager; if she can
take Simon, she could handle anyone. I think she's getting
ready to retire, but for a job like that . . . I'll call her and
introduce you."

"Later," Giles said. "Thanks. But tell me, you seem
to dislike Simon. Why do you sell him your crosswords?
Why not sell yours to Kosgrow and Lindenmann?"

"First of all, I have very little to do with him. I don't
talk to him and he doesn't bother with me. If he wants
to change a clue, let him; that's his job anyway, and he's
pretty good. Second, he pays five dollars more than the
others. Ever since my husband passed away, every penny
counts."

"You don't make a living from crosswords, do you?"

"Who can make a living from crosswords? I work after-
noons as an assistant librarian, and that doesn't pay too
well either. Also I baby-sit. That's when I construct, so
it's like found money."

"How long does it take you to construct a puzzle, Mrs.
Goldstein?" Isabel asked. "These cookies are delicious.
May I have the recipe?"

"Finished already? Don't worry, Miss Macintosh; I
have plenty. Here. I'll give you the recipe later; remind
me. How long? A fifteen by fifteen, actual work, about
four hours. I could do it a little faster, but I like to be
very exact."

"How do you send it in?" Giles asked.

"First I make a copy—it's free for me in the library—
then I mail it."

"If you had a facsimile machine, you could save two

days, get your check that much faster."

"If I could afford an expensive machine, I wouldn't have to construct crosswords or bake cookies."

Isabel turned red. "Oh, I'm sorry. I didn't realize— I've been gobbling up— I'd like to buy some."

"While you're at my table, Miss Macintosh, you're a guest. Later, when you leave, if you want to, it's cheaper than in the store, and better."

Giles chafed at the interruption. "Does your library have one? A facsimile machine?"

"Sure, but I'm not allowed to use it. Besides, Simon would have to have one, too, one that's compatible."

"You've never been in his office, Mrs. Goldstein?"

"Why should I go to his office? Once, I was there, five years ago. Just to meet him; I was curious. Didn't even offer me a glass of water. Mildred was there; she was nice, but he's a creep."

"If you can construct a salable puzzle in four hours," Giles said, "you must do at least fifty a year."

"More like a hundred, almost. But I don't sell them all to Simon. He rejects three quarters of mine; why, I don't know. The rest I sell to Kosgrow and Lindenmann, and a few I sell direct to some specialized publications who know me. They don't have a very big budget for puzzles, but once a puzzle is made, what else can you do with it?"

"Did you construct this past Tuesday's puzzle?" Giles asked.

"Me? Never. I do *good* work. Let me show you what I'm working on now." She went into the next room and was back in a minute. "Here. Look at that. What do you think?"

Giles studied the puzzle for a minute. "Yes, this is quite good, very professional."

"So why did Simon print the one he did on Tuesday? I haven't sold to him in two weeks. And Wednesday's? Did you see Wednesday's? Absolute dreck. And Thursday's? You could vomit from it. He's probably found somebody who'll do the puzzles for free—to break in, I guess—but he's making a big mistake. No real crossword fan will stand for it; he'll be fired for sure."

"You're right, Mrs. Goldstein," Giles said. "But maybe the constructor had some—some constraint that required that particular layout."

"You don't use constraints, Mr. Sullivan. You should know that. Themes, yes. Interesting gimmicks, yes. Puns, anagrams, cryptos? Fine, I love them. But that's it; no constraints."

"So who do you think constructed this week's puzzles, Mrs. Goldstein? Whose style is it? One of the other three of your professional colleagues?"

"Never. Sometimes they do a little better, sometimes a little worse, like me, but always good. This crap—excuse the expression—doesn't look like anything I ever saw. If Simon is trying an experiment, I wish he'd explain it to me."

"Well"—Giles looked at his watch—"it's been very nice talking to you, Mrs. Goldstein, but we must run now. Please call Mr. Simon's secretary; tell her we'll see her this afternoon. And let me know what I can do to help organize the Washington branch of the Cruciverbal Club."

"Sure, Mr. Sullivan, glad to. I'll call Mildred later; the office doesn't open until twelve. Simon's crazy hours. About the cookies, Miss Macintosh, how many pounds did you want?"

23

"**D**ID YOU HAVE TO BUY *EVERYTHING* SHE HAD IN STOCK, Isabel?" Giles said.

"I didn't realize how much she had," Isabel said. "How was I to know she was preparing for the temple bazaar? But I'm glad I did. They're irresistible, and cheaper than in the store. Charge it off to what you still owe me. It's only two cartons. There's room for the two of us in the front seat with Oliver if we squeeze together a little."

"You'll never eat this much in a year."

"Wanna bet, Sullivan?"

"If someone will kindly tell me where I am to drive next," Oliver said, "we can be on our way."

"I'll navigate," Isabel said. "Hand me the map. Charles Hupper is next on the list if I remember correctly. What's his address, Giles?"

"We're not going there," Giles said. "Shut off the engine, Oliver. I want your thoughts on this too."

"But I thought," Isabel said, "we were in a hurry. Three other constructors to interview before we see Simon, and it's mid-morning already."

"It's not necessary," Giles said. "None of the four constructors worked with the spy."

"Just because Mrs. Goldstein looks like a Jewish mother who bakes delicious cookies, cheaper than in the store,

142

doesn't mean she doesn't have a fax machine hidden under the floorboards. She admitted she needed the money."

"If you believe her, and I do, how does she buy a fax machine without money?"

"I'm sure the spymaster who set this up was very generous with equipment. Nothing but the best for his spies."

"If you were a spymaster," Giles said, "setting up an elaborate long-term operation such as this one, for which you needed the services of a crossword constructor, would you pick—look at it this way. Your spy, Fitzgerald, will get information whenever the President decides to see him; it could even be in the middle of the night. Fitzgerald then rushes home, condenses it into twenty-eight consonants, transposes the letters, and transmits it. The crossword constructor, Constructor X, must have it in his hands as soon as it is sent, or shortly thereafter. He must have it done in two hours, more or—"

"Not always, Giles. Sometimes he will have eight hours, which is plenty for a dreck crossword, to quote Mrs. Goldstein."

"A dreck crossword, as she calls it, in which there are two adjoining diagonals of low-frequency consonants, could take a professional more than eight hours to construct. And for at least one of these dreck puzzles, this morning's puzzle, the constructor had only two hours at most; you figured it out yourself. I think that constructing a puzzle under these conditions would take Hannibal more than two hours."

"All right, yes." Isabel nodded. "I see your point. Our spymaster could not depend on, would not choose, someone with a job, even a part-time job. He would not even take a semi-pro like Mrs. Goldstein. He'd pick a real pro, a full-time constructor-editor."

"Exactly. Albert Kosgrow or Frederick Lindenmann. The question is, which one. I have a sudden feeling of running out of time."

"It isn't even eleven o'clock, Giles. We have all day to see Simon. If his office doesn't open until twelve, he must work until eight, at least."

"I'm not worried about missing Simon; he'll stay put. I just feel uneasy. The trouble is, Kosgrow and Lindenmann live far out of Washington, in opposite directions. We could lose an hour going through noonday Washington."

"Might I suggest," Oliver said, "that we go first to that one who is nearest Professor Fitzgerald's university. The constructor might have been the one chosen so that, all other means failing, the information could have been delivered to him rapidly by an intermediary, should the emergency make it necessary. Also, if the constructor uses the same area code for his telephone equipment as the university, it would be much harder to track down his calls to or from Professor Fitzgerald."

"Right, Oliver, Kosgrow it is. Navigate, Isabel."

"Right. Straight ahead, Oliver, to the next major road, then left. Giles, as long as I have to do the brain work, reach back and open a carton. One bag will do for the while."

24

ALBERT KOSGROW'S HOUSE WAS ACTUALLY A CON-
verted barn on what had clearly been a small farm. It had
the dull look of cheap red-lead paint slapped on to protect
rather than beautify, and the tiny windows had clearly
been cut into the siding as an afterthought. A beat-up old
Ford pickup stood on the cinder road near the highway.

"Why are you getting out, Oliver?" Giles asked. "I
think you should stay in the car."

"I sense danger here, sir," Oliver said. "I'll go in first."

"Have no fear, Oliver." Giles held up his gold-headed
cane. "I am well-armed."

"Now I am doubly concerned, sir. I'll scout out the
house, and if there are any problems, I'll take care of
them."

"That could be harmful to the Group, Oliver. Isabel
and I have an excuse for visiting Albert Kosgrow, but
you, an English butler, can only draw suspicion down on
us."

"Your logic is sound, sir." Oliver closed the car door.
"Do be extremely careful and alert. I sense something."

"I will, Oliver. If you see anyone approaching, honk
the horn."

Giles knocked on the front door; there was no bell.
The echo had the dead feel of an empty house. Giles
knocked again, harder. No answer. With foreboding he

145

tried the door. It was unlocked. The hinges creaked as they entered.

"Hello?" Giles called into the dark hall. "Hello? Anyone home? Mr. Kosgrow?" Not a sound.

"He's gone," Isabel said. "Somehow he knew we were coming. We should have had the sense to come here first." A thought struck her. "Maybe Mrs. Goldstein called him?"

Giles took two more steps in. On his left was a sort of living room. He looked in. It was more a library, actually, shelves of books on all four walls. The low table was piled high with books. There was a faint odor of mildew.

They went deeper into the house, past some closed doors on the right, then a ship's ladder to a second floor. Another door on the left at the end of the corridor, open.

There was a full computer setup against the far wall, the screen casting a bright green light on what had to be the body of Albert Kosgrow, slumped over the keyboard, a big kitchen knife in his back.

25

"MOVE OVER, OLIVER," GILES SAID. "I WANT ISABEL to drive."

"I'm sorry, sir," Oliver said, "but Barca instructed me to protect your life on this mission, as well as Miss Isabel's."

"Did Barca also instruct you," Isabel said, "to provoke me into going to jail for strangling a male chauvinist butler?"

"We really must hurry, Oliver," Giles said. "I cannot afford your cautious pace."

"I have not scratched the car once, sir, in over thirty years of driving in New York traffic, and we are still alive. Miss Isabel's jeep, on the other hand, has had the equivalent of a full body replacement, piece by piece, every three years."

"Move!" Isabel yelled in Oliver's ear. He moved.

"Sit on the outside, Oliver," Giles said. "I'll navigate."

"I know the way back," Isabel said. "Don't worry."

"We're not going back to the Institute," Giles said. "Go straight ahead and turn right at the next highway. Drop Oliver off at the first phone you see." He turned to Oliver and said, "After you phone Barca, call a taxi and go back to the Institute. We'll meet you there when we're done."

"I'm sorry, sir, but I must stay with you. You are evidently going where there may be some difficulty, so I must go along to take care of any problems."

"I don't expect any problems of that sort, Oliver. Besides, I am armed."

"Exactly, sir. That is why I must stay close to you and Miss Isabel."

Giles flushed. "This is not the time to discuss my cane, Oliver. When we get to a phone, call Barca and have him remove the surveillance team from Eugene Simon's house in"—he looked at his watch—"at exactly twelve-twenty. I don't want the FBI to associate us with this affair."

"I will be pleased to make the call, sir, but I will insist on taking the keys with me."

"Oh, very well, Oliver, I give you my word we will not drive off without you."

"I am a gentleman's gentleman, sir, and you are, therefore, a gentleman whose word is his bond. Miss Isabel, I have observed, does not hesitate to take advantage of any opportunity to gain her ends, however laudable, using any means at hand. I will take the keys, sir, with your permission."

"You'll pay for this, Oliver," Isabel said, "when you least expect it. Don't say I didn't warn you." She pressed the accelerator to the floor. "I understand, Oliver, that the most dangerous seat, in case of an accident, is the one to the right of the driver."

"Slow down, Isabel, for God's sake." Giles had his feet forced tightly against the floor. "I'm on your right, too, and I have no steering wheel to hold on to. If Oliver goes, I go too. We'll never be able to stop in time for a phone. We can't go near Simon until we're sure the FBI is gone."

She slowed down a bit. "Why are we going to Simon's house? I thought we were to go back to the Institute after we found out who Constructor X is. Was. Did you notice the beautiful computer system he had? Expensive."

"Of course. Completely out of place in that shabby house."

"And did you notice what was next to the phone answering machine and the modem? A facsimile transceiver, the same one I have in my office. That machine can transmit a letter-size sheet in twenty seconds flat.

148

Remember what we were talking about before? We don't have to go to Simon's house to check; I *know* he has one exactly like that. *The Capitol Gazette* has to have one, too, that's either the same or compatible, no doubt about it. So why are we going to Simon instead of back to Barca to plan the next move?"

"Because—let me ask you a question, Isabel. And keep your eyes on the road. You drive; I'll watch for a phone."

"Yes, sir, sir," she said.

"Don't get smart, Isabel, this is important." He hesitated, trying to present it properly. "Who killed Albert Kosgrow?"

Isabel took several seconds. "Well, it wasn't what's-his-name, the other professional constructor, Lindenberg? No, Lindenmann, trying to take over the Maryland crossword business. And it couldn't have been Eugene Simon. Not only is he old and sick—Mrs. Goldstein says he never leaves the house—but he had full FBI coverage twenty-four hours a day. If he ever came here, even to hunt for mushrooms, there would have been twelve dozen FBI agents behind him trampling down the weeds. The killer also wasn't Professor Horton Fitzgerald, since the whole crossword deal was to keep him invisible, not only invisible, but to keep anyone from suspecting a spy existed at that level. Besides, although it would take an autopsy to prove it, I have a feeling that Fitzgerald was killed right after Kosgrow, by just the time it would take to drive from here to Fitzgerald's house. Further, unless our analysis is wrong, Kosgrow didn't even know he had a spy's message to conceal in the crossword. So," she concluded, "it has to be the Russians. A Russian. The watchman you mentioned before."

"Exactly, Isabel. Before, when I hypothesized a watchman, I was guessing; now I'm sure. Let me follow the logic through; when I tell this to Barca, if there's the slightest hole, he'll tear me to pieces. We agreed, and I feel we were right, that the spymaster set up this team some years ago and then went back to the Motherland.

He did his work so secretly that no one in the Russian Embassy, nor any other spy in the United States, knew of the existence of this operation. All they would know is that Zulkov would give them high-level information that was absolutely accurate. How he got it, from whom, was none of their business. And even Zulkov, the decoder, didn't know who the spy was. If not for a lucky accident ... Even if Zulkov were to defect before he turned over the message, where would we be? Trace our way back to Simon? No problem. From Simon to Kosgrow? Yes, in a short time. But after that? A truly dead dead end. Turn left at the next intersection."

"Suppose Zulkov defected *after* he decoded the messages?"

"Highly unlikely, but possible. Don't think our spymaster neglected anything. You'll see."

"All right, Giles, we'll stick to Zulkov defecting early. Simon, and then Kosgrow, would be arrested. That would kill the whole operation, wouldn't it?"

"Not necessarily. Temporarily, yes, but how long would it take to set up another team? Not using the crossword code, of course, but I'm sure some other means might be found. Then the spy would still be available for a second operation, if not a third and a fourth, and so on. In another city, probably; New York, for one, plenty of Russians at the U.N. The reason this operation was set up in Washington is obvious. Horton Fitzgerald's university is near here, a local phone call's distance from Kosgrow's home. Same area code; not as easy to check who called whom and when as with a long-distance call, but, if it were necessary, it wouldn't be hard to get the coded message to New York."

"Would they still use the crossword code if Simon and Kosgrow were arrested?"

"Not necessarily, but if they did, who can check all the crosswords published in the U.S., especially if the key were not the date but some other simple item?"

"Do you really think any New York newspaper crossword editor would be that—that venal?"

"Not the ones I know, but there may be an assistant features editor planted there, and one day the features editor falls in front of a subway train . . . Actually, it would not be too hard to become the crossword editor of a small neighborhood paper or a local suburban paper; just offer to do it for nothing but the experience. No one would ever suspect. It's just as easy to phone New York as to make a local call, and it's only more dangerous if someone suspects you."

"Are you sure it was done by phone, Giles?"

"Not *sure*, but I'm sure. We've already agreed that any kind of personal contacts, intermediaries, drops, are possible leads to the identity of the spy. We've ruled out radio transmission or any kind of signal from the spy's house, office, or car. So what else is left? No, it has to be by phone, although I'm damned if I can tell how he did it with his phone tapped. Phones are the method our spymaster favors. He bought, or rather gave, Kosgrow the money to buy not only a computer but a modem and a facsimile transceiver. I'll bet Simon has a matching setup, brand for brand. So, back to my question, who killed Kosgrow?"

"If it wasn't the spymaster himself, it had to be someone the spymaster left behind to keep an eye on things. A watchman who didn't know the setup but knew he had to watch for things that could cause trouble for the spy."

"Which things? Who was the Watchman supposed to watch?"

"Well, not Fitzgerald, since no one, not even the KGB, was supposed to know about him. And it wasn't Zulkov; he, too, was to have not the slightest smell of suspicion about him. Although, if any of their spies in the intelligence agencies even heard Zulkov's name officially, I'm sure there was some way of informing the Watchman— another ad, perhaps, and Zulkov would have gotten the chop. So it had to be the intermediate links of the chain the Watchman was checking, Kosgrow and Simon, and maybe someone at the *Gazette*."

"Why? Why was the Watchman watching them? Kosgrow and Simon?"

"If anything went wrong, they were the only ones who could be traced. And since they were expendable, he"—she took a deep breath—"he expended Kosgrow. So that's why you're rushing to Simon, Giles. To make sure he isn't also, uh, to protect him." She drew a deep breath. "You know, Giles, we've just had three murders, and it isn't even lunchtime. I don't think I could stand a fourth."

"Don't worry, Isabel. Simon doesn't need me to take care of him. He's already protected far better than I could protect him. They have an airtight shield around him, four men, at least, maybe six. No one can even get near him. No, what I want is to sit down with him, tell him that Kosgrow was murdered just a short— How long ago was it done, Isabel? You felt his neck."

"Several hours, three or four, I'm sure. His skin was somewhat cool, and his muscles were beginning to stiffen."

"Figure early this morning. So I will tell Simon the truth; that Kosgrow was killed by the Watchman, and that if we hadn't had a team around his house, Simon would be dead by now too. I'm going to tell him that we've removed his shield, that he's vulnerable to the Watchman, and his only hope is to tell us everything he knows and let himself be taken into custody. Otherwise I just leave, and one hour later Simon has a knife in his back too."

"What happens, Giles, between the time the FBI leaves and the time we arrive?"

"I've timed it so there will be only a ten-minute hiatus; that's why I wanted you to drive rather than Oliver. The FBI must be gone by the time we get there; otherwise they will connect us, and, through us, Barca, to this operation. Once they know, the world will know and, at best, the Group will be out of business."

"And at worst, Giles? Don't answer that; I don't want to know. I'll make sure to be there exactly as scheduled. You don't think the Watchman is hanging around, waiting for the FBI to go away, do you? In ten minutes he could stab Simon and his secretary and disappear again. Oh, God, Giles, is it possible? I've had three murders today, Giles, in one hour. I couldn't take a fourth." She looked sick.

"Nobody is going to hang around Simon's house or do anything else suspicious in that neighborhood. The way I figure it, after killing Fitzgerald, the Watchman drove to Simon's house and circled the block. He must have noticed a van, a parked car, a telephone repairman, whatever, hanging around and, as an experienced spy, he knew what that meant and went away, intending to try again another day."

"Do you think Simon will talk?"

"He has no choice as I see it."

"But according to our analysis he doesn't know anything."

"About the secret messages, no. But what he does tell us, added to everything else we know, may lead us to the spymaster."

"Not to the Watchman?"

"Not a chance. Simon won't even know the Watchman exists until we tell him about Kosgrow. Let him assume that the spymaster killed Kosgrow."

"Which may be the truth, as far as we know."

"Very doubtful. People who plan operations like this never go into the field. But more important, Simon can tell us about the man who approached him, the man who gave him the money for the modem and the fax machine. That could lead to the spymaster."

"Do you think the spymaster did the recruiting himself?"

"No, but if we find who did, that's another step closer."

"Could it have been the Watchman who recruited Kosgrow and Simon?"

"I don't think so. Everybody connected with the original setting-up operation must be out of the country by now. It's doubtful that the Watchman is the one who recruited Kosgrow and Simon."

"Then what good would it be to talk to Simon? Even

if we find out who the spymaster is, you said he's in Russia now and has been for several years."

"No matter. If Barca wants to use the information, or to try to turn the spymaster—he did lose a major spy in Fitzgerald, and if we publicize it, that's unforgivable to the Russians. If they don't kill him, Barca may decide to have it done; a brilliant man like that is too dangerous to leave around. Or the information Simon gives us may lead us to the Watchman. At the very least, even if he has a diplomatic passport, he should be exposed as a murderer." Giles's head snapped right. "Wait. There's a phone. Slow down. Back there. Make a U-turn, Isabel. On the left. Oliver?"

"No need to give me the keys, sir. Miss Isabel will not leave me behind. I believe she is beginning to understand—forgive me, Miss Isabel—that an operation is not all fun and games. Not the least bit chocolate-coated."

26

ISABEL GUNNED THE ENGINE. "WE LOST FIVE MINUTES on your call, Oliver. Don't complain about how fast I drive."

"You can slow down a bit, Miss Isabel," Oliver said. "Barca said we must not get there before twelve-thirty, to make sure no FBI people are left to identify us. He can't just call up and get them removed, you know; he has to use roundabout channels."

"Just as well," Giles said. "I want to discuss something that's troubling me, and I hesitate to disturb you when you're driving at high speeds."

Isabel eased off the gas a bit. "Don't let that bother you, Giles. Two separate sets of brain cells are involved."

"All right," Giles said. "Put your other set to work on this: Why was Albert Kosgrow killed?"

"To keep him from talking, of course."

"What about?"

"The spy ring. No, I'm wrong. He couldn't talk about Fitzgerald; he didn't know Fitzgerald existed. Same for Valentin Zulkov. And he didn't know about the Watchman. So the only one it could be is Simon. But that's pointless. If anyone was following a trail, he'd have to *start* with Simon, same as we did. I give up, Giles. Whom was Kosgrow going to talk about?"

"It could still be Simon, you know. It's one thing to be sure Simon is involved; it's another thing to prove it. With Kosgrow dead, no one could prove Simon knew he was transmitting secret information."

"Aren't those klutzy puzzles enough?"

"Not as evidence; a good lawyer could show a dozen harmless reasons why Simon accepted them. You can't sentence a man for stupidity. Or senility."

"So what does that leave, Mildred Burdock? I get the impression that she's as likely a suspect as Helen Goldstein."

"Well, she's the one person who could go in and out of Simon's house without suspicion, so leave her on the list. No, what is more likely is that Simon had an emergency number to call, an apparently innocuous number. And an apparently harmless message to give, such as 'Get me a photograph of Albert Kosgrow; I'm going to write an article about him.' Or 'In answer to your question, I would put Albert Kosgrow twenty-third on the list of the best constructors in America.' That would be the signal for the murder of whoever was named. We can check Simon's phone calls for the past few days."

"All right, it's possible Simon ordered Kosgrow's death and can give us a lead to the Watchman. But how did Simon learn we were going to interrogate Kosgrow? You didn't make that decision until after we left Mrs. Goldstein's house. Even Barca didn't know."

"Simon didn't find out, obviously; it must have been done as a precaution, a prophylactic measure."

"That doesn't make sense either, Giles. Why waste a valuable asset like Kosgrow just as a precaution? Could Simon be sure that there would be no more messages from the spy? Possibly the most important message of all would have come today. Simon couldn't contact the spy and the spy couldn't communicate with Simon, except through Kosgrow."

"There is always the possibility, sir," Oliver said, "that there is a second constructor, Constructor Y."

"If there is, it could be only Frederick Lindenmann,

and that doesn't make sense. Since there was no contact between Fitzgerald, the spy, and Kosgrow, the constructor, there can be no contact between the spy and Lindenmann either. So Lindenmann would also be constructing puzzles with secret messages in them for Simon, and he, too, would be a key to Simon. Therefore, if Kosgrow had to be killed to protect Simon, Lindenmann is dead, too, shutting off all communication between the spy and Simon."

"Lindenmann *may* be dead, for all we know, Giles. We should have checked."

"No, no, it's too improbable. The problem is—"

"Possibly Mr. Kosgrow was killed," Oliver said, "not to protect a person but to conceal the method, the crossword code."

"That doesn't fit either," Giles said. "If anyone was going to question Kosgrow, it could be only because someone was suspicious of the crosswords first. Killing Kosgrow could only intensify the belief that there was something fishy about the crosswords."

"The call that the features editor made," Isabel said, "Warren, the features editor at the *Gazette*. Barca told us that Warren called Simon and criticized the puzzles; told Simon never to use that constructor again. Maybe Simon had to tell Warren—there's really no way to avoid it— that Kosgrow constructed those puzzles."

"Assuming he did, Isabel, why would it be necessary for Simon to kill Kosgrow?"

"Warren's next question to Simon would be 'Why would Kosgrow, your rival, send you a puzzle? And what possible reason could Kosgrow have to send you two such puzzles in a row? Having accepted the first one, which was pretty bad, why didn't you edit it, clean it up? That's what we pay you for, isn't it, Simon? How could you accept the second one?' What could Simon say to that?"

"Made some kind of excuse, I suppose."

"Maybe. But what happens next, Giles, when he accepts the third puzzle? And the fourth? How to explain those? Wouldn't Warren have become suspicious? Maybe even asked another crossword expert to check those puzzles?"

"No one would have found the secret message; look at all the trouble we had."

"Maybe not, but wouldn't Warren, sooner or later, have a talk with Kosgrow?"

"Probably, but what could Kosgrow tell him, especially if Kosgrow didn't know there was a spy involved?"

"Innocent or not, Kosgrow would have had to tell Warren about the concealed message; there is no other acceptable explanation for those crosswords. Tell Warren not only where it was concealed, but show Warren the message as Kosgrow received it. Warren, anybody, would see that it was in code. A cryptanalyst would break it in a minute. That's about what it took us once we had the original message in front of us. This would immediately lead to the arrest of Kosgrow and Simon. So Kosgrow had to be killed."

"Yes, Isabel, but more than that. Kosgrow, sooner or later, would tell how he received the secret messages, which would lead to the exposure of the spy."

"You're right, Giles. Simon had Kosgrow killed by a professional, the Watchman, to protect both himself and the spy."

"Why do we keep saying 'the spy'? We know it was Fitzgerald."

"Simon didn't."

"Sorry. But now we've disposed of the idea that Simon was innocent of any complicity in the spying," Giles said. "But if you're right, wouldn't the killing of Kosgrow itself draw attention to Simon?"

"Not necessarily, Giles; as far as anyone else knew, there was no connection between Simon and Kosgrow other than that they worked in the same trade. Further, if we hadn't stumbled across his body, no one would have known Kosgrow was dead for a week; that little farm was not exactly in the middle of Times Square, and that little house didn't look like a center of society."

"What you say, Isabel, makes sense, but I can't help feeling that there must be more to it than that." He checked the map. "Slow down a bit more; we're approaching Simon's house. It should be on our left, next block. Oliver, do you see any signs of surveillance?"

"All clear, sir."

"Good. There it is, Isabel; go past a half block. Here. Park here. Oliver, you stay with the car."

"I'm sorry, sir, but I must go with you. Remember what you found at Mr. Kosgrow's house?"

"Nothing. He was dead."

"The killer might still have been there."

"I had my cane, Oliver."

"Exactly, sir."

Giles grew red. "I was an expert swordsman, Oliver. I can defend myself quite adequately, thank you."

"And Miss Isabel, too, sir? I am sorry, sir, but I must insist."

"There is no danger there, Oliver. An old man and an old lady."

"If you are certain of that, sir, that the killer is not inside already, why not leave the cane here, sir?"

"The FBI was watching until ten minutes ago, Oliver. I feel undressed without my cane."

"You are not wearing a cloak and topper, sir; the cane is inappropriate for summer slacks and shirt. Quite inappropriate, sir."

"Oh, very well, then, Oliver, I'll leave it in the car. There is no way I can explain to Simon why I am bringing my butler to visit him."

"Quite right, sir, and since you are willing to leave the cane, I believe there is truly no danger and so there can be no harm in your carrying it." Giles and Isabel started off. "Just one more thing, sir. Should Mr. Simon ask you who your valet is, please don't give my name."

✖✖✖✖✖✖✖✖✖✖✖✖✖✖✖✖✖✖✖✖✖✖ 27 ✦✦✦

"**H**E'S IN THERE," MILDRED BURDOCK SAID—WHO ELSE could it be?—"in the bedroom. Hurry." She half pushed Giles toward the door on the left side of the hall. The little one-story house was old, as old as Albert Kosgrow's house, but everything was neatly arranged, everything in its place, the difference Mildred's touch; it had to be. The second door on the right was open, showing what was clearly Mildred's crowded little office. Giles noticed that next to the computer, the same one he had seen in Kosgrow's house, was a facsimile machine, a carbon copy of the one Kosgrow had.

Giles had reached the bedroom door when Mildred stopped pushing. "You're not a doctor," she said accusingly. Noticing Isabel, she asked, "And who are you?" Mildred Burdock's small plump figure was quivering, her glasses fogged, her hair straggling from the once neat bun. She saw Isabel staring and attempted to smooth her out-of-fashion dress.

"I'm Giles Sullivan and this is my associate, Isabel Macintosh. You must be Mildred Burdock." He put out his hand.

She took it hesitantly. "Yes, Helen Goldstein called me. But this is not—I'm, waiting for a doctor and the ambulance, whichever comes first. Mr. Simon is, I'm afraid—" Tears filled her eyes. "Do you know anything about—?"

"I don't think I should—" Giles said. "How long ago did you call?"

"About fifteen minutes. When I came—I always come a little before twelve; Mr. Simon doesn't like lateness—his office door was closed, so I went into my office and started work. But I didn't hear anything and I had a feeling ... So I knocked on the door, but there was no answer. When I opened it, he wasn't there. I knocked on the bedroom door and he didn't yell or anything, so I looked in and he was lying very still. When I called him, he didn't move. I got scared and called his doctor, Dr. Chertnow. The nurse said he was not available, but she'd send another doctor who was covering for him. She told me to call an ambulance, so I did. Do you think—?"

"I think we should wait," Giles said. "A layman could do more harm than good. Miss Macintosh will take a peek. Isabel? Take a look but don't touch anything. We'll—let's sit down in your office, Miss Burdock. Can I get you a drink of water?"

"No, thank you, I'll be all right. There's very little room in my office; wouldn't you rather sit in the library? Mr. Simon doesn't have a living room."

They sat on the hard wooden chairs at the plain plastic-covered table surrounded by walls of books. Isabel returned, walked around the table until she was behind Mildred Burdock, and slowly shook her head at Giles before sitting down.

"I came here to visit Mr. Simon," Giles said. "I'm on the board of the New York Cruciverbal Club"—Mildred nodded recognition—"and I wanted to discuss setting up a Washington branch. Do you mind if we talk about it, Miss Burdock?"

"I don't know." She twisted her damp handkerchief. "Isn't there something we could do now? For Mr. Simon?"

"I wish there were," Giles said, "but I'm in the wrong profession. Why don't we just talk, Miss Burdock; it will help to pass the time until the doctor comes. May I call you Mildred?" She nodded and sat back in her chair, seeming to relax a bit. Giles paused a moment, then asked, "How long have you worked for Mr. Simon?"

"Over five years. He used to do it all himself, then he found he was spending so much time on records, billing, and correspondence, and I needed a job, so he hired me." She looked worriedly at the bedroom door. "Are you sure we can't—?" she asked nervously. "Maybe if you . . ."

"I wouldn't know what to do, Mildred," Giles said. "We must wait for the doctor. Now, tell me, do you also edit crosswords? Or construct them?"

"He wouldn't teach me. I love crosswords; it's my hobby. I make copies of all the crosswords that come in and I do them all, even the ones Mr. Simon rejects, but he never would let me edit. That's where all the knowledge and skill comes in." She started crying. "He didn't move at all when I called to him. Do you think . . ."

"We'll find out when the doctor comes," Giles said soothingly. "I didn't realize that editing and constructing crosswords paid well enough to warrant a secretary."

"Oh, yes. The time I spend on clerical and bookkeeping and keeping things in order and sending out puzzles and billing—all that time he can do the editing." Giles was pleased to see that as she talked about her work, Mildred seemed to relax. "He doesn't do construction anymore—it takes too long—but now he has accounts all over the country. Not just crossword books, but magazines, the specialized magazines, house organs, flight magazines; you have no idea how many crosswords are published every day. And, of course, the *Gazette*."

"You send everything out yourself?"

"I do *everything* around here but the editing and negotiating the fees. That he does himself. It's not easy keeping track of who gets what, who is due a puzzle and when, who hasn't paid us yet, who gets paid—the constructors get very nasty when their checks are late one day and I get yelled at as though it's my fault; he never talks to anybody. I work very hard."

"The computer helps, doesn't it?" Giles was trying to

keep her talking, to take her mind off Simon. Mildred seemed grateful for the opportunity to talk about mundane things. She wiped her eyes with her damp handkerchief and said, "Oh, yes, I couldn't do without it. At first I didn't like the idea, sort of like I'm at the mercy of a machine, but our business has grown so that it would take more people if I didn't have it, and you see how little room we have in here."

"You do your own mailing? A postage meter?"

"We're fully mechanized, much faster than pasting stamps. What I'd like better is if everybody had a facsimile machine. That really saves time and money. You could send a letter and a puzzle to anywhere much faster than you could put it in an envelope and stamp it, and you wouldn't have to type the envelope either. But only our big customers can afford them; they're very expensive."

"*The Capitol Gazette* has one, I take it?"

"All our big clients, yes."

"Do any of your constructors use a facsimile machine to send you their puzzles?"

"No, the average constructor doesn't have enough volume for that; they all use mail. The only one who ever sent us anything on the machine is Albert Kosgrow, this past week."

"Kosgrow is an editor himself," Giles said. "Isn't it unusual that he would send a puzzle to a rival?"

Mildred looked at her watch. "The doctor should have been here by now; the nurse said it wouldn't be long. I wonder what's keeping him." She shook her head and returned to Giles's question. "Yes, it's very unusual. Neither Mr. Lindenmann nor Mr. Kosgrow had ever sent us anything before. They're our competitors, you know. The only reason I can think of was to make Mr. Simon look bad so Mr. Kosgrow could get our business. We got a call from Mr. Warren; he's the features editor of the *Gazette*. Several people had called in on Wednesday, complaining about Tuesday's and Wednesday's puzzles. I can't imagine why Mr. Simon used them, they were so terrible, unless he owed Mr. Kosgrow a favor."

The doorbell rang. Mildred Burdock jumped up and answered the door. A short middle-aged dark-skinned man carrying a little black bag bustled in. "I am Dr. Patel," he said, "taking calls for Dr. Chertnow. Where is the patient, please?" Mildred led him to the bedroom. He went in and closed the door behind him. Mildred waited in front of the door for a moment, then resumed her seat.

Giles took up his questions again. "When Mr. Warren spoke to Mr. Simon about Tuesday's and Wednesday's puzzles, what did Mr. Simon say?"

"I answer the phone, Mr. Sullivan. I told Mr. Warren that I'd give the message to Mr. Simon and ask him to call back."

"And Simon said—?"

"Forget about it; he'd take care of it."

"Did you solve those puzzles?"

"Oh, yes, I always do the *Gazette* puzzles. They were really—not very nice-looking."

The doctor came out of the bedroom, shutting the door carefully. "I'm sorry," he said to Mildred Burdock. "He was an old man, and very sick. I'm sure he didn't feel anything." Mildred burst into tears.

Giles approached the doctor. "Is there anything I can do?"

"Thank you, sir, but that is quite all right. I am covering for his personal physician. Dr. Chertnow gave me complete instructions concerning all his critical patients. He was expecting something like this, you know, at any moment. His office will do all that is required."

"What was the cause of death, Doctor?" Giles asked. The doctor looked at him sharply. "I'm an attorney," Giles said. "I guess it's a typical attorney's question. Sorry."

"That's all right." The doctor softened. "I'm not certain, you understand, but it appears to be heart failure, although it may have been a combination of things, possibly complicated by an acute hypoglycemic episode. Dr. Chertnow might be more specific when he returns. The patient was a diabetic, you know, and his kidneys were not in very good shape either."

Giles turned to Mildred Burdock. "Did Mr. Simon tell you how he wanted things handled?" She shook her head. "You'll have to get in touch with his next of kin. Who are his closest relatives?"

She looked bewildered. "I don't think he had any. He never mentioned anyone."

"Would you be his heir, then, Miss Burdock?" Isabel asked. "Or executor? Does he have a burial plot? Does the body have to be shipped anywhere?" Mildred looked confused.

"Do you have his attorney's name and phone?" Giles asked. Mildred went to her desk, came back with a card, and gave it to Giles.

"He might know," Mildred said. "He never told me anything. I don't think he left me anything; he never really liked me, you know. Or anybody. I guess—do what you think is right, Mr. Sullivan, whatever is best." She burst into tears. "I want to go home now, please. Everything is taken care of; I'm always up-to-date. I'm so tired. You take care of everything. Ask the lawyer; he might know. I'll be in tomorrow and clean up. He'll be gone by then, won't he?"

"What about the business, Miss Burdock?" Giles asked. "Your paycheck? Who's going to take care of everything? Can you?"

"Me? No, I can't. I'm not an editor. Maybe Mr. Kosgrow? Or Mr. Lindenmann?"

"Can I give you a lift home, Miss Burdock?"

"Thank you, Mr. Sullivan, I have a car. I'll be all right, thank you." She walked slowly out the front door.

Giles looked at the doctor. "There's a good deal of work to do, legally, to end or transfer a business, which I'm sure Miss Burdock doesn't fully comprehend. I'm going to be in Washington for a very short time, Dr. Patel, and I won't be able to . . . Would you be kind enough to get in touch with Mr. Simon's attorney?" Giles handed the card Mildred Burdock had given him to the doctor.

"I'll ask Dr. Chertnow's nurse to do it," Dr. Patel said. "It's not quite in our line of work, you understand, but under the circumstances..."

"One more thing," Giles said. "Forgive me for asking, but was there any evidence of foul play?"

The doctor raised his eyebrows. "Do you have any reason for asking, Mr. Sullivan?"

"Not really, Doctor, just that with diabetics, one's mind automatically goes back to the von Bülow case."

"Well, I won't rule it out," the doctor said, "because I wasn't really looking for anything like that; a man in his condition, death was a constant companion. But since you've asked the question, I'm going to have to leave the death certificate open for a while and see if I can get an order for an autopsy. Are you an interested party, Mr. Sullivan?"

"No, no, actually I came to visit Simon, and stepped into—I never expected—I had better leave now too. Really, quite unexpected."

28

"LET OLIVER DRIVE US BACK," GILES SAID. "I NEED your full attention. Can you do your own navigation, Oliver?"

"Have no fear, sir," Oliver said. "Just give me a moment to study the map."

"You can drive as slowly as you want," Isabel said. "I don't care how many accidents you cause as long as we get back in one piece."

"Defensive driving is not necessarily slow, Miss Isabel, but you are right; one's first obligation is to avoid damage to oneself and one's passengers, not to protect the insane, the incompetent, and the dangerous."

Isabel settled back, snapped on her seat belt, and said, "Do you really believe in fairies, Sullivan?"

"Not since I was your age, Macintosh, but what would you have me do? Tell the doctor about Kosgrow? Or Zulkov? Fitzgerald? *Barca*?"

"You could have insisted on an autopsy right off."

"And if he finds Simon was murdered, what then? I can just hear the police now: 'Who told you, Doctor, that Mr. Simon was murdered? Where does he live? What reasons did he give you for his suspicions?' And when the police got to me? 'You say you never saw Mr. Simon in your life, Mr. Sullivan? But you were sure he was

167

murdered? I think you'd better tell us on what basis you made your accusation, Mr. Sullivan. No, not here; downtown. And bring Miss Macintosh with you.'"

"All right, Sullivan, you've made your point. But you do agree he was murdered, don't you?"

Giles hedged. "We can't be sure of that, Isabel. Simon was old and sick. Barca made that point himself, remember? Congestive heart failure, kidney failure, glaucoma, severe diabetes, and old age; it could have been a coincidence."

"Coincidence? That it happened on the morning Kosgrow and Fitzgerald were murdered? When Kosgrow and Simon were the only links we have with the spymaster? Come on, Sullivan, grow up."

"First answer a few questions for me, Macintosh. When did Simon die?"

"Do I have to go through another of your defense-attorney interrogations before you admit the obvious? If that's what it takes... Simon died before we got there, probably an hour or two. He had that sort of blue-gray look that dead people have."

"Did he die before or after Kosgrow died?"

"It's hard to tell; the blood on Kosgrow's back looked sort of fresh."

"Just as I thought. Now, listen carefully. When was Simon *killed*?"

"That's the same—Oh. I see. I don't know when he was killed. First—"

"Correct. First you have to know *how* he was killed. So tell me, Macintosh, how *was* Eugene Simon killed?"

"It wasn't by anything obvious, a knife or a gun; the doctor examined him. Nor asphyxiation or any other violence; the bedclothes were fairly neat. No obvious signs of poisoning, though we'll know better after the autopsy. Given that he was a diabetic, I'll put my money on an insulin overdose. A big one."

"That's what I guessed, although we can't be sure until the autopsy. Oliver, stop at the next place there could be a public phone; tell Barca that Simon was dead when we got there. Ask him to use his influence to get an autopsy done right away."

"I will do as you say, sir," Oliver said, "but it seems unnecessary to me. It is almost certainly as you described."

"I'm glad you agree, Oliver. So, Isabel, when was Simon murdered?"

"If it was an insulin overdose, Giles, several hours before, at least, depending on the amount of insulin injected and how much sugar and carbohydrates Simon had eaten, how much exercise he had performed, had he taken a cold bath and burned energy to create heat, and so forth. Too many factors unknown to allow for a definite answer at this time."

"I'll put it another way, Isabel. Was Simon killed in the five or ten minutes between the time the surveillance team was pulled off and the time Mildred Burdock arrived?"

"No. Impossible. Two reasons. First, insulin shock doesn't work that way; I've read about it. An overdose of insulin must first burn up all the sugar in the body, including the stored glycogen. Then the victim goes into coma, then he dies. It takes *hours*. Second, the killer had no way of knowing that the FBI team would be removed, much less when. He couldn't have hung around the house waiting for them to go so he could sneak in and inject— there's a phone, Oliver."

"I see it, madam. I'll be right back."

"So when was Simon killed, Isabel? Did Mildred Burdock do it in the half hour or so—we can check the FBI reports for the exact time—she had before we got there? Or, more like twenty minutes, assuming she arrived five before twelve and phoned the doctor at a quarter after?"

"No, for the same reason. But if she did do it, she could have done it the night before; Helen Goldstein said Simon worked from twelve to eight."

"That is possible, but remember, the house was bugged

and the phone tapped all the time."

"While Simon was in it? He never left the house, you know."

"It could be done while he was asleep, even if he was a very light sleeper. If you don't want to drill in a spike mike from the outside, you can pick up vibrations from a window, or even fix a tiny sensor to the windows. So if Miss Burdock suddenly stuck Simon with a hypodermic, wouldn't he have said 'Ouch'?"

"I'd like to hear those tapes myself."

"You can if you wish, but these tapes are monitored, not just recorded. I assure you that if there had been anything unusual in the Simon household, Barca would have known about it one hour later."

Oliver returned. "Barca said he will take all necessary steps. We are to see him as soon as we get back." He started the car.

Giles continued. "I am sure the tapes will show that Mildred Burdock left at precisely two minutes after eight and that she said 'Good night, Mr. Simon,' and he said 'Did you finish everything?' and she said 'Yes, Mr. Simon' and left. And that the outside members of the surveillance team will bear this out."

"Are you trying to tell me that Simon was *not* murdered, Giles?"

"No, no, I believe he was. But I don't see how it is possible to kill a man with an insulin injection in a small house which is completely bugged and surrounded by a group of FBI agents and they don't know it. Until I know *how* it can be done, I have to keep open the possibility that Simon died a natural death."

"This is going to be fun," Isabel declared. "If our luck keeps on running the way it has up till now, there's going to be a new secret message in Saturday's paper, the autopsy will show that Simon died of a massive overdose of insulin, the hypodermic next to Simon's bed will have his fingerprints on it in the proper places, as well as the insulin bottle in the refrigerator, and Barca will carefully, and in great detail, explain to us what idiots we are and ask us why we wasted the plane fare to come to Washington when he had five mentally handicapped daughters who could have done just as badly for less money." She took a deep breath. "Giles, I need a vacation. Desperately. Reach back and get me another bag of chocolate chip cookies."

 **29**

"**O**F COURSE HE WAS MURDERED," BARCA SAID. "ANY-one who would doubt that would invest in government-run lottery tickets. Please pass the tomatoes and anchovies, Kitty. And the capers too."

"It's the logical solution, Father," Jane said, "but it also sounds impossible. Have some sweet onion too."

"I'd like to get the results of the autopsy first," Giles said, "before we make our minds up."

"We'll have that by the time lunch is done," Elizabeth said. "I phoned our friend right after Oliver called and told him to rush it."

"It's certain to be insulin shock," Kitty said. "That's what I would have done under the circumstances."

"Simon was alone for sixteen hours," Barca said. "Is that enough time, Mary? Please pass the corn bread and the butter. No, the one with the Russian caraway."

"It depends on his body weight," Mary said, "his state of health, the amount and concentration of insulin injected, what he ate for super and breakfast, how much exercise he did, and other variables, but if I were the killer, I'd make sure to give him enough insulin to kill a horse. Try the pimientos, Father."

"You've been unusually silent today, Lydia," Barca said. "Is something bothering you?"

172

"We had breakfast at six," Lydia said, "and it's now after two. When I've regained my strength, I'll talk."

"After lunch," Barca announced, "I intend to take a siesta and leave the thinking to you young folk. What I'd like by teatime—yes, we'll have tea at five, no, make that five-thirty; must have time for proper digestion, so that Lydia will not waste away to a shadow—is the answer to some simple questions. One: Who killed Albert Kosgrow? Two: Who killed Eugene Simon? Three: *Why* were Kosgrow and Simon killed? Four: *How* was Simon killed? Five: How did Fitzgerald transmit his secret messages to Kosgrow? Six? Who killed Fitzgerald and his housekeeper? And seven: If all four were murdered in one morning by the same person, which is highly probable, where does he keep his roller skates?"

"Why the rush?" Isabel asked. "You're always setting deadlines for us, impossible deadlines. What difference does it make if we get the answers today, tomorrow, or never? The spy ring is broken."

"In this business," Barca said patiently, "you can never be sure you have accomplished your task. Intelligence organizations are like the Hydra, cut off one head and two others spring up to take its place. Worse, you are never sure that the head is completely cut off, nor even that it is the right head. For example, after analyzing this operation exhaustively since Tuesday evening, and with you and Giles since Wednesday afternoon, we have just determined that there is at least one more person, the Watchman, who is part of this particular spy team. If we find him, he may lead us to the spymaster."

"Do you really think a KGB thug would know the identity of the spymaster?"

"I'm sure he doesn't, but he may know something or someone who can give us a better lead. So question eight is: Who is the Watchman?"

Giles ignored the question. "What about any circumstantial evidence, Ackroyd? Do you have the reports on the inside of Simon's house? Now that it's empty, it should be child's play to get in, take pictures, make a complete inspection, the works. They have to remove the bugs anyway, don't they?"

"That will come," Elizabeth said, "with the autopsy report, right after lunch. We're getting the reports of the surveillance teams, too, but I can tell you right now, nothing unusual happened."

"Could there have been someone hidden in the house," Jane asked, "before the surveillance teams were put in place? Who stayed hidden until after the doctor and the ambulance left and then just walked away?"

"It's theoretically possible," Giles said, "but it doesn't fit. It's a small house; the killer would have had to have the cooperation of Simon's secretary as well as of Simon himself. If he was a houseguest, which, given what we know of Simon's disposition, is extremely improbable, I'm sure Miss Burdock would have mentioned it, especially after she found Simon's body. And she would have introduced us as well. But why should anyone move in there—there was only one bedroom—and expose himself to Simon and Burdock four days ago? The whole idea of the Watchman, of this whole operation, was to remain invisible. In fact, we're still not certain, although it's probable, that Simon knew he was part of a spy ring. Even more important, *when* was it decided that Simon should be killed? Certainly not four days ago. There was no way to be sure the operation was completed; the President might have called Fitzgerald and the other Adversaries in and revised his whole policy today. You don't destroy an asset as valuable as Simon on a whim."

"Then why did they kill him?" Isabel asked.

"I believe it had to do with Warren's call; Wesley Warren, *The Capitol Gazette*'s features editor. He called to complain about the first two puzzles, Tuesday's and Wednesday's. Whoever knew about it, or overheard Warren, must have passed that information on to the Watchman, or his controller. The Watchman guessed that this might lead to an investigation of Simon and the puzzles which, sooner or later, might show that there was a spy among the President's Adversaries. Knowing this, it would be relatively easy to determine it was Fitzgerald, just as we did. So a decision was made: It would be safer to remove Simon, with all the risks it entailed, than to leave Simon alive and able to talk. I mean, can you imagine Simon trying to give three good reasons why he published those four clumsy puzzles? Which came from a competitor of his who had never submitted a puzzle to him before? Impossible."

"Then that was the signal," Isabel said. "Whenever a puzzle came in from Albert Kosgrow, Simon had to send it in to be published the next day. And that's why Simon and Kosgrow were equipped with those identical fax machines, so they could transmit puzzles instantly, no time lost. Kosgrow, as soon as he had constructed the puzzle, sent it to Simon. Simon didn't have to edit it at all; he just sent it on to the *Gazette*. Perfect."

"Exactly," Giles said. "And that gives me an idea. Isabel, explain to me in detail how that machine of yours, the facsimile machine, works."

"I don't know too much about it, Giles, just roughly what it does."

"I know," Kitty said. "You need a compatible machine on the other end, not necessarily the same make or model, though that makes life easier. You put the document you want to send into the machine, call the receiver, the other party, on the phone. He puts his phone in a cradle, or even keeps a permanent connection open all the time, you press a button, and twenty seconds later a copy of what you sent comes out of the receiver's machine."

"What happens at the receiving end, Kitty? What do you see?"

"The phone rings, two short rings, you press the Receive button, and zip, you have it."

"Any noise?"

"A slight hum; that's all."

"If it sends a whole document in twenty seconds, how fast will it transmit twenty-eight letters?"

"The machine operates at ninety-six hundred baud, that means nine hundred sixty letters a second, or any of the lower speeds down to two hundred forty letters a second. But you need a special telephone line to transmit at ninety-six hundred baud, so the machine falls back to whatever speed can be used on the connection. Also, though the message may be twenty-eight letters long, there is a recognition signal sent first to activate the receiving machine. For simplicity, let's figure thirty-six letters, sent at two hundred forty letters a second, which gives us a transmission time of a bit less than a sixth of a second."

"That's how," Giles said triumphantly. "That's how Fitzgerald sent his coded message to Kosgrow. Check the phone tap tapes. You'll hear a short high-pitched sound, like a beep. Remember when we discussed a burst transmission? The kind where you slow down the tape so you can hear the message? Well, we didn't have a burst transmission of a clear message, we had a standard transmission of fax to fax which, when slowed down, wouldn't sound like anything at all."

"I'm sorry, Giles," Kitty said, "but that's *not* how it was done. I thought of it before, but it won't work. First of all, we agreed that the spy, Fitzgerald, could not know anyone else in the spy ring, just as none of the others could know him. To send, you have to know the phone number you are sending to. Once you know the number, it's easy to find the name and address that go with it. Second, this machine automatically imprints on the received message sheet, the sending terminal's name, address, and date."

"Third," Elizabeth said, "there were no outgoing phone calls or transmissions from Fitzgerald's phone during all the time he was tapped, not even when he wasn't home."

"And last," Jane said, "Fitzgerald didn't have a fax machine. Sorry, Giles."

"I'm afraid," Barca said, "that prolonged association with my offspring has had a deleterious effect on your normally acute intellect. Or possibly it is the unbearable chill imposed on this house and its occupants by overly hot-blooded meddlers with the air-conditioning system which has frozen all the higher thought centers. 'Oh what a mighty mind is here o'erthrown.' I had hoped that under Oliver's benign influence, and by association with the promising Miss Macintosh, the effects would be overcome, or, at least, allayed, but in vain. Go, Giles, do your best to think clearly, if you can remember how once it was done. I expect results by teatime. Lydia, my dear, if you wish to get back in my good graces again, please pass the gooseberry fool."

"Okay, everyone," Elizabeth announced, "synchronize your watches. We assemble in the workroom for a briefing at exactly two-thirty."

XXXXXXXXXXXXXXXXXXXX **30** ⬥⬥⬥

ELIZABETH READ FROM HER NOTES. "EUGENE SIMON died of"—she stopped and smiled evilly all around the table—"heart failure."

"No," gasped Isabel, "it can't be."

"Brought on"—Elizabeth was still smiling—"by a massive overdose of insulin, administered at least eight hours prior to his death, and possibly as much as twelve hours before."

"That means he was injected between midnight and four A.M.," Kitty said. "That's impossible."

"I asked if it could have been as much as sixteen or eighteen hours," Elizabeth said, "and I was told that it's impossible to say no, but given Simon's condition and the amount of insulin found in him, it's highly improbable."

"But the house was empty at that time," Lydia said, "wasn't it? Was anything picked up on the bugs, Lizzie?"

"I'm coming to that," Elizabeth said. "After MIldred Burdock left, which was at three minutes past eight P.M.— the observers verify that—there were the normal sounds of Simon working. At eleven P.M. he opened the refrigerator and, from the noises, or, rather, lack of wrong sounds—there were no sounds of opening bags or eating or cleaning up—Simon gave himself an injection of insulin. About thirty minutes later he had supper, which had

178

been delivered in a paper bag—more about that later—
cleaned up, and went back to work. Just before he ate,
right after he opened the paper bag, he went back to the
refrigerator and, they are sure, from the sounds, gave
himself another injection of insulin."

"Couldn't they have counted the used hypodermics in
the garbage pail?" Isabel asked.

"They did. There were three, which means that on that
day Simon took three injections or that Mildred Burdock
threw out the garbage from the day before in midday
without anyone seeing her do it. There's very little doubt
he gave himself three injections yesterday."

"Were the remnants of what was in the syringes
checked?"

"Of course. You think he injected cyanide, or something slower-acting? No, nothing in the syringes but tiny
amounts of U-100 insulin, and no traces of any foreign
substance in Simon's blood. An hour after supper Simon
went to the refrigerator and, the sounds show, he drank
something from a bottle—more about that later too—and
went back to work. At about three-thirty A.M. he undressed,
went to the bathroom, had another drink from the bottle
in the refrigerator, evidently emptied it, threw it into the
garbage pail, and went to bed. He slept restlessly for about
two hours, then slept soundly or, more likely, was in a
coma."

"No one entered the house?" Jane asked. "No way
anyone could have sneaked in?"

"There were lights at the front and back doors," Elizabeth said, "and two of the observers had night-sighting
equipment. Nothing on the tapes, either, until Mildred
Burdock came in at eight minutes to noon. She put the
breakfast bag into the refrigerator, fussed around for a
while, and at eight-fourteen she knocked on Simon's door.
She knocked three times and called to him, louder each
time. After another minute, presumably wondering
whether or not she should risk waking him, she opened
the door. She called to him from the open door and, when
he didn't respond, walked over to the bed. She must have

touched him, because she made a funny sound, like a half scream, ran out, and phoned his doctor. The nurse told her to call an ambulance right away, and said she'd find a doctor. Burdock called for an ambulance and spent the time walking up and down, moaning, until Giles rang the bell."

"Are you saying," Isabel asked, "that Simon killed himself?"

"I'm not saying anything," Elizabeth replied. "I just presented the facts as we know them; and everything I said checked with everything reported, perfectly consistent. But suicide is out of the question. The reason is that what was in the bottle Simon drank from twice, was eighty grams of Instant Glutose. Diabetics keep that, or something similar, handy in case they feel that their carbohydrate intake is not in balance with their insulin injection, and they have taken too much insulin. The usual dose is one third of a bottle. Simon evidently drank two thirds of a bottle or more. He wouldn't do that if he were trying to kill himself."

"How do you know it was the Glutose he drank?" Isabel asked. "And shouldn't that be 'glu*cose*'?"

"It's a trade name for a popular brand of glucose solution," Elizabeth said. "We know he drank from a bottle. There were no other bottles in the house, either in the refrigerator or in the garbage pail."

"I need some technical information," Mary said. "What did Simon weigh? How much insulin did he usually take? What kind of insulin was it?"

"Simon weighed one hundred forty pounds. He had Type I diabetes, which means his body produced no insulin at all and he always needed insulin to stay alive. He used one hundred eighty units of insulin a day, a tremendously high dose. He gave himself two injections daily, one before breakfast and one before supper, ninety units of U-100 insulin, mixing short-acting insulin with intermediate-acting insulin so he would be in balance all day and all night. If he occasionally binged on sweets, which was most unusual because Burdock warned the few visitors he had never to bring cake or any carbohydrates or alcohol, he would take a proportional amount of short-acting insulin a half hour in advance."

"He ate sweets?" Isabel asked. "He drank? As sick as he was with diabetes?"

"If you couldn't have your chocolate fix every day, Isabel," Jane said, "you'd be climbing the walls in one week. Well, imagine, if you can, *never* having any choc-olate, or sugar, or vanilla or ice cream, or cake, or—"

"Stop!" Isabel screamed softly. "I'll talk."

"Exactly. So if he could cajole a visitor into sneaking some candy, or a small bottle of anything, past Burdock, he'd shoot up, drink the cognac, and most of the time no one would notice."

"But it didn't do him any good," Mary said, "did it? He lost three toes to gangrene, I remember, and he had glaucoma and all sorts of other problems. Did he smoke too?"

"When he could get away with it," Elizabeth said. "He had a real death wish. It's a wonder he lived as long as he did. You really can't blame the doctor for thinking it was heart failure, since it really was."

"What else was in the refrigerator?" Mary asked.

"Two partly used 10 cc. bottles of U-100 insulin, one regular short-acting, one intermediate-acting. A head of iceberg lettuce. Four stalks of endive. An escarole. That's it."

"No food?" Lydia asked. "Nothing?"

"Doctor's orders," Elizabeth said. "And Burdock was very strict about it."

"It isn't just sugar that diabetics can't eat," Mary pointed out. "Carbohydrates of any kind are almost as bad for you. Not really bad, but they have to be kept in balance with the insulin intake. Fat and protein should also be measured to keep the proportions of food and food types in balance. The balancing of food with insulin must be done accurately at all times."

"His doctor found," Elizabeth said, "that if any food was kept in the house, Simon would eat it all at once. He worked out an arrangement for Simon which would keep Simon out of the hospital, with Burdock's help. A local diner a couple of miles down the road would deliver a meal of exactly measured calories and balanced food types in a sealed white paper bag shortly before mealtimes. The doctor would plan the meals a month in advance and Burdock would make the arrangements. She usually picked up the breakfast on her way to work. It was expensive, but Simon's life depended on it, so he had no choice."

"What about weekends?" Isabel asked. "Couldn't he cheat then?"

"Burdock told the diner that if she found out they gave Simon as much as one grape that wasn't on the menu when she wasn't there, she'd cut them off."

"No wonder he hated her," Isabel said. "Couldn't he sneak away on his own on weekends or nights?"

"Boy," Lizzie said, "the idea of living on a strict diet really disturbs you, doesn't it? Your mind automatically jumps to ways to cheat. Well, you're not alone, Isabel; Lydia looks a little worried too." She smiled sadly. "I am too. I think we're all prediabetics; I've been reading up on it. Father especially. You should adjust our meals, Jane, gradually, so Father doesn't notice."

"He'll notice," Jane said. "And after Lydia, you'd be the third to complain, Lizzie. But I'll do it. You'll all have to back me up when he screams."

"We will," Kitty said.

"Simon couldn't sneak away weekends, Isabel," Elizabeth responded to the question, "because he had no car and the nearest store was two miles away. He had difficulty walking even before the operation, and he was even worse off without his toes."

"What did he have for supper?" Mary asked. "Last night, I mean."

Elizabeth checked her notes. "Six ounces of unsweetened cranberry juice, two ounces of turkey breast and one slice of whole-grain bread, with lettuce, one-half a medium-size papaya, and six ounces of skim-milk yogurt."

"Yuch," said Isabel.

"Double yuch," Lydia said.

"Takes a lot of guts to be a diabetic," Kitty said. "I don't know if I could do it."

"You could if you had to," Jane said. "Think of the 'or else.' Our diet starts tomorrow. Better safe than sorry."

"Can't you start after I'm gone?" Isabel asked. She looked at Jane's stony face and shut her mouth.

After a moment's silence Jane asked, "What about Fitzgerald? What did you observe in his house?"

"A typical bachelor academic's house, with a modern computer, fully equipped. His study looked very much like your father's."

"I still believe that Fitzgerald transmitted the message to Kosgrow by phone," Giles said. "There is no other way."

"His computer did have a modem," Isabel said, "so he could work at home and send data to his computer at school. Could he have transmitted the secret message to Kosgrow through the modem?"

"We thought of that," Kitty said, "but he made no calls, not one, during the period he was watched and tapped, and still Kosgrow got the message last night, the one that trapped Fitzgerald."

Giles thought for a moment. "You're sure Fitzgerald made no calls at all while he was being watched?"

"None."

"Did he *receive* any calls?"

"Not really. The call-forwarding phone, somebody rang Fitzgerald's office about four o'clock and hung up when the machine answered."

Giles looked agitated. "What did Fitzgerald say? On his answering machine, I mean. Does he say 'This is Professor Fitzgerald. I am not at home now, but if you,' etc.? Or does he say 'This is seven two six four. Please leave your name and number and,' etc.? Or what?"

"Actually, *he* doesn't say anything; he uses a computer-generated voice, synthesized, sounds like a robot. I guess he does it so anyone who accidentally dials his office number won't know whom he's reached; he does have a distinctive voice, you know, and he's been on TV a lot lately."

"Yes, but what does he *say*? The answering machine message? Verbatim."

"It says, 'When you hear the tone, please leave your name and phone number and a short message. Beep. Hum. Click.' That's it, Giles. Verbatim."

"A short message? Beep. Hum. Click." Giles sat back. "A short message? Beep? That's it! Did you slow down the 'beep'?"

"Of course, Giles," Kitty answered patiently. "It wasn't a burst transmission. No message."

"Did you run it as an input on a facsimile machine?"

Kitty stared at him. "Give me the tape, Lizzie. Quick." She grabbed the tape and ran into the study.

Two minutes later she came back with a sheet of paper. She placed it on the table. On it was printed: "SUNWTTXECPLNRTRLCDLTPWSNTSTS." "This morning's message," Kitty said. "I think you've got it, Giles."

"Not so fast," Isabel said. "Even if his answering machine used a computer voice, Kosgrow had to dial Fitzgerald's office at the university. He had to know that phone number and he could have found out who Fitzgerald was from that. The whole idea was to make sure no one could find out Fitzgerald was the spy."

"Somewhere in D.C.," Kitty said, "is one of those use-our-prestigious-address-and-phone services where the John Q. Smith Company, fee paid a year in advance, has a dusty phone that never rings which, when it is called, has its call forwarded automatically to Fitzgerald's second phone, at the university, from which it is *again* forwarded to Fitzgerald's home answering machine. The perfect cutout."

"Yes," Jane said, "and Kosgrow didn't make the call himself; he had his facsimile machine make the call for him. The fax machine ignored the voice, which it couldn't understand, but the beep generated by Fitzgerald's computer was in a language it could understand, so it printed out the twenty-eight-letter message contained in the beep."

"Can a facsimile transceiver do that?" Isabel asked.

"I don't know if it's built in," Kitty said, "but if it isn't, it would take me, or any repairman, five minutes to make it work that way. I know that our computer can talk directly to our facsimile machine or any compatible fax machine that uses the same CCITT electronic code."

"Congratulations, Giles," Elizabeth said. "And you, Kitty, hang your head in shame. You could have done it."

"Should we wake Father from his nap," Lydia asked, "to tell him?"

"Not now," Jane said. "There's nothing important enough in this to disturb him for. It's interesting, but it doesn't require any action. Besides, I can very easily wait another two hours to have him tell me that I'm a low-grade moron."

"Yeah," Lydia said. "And he'll be rested from his nap. We'll never hear the end of this. We owe you one, Giles." She didn't elaborate.

31

"THAT'S ALL VERY WELL, GILES," BARCA SAID, "BUT
I gave you seven other problems, six actually, childishly
simple problems, which, I take it, in the flush of ecstasy
at having stumbled on the simple mechanical solution to
the easiest question, you did not address at all. Perhaps
you forgot them? With advancing years, certain persons
of lazy habit, having neglected to exercise their minds
fully in their youth, tend to lose the faculty of recollection.
Would you like me to repeat those questions I asked only
a few hours ago?"

"That is quite unnecessary, Ackroyd."

"Good. I am relieved that you have retained, at least,
your short-term memory. But perhaps, in the future, a
notebook? Comes in very handy, I hear; frees the remaining brain cells for more important functions. You had three
hours, Giles, three whole, uninterrupted hours. One
hundred eighty minutes. Divided by six that is, Mary?"

"Thirty minutes per question, Father."

"Precisely. And these questions, the six forgotten questions, are all related. One question, really, Giles. Almost
two hundred minutes for one question. Now, really, Giles."
He turned to Jane. "Isn't the tea steeped enough, Jane?"

"It will be ready just about the time you finish speaking,
Father."

He glared at her suspiciously. "But I forgive you, Giles. It's the atmosphere here. I understand how difficult it is to think clearly under these conditions. I should never have brought you into this house in the first place; I do hope the effects are not permanent. Why, there have been times when I, even I, was unable to solve a problem, to know the best way to accomplish my ends, for several seconds. There is a miasma given off by these daughters of mine, a radiation that short-circuits the neural pathways and makes it impossible to think rationally, to solve the simplest of puzzles. For this I apologize, Giles, most sincerely."

"No apology is necessary, sir," Giles said, not smiling. "I volunteered, knowing the danger."

"And you, Isabel. It is especially unfortunate that you have been exposed to the evil influence at a time when you will be the center of attention, watched from all sides, as the acting president of Windham University. Perhaps, before you go back to consort with your judging peers, you might stop off in New York and take a course in remedial logic? Memorize a few of the more popular catchphrases, use them judiciously, to confound your critics? If you are careful, you might just carry it off."

"An excellent suggestion, sir," Isabel said seriously.

"And you, Kitty, having turned to technology in compensation for your lack of intellectual stature, should it not have been *you* who discovered Fitzgerald's mechanical method of transmitting the secret messages rather than annoying our guest with such trivial problems?"

"It should have been, Father," Kitty said.

"Is it not reasonable to assume, Mary, that five perpetual students who have never even tried to earn their keep and on whom I have spent my best years training in the rudiments of communication might possibly have deduced, from the evidence in front of their very eyes, how a *poseur* such as Fitzgerald could have transferred information when he was phoned?"

"Perfectly reasonable, Father," Mary said.

"Don't you agree, Lydia, that if I ask six questions of

187

six people, six people and six questions, isn't it logical to assume that I would get one answer from each person?"

"Supremely logical, Father," Lydia said.

"Do you realize, Elizabeth, the shame you have brought on my head, the dishonor to the name of Ackroyd? It will be spoken of, and, yes, they *will* speak of it, noticeably hushing their whispers when I enter the club, as Ackroyd's folly, nay, Ackroyd's *disgrace*. The House of Ackroyd will resound through history along with the House of Atreus. Plays will be written, epic poems, to keep my shame alive. Atreus was cursed by Thyestes; I must have been cursed by all Olympus. Can anything wash out the stain?"

"Regrettably, nothing, Father," Elizabeth said.

"And you, Jane, my firstborn. Is it possible that—? Isn't that tea ready yet?"

"Are you finished speaking, Father?" Jane asked. "I didn't want to interrupt you. Whatever my faults, I remember my manners, which I learned at your paternal knee."

He looked at her, wounded. "Serve the tea *now*, Jane; I will discuss this fiasco with you later. No need to involve our guests in family matters. Miss Macintosh first, please, in case you had forgotten the appropriate protocol."

"Indian tea on the left"—Jane offered the tray to Isabel—"Chinese on the right. Cucumber sandwiches this end, watercress that. Cream and sugar? Lemon?"

"White bread and butter?" Isabel drew back. "Cucumber and watercress? No offense intended, Jane, but I can't function on that. Even the crusts are cut off." She stood up. "Hold the tea ceremony for a minute, Jane. I shall return."

Isabel was back in less than a minute, slightly out of breath. "Here," she said, handing a small white bag to each one, "they're good, and cheaper than in the store."

"Chocolate chip cookies," Lydia squealed. "I was just in the mood."

"I have tons," Isabel said. "Two huge cartons. It would

cost a fortune to fly them back. There's only a half a pound in a bag. Enjoy."

"They are very good," Barca said. "Mrs. Goldstein's?"

"I'm thinking of inviting her to be resident baker and crossword constructor at Windham U. I'd kill for an unending supply of these. I'll bet when the kids hear of it, we'll have no trouble raising our fees."

"If you dare take her away from Washington," Lydia said, "I'll—Jane, put in a standing order with Mrs. Goldstein. Isabel, do you—? Would you mind—? Do you really have tons? These are irresistible."

"Of course," Isabel got up. "I'll get another batch. Take this one while you're waiting."

"God bless you, Isabel," Lydia said. "I've always liked you, you know, in spite of everything."

"Wait," Giles said. "I know. *Now* I know." He jumped up. "I have to go. My God, it's almost six o'clock. Excuse me; I have to go into the workroom."

"Whatever for, Giles?" Ackroyd asked.

"To construct a puzzle, of course." He walked quickly to the door. "Jane, do we still have that safe house, apartment, on Ordway?"

"It's always available, Giles, on a few hours' notice. Why?"

"There's not enough time; I'll talk to you later. Don't disturb me for *anything*."

32

"GILES HAS BECOME EXTREMELY SENSITIVE OF LATE,"
Barca said. "There was a time when I could point out his
more egregious failings in far stronger language than the
mild constructive criticism I offered today, and he would
accept it in the spirit in which it was intended."

"I don't think," Isabel said, "he was personally
offended, Ackroyd, knowing that from you even faint
praise is an accolade bestowed only reflexively. God, listen to me. Is your manner of speech catching?"

"I should hope so, my dear; keep trying. Then why
did he run out so quickly and, not that I wish to carp, so
impolitely, without so much as a by-your-leave?"

"He's going to construct a crossword puzzle."

"I thought that's what he said. Does this urge strike
him very often? And so suddenly? Has his physician diag-
nosed the underlying illness or malfunction?"

"No, I'm sorry. I'm not explaining it well. The Brun-
dage case, you must know about it, although the details
were never publicized—Giles trapped the killer by means
of a crossword puzzle he constructed. And in the Humboldt case he used the same technique. Well, he seems
to be repeating the same pattern here. He's constructing
a puzzle to trap the killer, or the killers, of Albert Kosgrow, Eugene Simon, and Horton Fitzgerald."

"I see. Or, rather, I don't see. In the other two cases, which Oliver told me about in detail, he knew who the killer was, did he not? That is, he used the puzzle he constructed to trap, as you said, the killer, not to determine who the killer was. Isn't that so?"

"Yes, exactly, Ackroyd."

"That means he knows who the killer is, without any doubt."

"Not necessarily, Ackroyd, but I'd bet on it."

"Very well, then, I'm proceeding slowly, step by step, you understand, in order not to confuse my slow-witted offspring. We, one of us, must have said something immediately preceding Giles's unseemly jumping up at the table."

"Well, not necessarily *immediately* before; Giles is not very quick-witted, you know. There could have been something said, or that he realized he understood, much earlier, even yesterday, that was the clue but lay dormant, until someone said or did something at teatime that triggered the connection that gave Giles the clue he needed to complete the solution to the puzzle."

"Exactly. So," he addressed his daughters, "who spoke last before Giles ran off?"

"I think I did, Father," Lydia said. "I remarked how I had always liked Isabel. A slight exaggeration."

Barca thought for a moment. "I see nothing in that to warrant . . . Do you, Isabel?"

"Not for the life of me."

"Perhaps something earlier, ladies? Since you said it, Isabel, I might as well agree: Giles was never very quick, I'm sorry to say. A sound thinker, but cautious. What happened at the beginning of tea?"

"You were discussing our incompetence, Father," Jane said.

"Ah, yes, I do recall. In a most restrained manner, as I remember; it does not do to embarrass one's guests. Was there anything I said that might have stimulated Giles into unexpected brilliance?"

"Not that I noticed, Father," Elizabeth said.

"It couldn't have been anything you said, Elizabeth, obviously, since you were admittedly baffled by the mechanism of a familiar device that even a professor of political science could understand. You, Isabel, think back. What did you say that was of import?"

"Not a thing, Ackroyd; I don't know any more than you do. I'm afraid we will have to wait until he comes out."

"Which may not be for—How long does it take him to compose a crossword?"

"You heard what he said the other day; anywhere from two to eight hours."

"Perhaps if I opened the door a crack?"

"Don't even think of it, Ackroyd; the interruption may cost an hour or more. He gets very jumpy when he's constructing, and he has his sword cane with him. In the Humboldt case he almost stabbed me when I just said hello."

"Then I'll send Oliver. Surely he wouldn't stab Oliver, would he?"

"He might try, under these conditions, without thinking. But Oliver is too dangerous to—well, you know. He might break Giles's arm automatically while he was defending himself, and then who'd trap the killer? No, we must wait for Giles to come out of his own accord, when he's finished."

"I accept your judgment of the situation, Isabel. Two to eight hours, you say? That would bring us past eight o'clock at a minimum, and possibly as late as two A.M. After midnight. We really should prepare, fortify ourselves for any eventuality. Jane, at eight, a light cold supper? Say, melon with prosciutto, jelled consommé, gravlax, curried kidney bean salad, and fresh raspberry sherbet?"

33

"Ah, Giles," Barca said, "just in time for dessert. Jane had a place set for you in the hope that you might finish in time. You *are* finished, are you not?"

"Yes. No, I can't stop now. It's almost nine. Here's the puzzle, Kitty. Send it to the *Gazette* at once. By your facsimile machine. Hurry. You, Barca, call your friend. Tell him to pressure Wesley Warren to run it in tomorrow's paper. It must be tomorrow."

"I can't call my friend to press—not pressure, Giles, watch your language—press Warren; it would arouse his suspicions about the crosswords, including this one. He's upset about this week's puzzles already; I don't want him putting two and two together."

"I can't send it," Kitty said. "Every transmission has our name and address printed on it automatically, remember? We can't risk exposing the Group under any circumstances."

"Can't you defeat that function, Kitty?"

"Probably, given enough time, but what if it took hours?"

"Then I'll bring it to Warren myself. I'll tell him it was done by Hannibal, as a special favor in honor of Eugene Simon. Free. He won't be able to resist that. I'll even promise him a twenty-three by twenty-three puzzle by Hannibal for the Sunday edition."

"I'm sure he would be very grateful, Giles, but how would you explain rushing in at ten o'clock—the presses roll at eleven—and insisting that he tear out what he has already set and substitute this puzzle? What reason would you give? And I'm sure he's no fool; he might even get the idea that *you're* Hannibal. No, Giles, it's just too late. Can't it wait another day?"

"No. There's no way; this is not a Sunday puzzle. Sunday's puzzle is already printed. This must be in Saturday's paper. Tomorrow. Another day gone, and everything could be lost."

"I'm sorry, Giles," Barca said. "Perhaps if you explained what you want to accomplish, we could suggest another method."

"There is no other— How can you sit there eating ices while—? I don't care what we risk, Barca; you have to."

"I know what to do," Isabel said. "I'll drive you to Simon's house, and I'll send it to the *Gazette* by Simon's fax machine. At this time of night I'll get you there in less than a half hour; just don't complain about my driving. I'll mark it, add a note, that it was Simon's dying wish that this be in tomorrow's paper. That's the best I can do. Okay, Giles?"

"Yes. Great. Thanks. Let's go."

"Take Oliver," Barca said.

"I don't need Oliver," Giles said. "I have my cane."

"Oliver will open the back door for you in one minute, Giles, as well as take out anyone who may be on guard. Such as the police. Don't argue, Giles; go. I'll have Oliver meet you out front. Good luck. And when you come back, whatever time that is, please wake me. I have been supporting you unstintingly, albeit blindly, out of loyalty to your past endeavors, but there *are* limits, and given an explanation of what you hope to accomplish, I will be able to direct your efforts to productive ends. Go."

"Yes," Giles said. "It will be a pleasure to wake you. I'll need lots of help tomorrow. Good night."

34

BARCA WAS WRAPPED IN AN ANKLE-LENGTH PORT-colored robe so heavily embroidered that, Isabel thought, had he been wearing a crown rather than his usual fez, he could have passed for Boris Godunov.

The five Ackroyd women were dressed in reverse chronological finery, from Jane in a lacy negligee to Lydia in a ratty old flannel bathrobe, each looking more unattainably beautifully begrudgingly sexy than Isabel could ever hope to be. "But it isn't even ten," Isabel said. "Why the—?" She waved her hand at the nightclothes.

"I have found," Barca said, "that impromptu actions, not fully thought out and lacking proper logistic support, often require immediate salvage efforts, usually at three o'clock in the morning. In view of Giles's explosive behavior earlier this evening, I felt we should all get whatever rest we could, while we could, in anticipation of a Mayday call before dawn. I take it, Isabel, that Giles's new crossword was sent in time?"

"Well before the deadline, Barca, but we don't know if they'll print it."

"The presses will roll in an hour, Isabel. It is too late now to change anything, even if I were willing to risk an investigative reporter's curiosity by having my friends press a newspaper to stop the presses in order to substitute one crossword puzzle for another. While I do trust Giles's judgment, usually, I doubt if the possible gain would have been worth the risk. We will learn at five-thirty tomorrow morning if you were successful. Any trouble, Oliver?"

"No, sir," Oliver said. "Piece of cake."

"Then let's go back to bed. Giles can tell us all about his mysterious puzzle at breakfast."

"Good idea," Kitty said. "After you, Father."

"But," he sputtered, "but aren't you—?"

"Not a bit," Lydia said. "Good night, Giles, Isabel, Oliver. Come, Father."

"You are dissembling, Lydia," Ackroyd said. "Trembling at the thought, all of you—I can tell—of not hearing right now what Giles—. Especially you, Kitty; curious as your namesake. Typical female trait. Well, if you insist. As a loving father, I would not have you tossing and turning all night in the agony of your ignorance. Giles, you might as well go into the study and enlighten these fluttering chits. I may as well join you. Jane? Order tea, please."

"I'll have chocolate milk, Jane, if you don't mind," Isabel said. "I'm completely pooped and I need to soothe my nerves. I don't know if you realize it, Ackroyd"—her voice rose—"but it's Friday night, only Friday night. I started out from Rockfield, Vermont, early Wednesday morning, after a difficult meeting with my board of trustees, and I've had three days of solid— In these three days I've been involved in one accidental death, four murders, one spy, one spymaster, one Watchman, four coded crosswords—five, counting Giles's latest creation—I've broken into a house, two houses, gotten practically no sleep, and I've *had* it. Plus too much bullying." She glared at Bennet Ackroyd.

"Yes, Isabel." Ackroyd's pompous manner was shut off; it was Barca responding. "I do realize it. You're not alone, Isabel; we've all been driving ourselves. It's the nature of the trade; long periods of inactivity broken up by short bursts of continuous action, pressure, and danger. You are in the midst of one such affair right now, and you cannot leave the game. We may need you at any moment; we're all totally dependent on each other. But when this is over"—his voice grew cold—"if you really feel that the Group is not for you"—Jane looked sharply at her father—"if you feel you are not equal to the task, we will give, all of us, since *all* our lives are at stake, serious consideration to permitting you to—to become an inactive member." There was dead silence; everyone was carefully not looking at Isabel.

"If she gets chocolate milk," Lydia broke the silence, "I want more chocolate chip cookies. Okay, Isabel?"

The tension relaxed. "I'll get a bag for each," Isabel said. "Don't start without me."

When she got back, Giles was seated in Barca's own chair, looking very tired. She realized, suddenly, surprised, that he was not young.

"I'd like to start at the end," Giles said. "The murder of Eugene Simon. How it was done."

"Not *who*, Giles?" Jane asked.

"That will become clear," he said. "But please challenge me if you find the slightest discrepancy in my reasoning. If I can't refute your cross-examination—. Let's hope I'm right, because if I'm not, we've lost this battle." He drew a deep breath. "Here are the facts as we know them. Eugene Simon awoke at eleven-thirty A.M. Thursday morning, went to the bathroom, went to the kitchen and got his paraphernalia from the refrigerator and injected his insulin, got dressed, and was at work in his office when his secretary, Mildred Burdock, arrived at eleven fifty-seven A.M. She brought with her the bag containing Simon's breakfast that she had picked up at the diner. The breakfast consisted of four ounces of orange juice, one slice of whole-grain toast, a package of unsweetened bran cereal, one small apple, eight ounces of skim milk, a container of coffee, and a packet of artificial sweetener. She placed the bag on the kitchen table and went to work in her office. Simon went into the kitchen without greeting her and ate his breakfast.

"Burdock and Simon worked without speaking until four P.M., when Simon called her in and gave her a batch of puzzles to send to various publications. At five past four P.M., the delivery boy brought Simon's lunch to the house and gave it to Mildred Burdock. She put the bag on the table and Simon ate his lunch, which consisted of four ounces of unsweetened grapefruit juice, one slice of whole-grain toast, a salad of two ounces of water-packed tuna with lettuce and celery, a quarter of a small cantaloupe, a container of coffee, and a packet of sweetener."

"He didn't take another injection of insulin before his lunch?" Isabel asked.

"Most diabetics," Mary said, "avoid taking more than two injections daily by using a mixture of rapid-onset and intermediate-onset insulin, so that their food intake and energy output are balanced over a twelve-hour period."

"And shouldn't he have drunk some water," Isabel asked, "and gone to the bathroom several times during the day? I thought that's one of the symptoms of diabetes."

"According to the reports," Elizabeth said, "he did, frequently, but we didn't mention every little detail. Is it important, Giles?"

"Not a bit," Giles said, and continued. "Mildred Burdock ate her lunch, which she had brought in her tote bag, in her office with the door closed, evidently so as not to drive Simon mad with envy."

"Sure," Isabel said. "I can imagine Simon tearing a bologna on white with mayo out of her hands in a frenzy of lust. I would do it myself on a diet like that. I'll bet it used to happen like that before Simon's doctor worked out this feeding-the-animals routine."

"We'll find out," Lydia said, "when the police take her statement."

"No need," Giles said. "We have all the information required." He went back to the narrative. "After lunch they both worked until six, when Simon gave Burdock a batch of correspondence to be answered. At six-eleven P.M. a document came in on the facsimile machine and—"

"That had to be Kosgrow sending in his coded puzzle," Isabel said. "Did any other calls come in? Or go out?"

"None," Elizabeth said. "There's no doubt it was Kosgrow's transmission. We'll have the proof tomorrow, when we check Kosgrow's phone times."

"Don't bother," Giles said. "It was the puzzle. Right after it came in Mildred went into Simon's office and said, 'Is this what you want for tomorrow's *Gazette*?' And Simon said, 'Of course, Burdock; don't you pay attention? Just do what you're told and don't bother me.' Mildred went into her office and faxed the puzzle to the *Gazette*. Both she and Simon continued working until seven forty-five P.M., at which time Simon's supper was delivered. Mildred put the bag into the refrigerator and told Simon she was leaving."

"We know the rest," Mary said.

"Not everyone has your photographic memory, Mary," Giles said. "Let me complete the story so it makes a coherent whole in everyone's mind." He cleared his throat. "Mildred Burdock left at three minutes past eight. Simon kept on working. At eleven P.M. he opened the refrigerator, took out his equipment, gave himself his evening injection of insulin, and went back to work. Thirty minutes later he took his supper bag out of the refrigerator, opened it, and put it on the table. Then he gave himself another injection of insulin, ate supper, and went back to work. An hour later he went back to the refrigerator, took a drink from a bottle, evidently the Instant Glutose, and went back to work. At three-thirty A.M. he undressed, went to the bathroom, had another drink of Instant Glutose, evidently emptying the bottle. He threw the bottle into the garbage pail and went to bed. He slept restlessly for about two hours, then went to sleep soundly or, more likely, fell into a coma."

"Are you saying nobody killed Simon?" Isabel was outraged. "That he killed himself?"

"Yes, of course. That's the only way it could have happened."

"Nonsense, Giles," Barca said. "Burdock killed him."

199

"But Burdock wasn't in the house then," Isabel protested. "She had left four hours earlier. There was no way for her to come back."

"No way at all," Giles agreed.

"Then if Burdock didn't kill Simon," Isabel asked, "who did?"

"Burdock was the murderer," Giles said. "But Simon killed himself."

"Of course," Barca said. "That's the only way it could have been done. That's why you jumped up at tea, Giles. Most impolitely, I might add."

"I know," Giles said. "Sorry."

"Are you trying to drive me crazy, Giles?" Isabel said. "Barca and I can't both be right."

"Of course we can," Barca said, "now that Giles has presented the events in their proper perspective. I think Lydia should be the one to put it into words; it may serve as an object lesson to keep her from getting fat."

"For that very reason," Lydia said, "perhaps you should tell the story, Father."

"Perhaps I'd better," Barca said.

35

"Let's start," Barca lectured, "with the impor-tant facts. Simon gave himself three injections of insulin: one at eleven-thirty A.M., before Mildred Burdock arrived with his breakfast; another at eleven-thirty P.M., three-and-a-half hours after Mildred Burdock left for the night, and a third at midnight."

"Are you depending on *sound* alone," Isabel asked, "on your low-fi bugs, for all this? Couldn't Mildred Bur-dock have killed Simon *before* she left, and had a tape recorder or a radio transmitter to make the sounds the FBI thought were made by Simon? He didn't speak, did he? Talk to himself? How hard would it have been to imitate the sound of a refrigerator door being opened and closed, of bottles, tearing bags, eating, walking around, flushing toilets, all these things, while Simon lay in a coma?"

"Not hard," Barca admitted, "but there are some dif-ficulties. Mary? Elizabeth?"

"Diabetics usually inject themselves," Mary said, "in the lower abdomen, buttocks, and upper thighs, where there is fatty muscle tissue."

"It is certain," Elizabeth said, "that Simon did not undress to allow Burdock to inject him. Nor did he yell, 'What are you sticking me with that hypodermic for?' He was not in a coma before Burdock left either; the surveillance team saw him passing windows several times, and observed lights going on and off at the appropriate moments to coincide with the sounds. His fingerprints were on the insulin bottles, the glucose bottle, and all three hypodermics, not sharp and clear as though someone had pressed his fingers to them, but in a way consistent with their normal use."

"*Three* hypodermics?"

"Diabetics always use a new hypodermic," Mary said, "for each injection, to avoid infection and contamination of the insulin. They even break the needle after one use to make sure they don't accidentally use the same hypodermic again."

"Sorry, Barca," Isabel said. "Didn't mean to interrupt."

"Quite all right, my dear, we want to leave no loose ends." He looked around. "Any more questions? None? Then I'll go on. The key is the third injection. Why did he do it? Here is a man who, for some years, has made a satisfactory adjustment, balanced his food intake with his insulin injections—very large amounts, true, but balanced nevertheless—by taking two injections a day, one before breakfast and one before supper. He mixed rapid-onset insulin with intermediate-onset insulin so that he could get through a twelve-hour period without major discomfort or danger. Why did he inject his insulin a half hour before each meal? Mary?"

"It takes time," Mary said, "for insulin to be absorbed and distributed through the body; twenty to thirty minutes. The technique Simon used makes available to the diabetic extra insulin to balance his food intake at mealtimes and makes available slower-acting insulin for the following time as well."

"Exactly," Barca said. "So, having taken a large dose, some ninety units of insulin, at eleven-thirty P.M., why should he take an *additional* injection only a half hour later? Just when the insulin he had injected a half hour before was ready to work?" He looked at Isabel expectantly.

"He forgot he took the earlier dose?" Isabel suggested.

"Not bloody likely," Barca said. "That is one thing diabetics *never* make a mistake about. Not live diabetics, at any rate. Besides, all he had to do if he was in doubt was to count the number of broken needles in the garbage pail."

"Alzheimer's disease?" Isabel tried.

"In a man who spends all day editing crossword puzzles?"

"Maybe when he saw his supper, he realized that he hadn't taken a big enough injection?"

"Two ounces of turkey breast and a slice of whole-grain toast? Come on, Isabel, say what has to be said."

"Father," Lydia said, "stop pulling teeth. It's obvious that Isabel is right. When Simon saw his supper—he gave himself the third injection *after* he opened the bag with his supper in it—he *did* realize he hadn't given himself a big enough injection to balance *that* supper. Therefore, what was in that bag was *not* turkey breast. It was a pound of chocolate chip cookies."

"Then why did he die?" Barca asked. "If he balanced out the chocolate chip cookies with additional insulin? Every diabetic carries the calorie and carbohydrate values of food tables in his head, and knows to the unit how much insulin he needs to balance his intake."

"Because they weren't chocolate chip cookies," Isabel said, suddenly understanding. "They were chocolate truffles, or something similar, which looked like candy but which were made with that cellulose stuff they give people with constipation. And artificial sweetner, bran, and other very low calorie, no-sugar, practically no food value ingredients. When Simon saw the candy, he couldn't resist. He knew that he would end up eating the whole bag; he could no more stop at half a bag than I could. Nor Lydia. Can you imagine the effect that had on him after all those years of eating cardboard and excelsior? He also knew he had to eat something to balance the insulin he had already injected. The lettuce and the celery he had in the refrigerator were practically worthless for that purpose, though if he had eaten them and drunk the Instant Glutose, he would probably still be alive."

"He couldn't eat that stuff," Lydia said, "any more than you or I could, under the circumstances. But he knew he would be safe if he took the appropriate amount of insulin in addition to what he had already injected to balance the turkey breast. Given what he took normally for toast and white meat, ninety units, I'll bet he took an additional ninety units, or even a full cc. of U-100 insulin before he ate one piece of the candy. So he gave himself a massive dose, in *addition* to his original large dose, of insulin, with no sugar to balance it. He killed himself, even though he did not commit suicide."

"You're leaving out a great deal, Lydia," Barca said. "Mary?"

"There is U-500 insulin," Mary said, "which is five times as potent as the standard U-100 insulin; five hundred units per cc. I am sure if I were trying to kill Simon, I would have substituted U-500 insulin for his U-100. I'd switch labels, and I'd fix it so any differences in clearness or cloudiness of the solution were approximated by any means at hand. Not that Simon would have noticed minor differences in appearance; he did have glaucoma."

"Can anyone get U-500 insulin?" Isabel asked. "Or U-100, for that matter?"

"U-500 requires a doctor's prescription," Mary said, "but it isn't terribly hard to steal a prescription blank and write a prescription; insulin isn't watched by pharmacists as carefully as a narcotic. Anybody can buy needles, in 1 cc. sizes. So, at eleven-thirty P.M. Simon injected not ninety units of insulin but four hundred fifty units, and at midnight he injected another five hundred units, more or less. A truly killing dose."

"But wouldn't he have noticed?" Isabel asked. "I mean, it's not like cyanide, is it? Aren't there symptoms? Doesn't it take some time?"

"The symptoms of acute hypoglycemia," Mary said, "are headache, anxiety, confusion, sweating, trembling, weak knees, poor balance, and rapid heartbeat. That's why he drank the glucose, and, when it didn't help, drank some more."

"Why didn't it help?" Isabel asked. "Even if it wasn't enough, given the huge dose of insulin, it should have . . . Oh, I see. It wasn't glucose."

"No," Lydia said. "It was a liquid that looked and tasted like glucose, but was something sugarless, artificially flavored, and sweetened with artificial sweetener."

"But didn't the police notice? Surely they examined the insulin syringes and the glucose bottle. And the bag the supper came in."

"During the twenty minutes Mildred Burdock had before she called the doctor," Lydia said, "she substituted an old bottle which had held real glucose, three hypodermics with a trace of U-100 insulin left inside, and two partly filled bottles of U-100 insulin, all with Simon's fingerprints on them in the proper places and properly smudged. Not faked, they were from the day before, when she didn't throw them out with the garbage. The bag from the diner, too, that held the turkey breast and toast supper, with the bill restapled."

"You mean"—Isabel was incensed—"that when Giles and I were there, she had all this in her tote bag? And we didn't know? Suspect? And the surveillance team, they didn't suspect either? From the sounds?"

"The way to be a perfect spy," Barca said, "is to act as though you are being observed at all times, and to live the part you are playing totally."

"And she did that for five years? The nerve!"

"Oh, yes," Barca said. "Nerves of steel. Especially since she had earlier that morning, killed Kosgrow."

Isabel was silent, shocked. "Then—then she was the Watchman?"

"Of course," Barca said. "And she was one of the few people who could approach Albert Kosgrow, even though they had never met. Possibly she suggested that Simon was thinking of retiring and had sent her to sound out Kosgrow on some business arrangement whereby Kosgrow would gradually take over Simon's accounts and, possibly, even continue using Burdock to help with the routine work. He'd have no qualms about turning his back on this sweet little middle-aged lady and, zip, right in the heart."

Isabel took a deep breath. "But why? She broke up the spy team all by herself. It would take a year to build it up again, maybe more. Why did she do it?"

"Her job was to do," Barca said, "precisely what she did: to protect the spy. Kosgrow and Simon were expendable. That the spymaster had another team set up is extremely doubtful, unless it exists in New York, but his primary goal was to keep Fitzgerald's existence secret, and were it not for Tom Burke's suspicious nature, Zulkov's accidental death, and Giles's brilliance, aided by Isabel's insights, Fitzgerald would, today, be in one way or another transferring vital secrets to the Russians."

"But it doesn't fit," Isabel said. "Burdock didn't know we had discovered the messages or had identified Fitzgerald when she killed Simon and Kosgrow. In fact, when she *decided* to kill them—it couldn't have been after Wednesday night—we didn't even know what the messages were, much less who the spy was. She might even have shut off another message from the spy for all she knew. So why did she kill them? When did she *prepare* to kill them?"

"It was evidently arranged," Barca said, "that it was more important to protect the spy than it was to get another message. Burdock had been ready, ever since the Aeroflot advertisement appeared, to kill Simon and Kosgrow if there was any danger of exposing the spy. Like the efficient killer she was, she was prepared with everything she might need for any eventuality from that time on. What decided her was Wesley Warren's call on Wednesday night. He's the features editor of the *Gazette* who complained about the quality of Tuesday's and Wednesday's puzzles."

"But Simon could have stalled Warren another day or two; by that time the conference would have started."

"Simon couldn't stall Warren," Barca said, "because

Burdock never gave him the message. Simon didn't know that Kosgrow's puzzles were being published in his space. He gave Burdock the puzzles he had edited for the *Gazette*. Burdock filed them somewhere handy, and would have sent them in only when a puzzle from Kosgrow did not come in on the fax machine. When a puzzle from Kosgrow did come in, she faxed it to the *Gazette* at once, never showing it to Simon. Burdock knew that Warren would call them about Thursday's puzzle, and might insist on talking to Simon directly. If he did, the jig was up. Simon would deny approving those puzzles and it would be obvious that Burdock had sent them. What explanation could she possibly give for substituting those puzzles for the ones Simon gave her to submit? This being Washington, the FBI might have heard about it, and the CIA too. Possibly they would not have decoded the secret message, but Burdock could not take the risk. She may have been willing to sacrifice herself, though I doubt it, but getting caught like that might lead to the spy. So Simon and Kosgrow had to be killed."

"Are you saying Simon never read the *Gazette*? Not even to check the crossword?"

"Obviously. Why should he? He'd already edited it. No one else would have changed anything. It never occurred to him that what he gave Burdock was not what she transmitted."

"All right. I can accept the necessity of killing Simon. But with Simon dead, and the police thinking it was a natural death, why kill Kosgrow?"

"To close the door fully. Warren might have followed through, asked Burdock who constructed those four puzzles. She could not plead ignorance, and if Warren questioned Kosgrow, the secret message would be exposed. A slight chance, true, but the Watchman's orders evidently were to protect the spy at any cost, and to close every loophole, no matter how tiny."

"No." Isabel shook her head. "You're wrong. You're forgetting something."

Barca raised his eyebrows. "Wrong? Then who do you

think killed Simon and Kosgrow?"

"I don't mean that," Isabel said. "She killed them both. But she also killed Fitzgerald, didn't she?"

"Of course."

"Then why . . . ? If she killed Fitzgerald, who was she protecting when she killed Simon and Kosgrow? And we always said that no one, even the KGB, knew that Fitzgerald was the spy. So how did she know whom to kill?"

"It seems," Barca said blandly, "that that assumption was not completely accurate. We based it on another assumption: that the Watchman's primary responsibility was to protect the identity of the spy. Up to a point that was valid. Certainly the spymaster, or whoever it was who persuaded Fitzgerald to pass on the information, told Fitzgerald that they would sacrifice anyone and anything to protect his identity. But the Watchman had a higher priority, to keep anyone from finding out that the U.S.S.R. knew our minimum position in the negotiations. If we even suspected that the Russians knew our walk-away terms, the President would have changed them at once, completely wiping out the tremendous advantage the Russians had. This conference is, in effect, the first phase of their battle for world domination. In such a case, the life of one spy, even one as important as Fitzgerald, is insignificant."

"So the spymaster did have someone in the U.S. who knew the identity of the spy."

"Given the priorities," Barca said, "it's what I would have done. You should have caught that, Giles."

"Sorry about that, Chief," Giles said.

"Learn from your mistakes, Giles, and all will be forgiven."

"I still don't see," Isabel said, "if Fitzgerald was to be killed, why—"

"Look at the timing, Isabel," Giles said. "Simon was killed yesterday, before eight P.M., when Mildred Burdock put the fake supper, the fake glucose, and the quintuple-strength insulin into the refrigerator. Kosgrow was killed early this morning. When was Fitzgerald killed?"

"I don't know exactly, Giles, but right after Kosgrow was killed. It depends on the traffic, I guess."

"But definitely after Kosgrow. The housekeeper was stabbed in the kitchen, not in her bed. Fitzgerald was stabbed in front of his computer, not at breakfast. They were killed not more than an hour before we got there. So when did Burdock decide to kill them?"

"It's clear," Isabel spoke slowly, "that had Burdock decided to kill Fitzgerald even a few hours earlier, she would have killed Fitzgerald first—he was much more important and much closer to the center of Washington—and then gone after Kosgrow. There was really no great hurry to kill Kosgrow; it could even have been done a day later. Simon was already dead, or as good as dead, and if it weren't for you, Giles, it would have been recorded as a natural death. So something happened, had to have happened, shortly after, almost immediately after, Burdock killed Kosgrow that made her decide to kill Fitzgerald, something that would have shown us that Fitzgerald was a spy and that the Russians knew what our position was in the coming conference."

"Not necessarily that certainly," Giles said, "but Burdock was, or her orders were to be, super-cautious, to take no chances. She had to wipe out the slightest chance of exposure. Now, where was she when she learned that there was a possibility that Fitzgerald could be exposed, or even suspected?"

"She had to be in her car, on the way back from— The radio! Something was announced on the radio that— But you were with me all the time, Giles; we didn't even turn on the radio."

"We did," Barca said. "Early this morning, Professor Emeritus Gadsden Wright Frazier was found dead in his home, apparently a suicide. He was quite old, and had been suffering from cancer, very painful cancer, for the past year. Although there is very little doubt, the police are investigating, and examining the professor's papers for more information."

"I take it," Isabel said, "that Professor Frazier was

ACROSS

1 Picket
5 Urban woe
9 20 ___ = 1 riyal
14 "___ that opened of
   itself": Krylov
15 Heavy reading
16 Salt of uric acid
17 In disagreement
20 Rod Hull's puppet pal
21 Tourney
22 More, to Browning
23 Avdp. units
24 Channel
25 On a roll
26 Pinkerton Agency logo
29 Assent from Coop
30 Bleachers phenomenon
31 Dollface
32 Mid-morning
35 Harder to get?
36 Monogram of The Duke
37 Half a 1939 film title
38 Big goof
39 Kadiddlehopper
40 Conditions
41 "___ Making Eyes at Me"
42 Castered platform
43 Washington didn't;
   Washingtonians do
44 Press piece
45 Beneke
46 Soapy prefix
47 Sun Yat-___
48 Emulate Parker and
   Barrow
49 AFB near Lompoc, CA
52 Half a painting
54 Azerbaijan's capital
55 E-O link?
56 What to do in Calaveras
   County
60 The end
61 Town in NJ or CA
62 "What'll ___now?"

63 Put a ___(squelch)
64 Endow
65 Dill, once

DOWN

1 Do the walls
2 Forceful weapon
3 Food for the indolent?
4 Outer: Prefix
5 Clog
6 Boudin inspired him
7 Sign
8 Kingly name: Abbr.
9 Not so loud
10 Coffeemakers
11 Carry on
12 Pou ___(HQ)
13 She tends to brood
18 Montreal arena
19 Sandpiper's cousin
25 NYC theater eponym
27 Hick
28 Black-hatted one
29 Bosox legend
30 Took the prizes, slangily
32 Works hard for the money
33 Bergen's Miss Klinker
34 Epistaxis
35 *Night of 100 Stars*
   mastermind
38 Flat-bottom, e.g.
39 Crew leader
41 First of 12 Playmates:
   Abbr.
42 Foil the eavesdroppers
45 What *tejer* means
48 Minsky's worries?
49 1970s Olympian Lasse
50 Crystal-lined cavity
51 Bunker, e.g.
53 Emilia's hubby
54 Benevolent bunch?
56 Hyperion's alter ego
57 UK record label
58 CCXI quintupled
59 Erstwhile Afr. federation

SATURDAY, JULY 3

Horton Fitzgerald's mentor in college? The one who enlisted him?"

"I think the police will find the FBI examining Wright's papers in a very short time. I'll bet they contain something interesting about several of his top students."

"And on the strength of this 'may,' Burdock decided to kill Fitzgerald."

"In this business, Isabel, you don't take unnecessary risks, especially when you play for such big stakes. What would you have done in her place? Don't forget what her punishment would be for failure. Or even success. She's the last link in the chain, from the spymaster's point of view."

There was silence in the room. Finally Isabel spoke. "I'm beginning to understand what you, the Group, do, and how well you do it. How important it is. I'm sorry I was so—so critical, so snide, before. I apologize."

"Not necessary," Barca said, "but accepted. We've all felt like that at one time or another. And you can say 'we'; it's all right. You played a very important part in this case, if you'll just think about it. And now"—he turned to Giles—"I assume that the puzzle you constructed so hurriedly earlier today, was for the purpose of apprehending Mildred Burdock?"

"But we can't," Isabel said. "She must be— She can't be sure that there will be no clues found, nothing the doctor noticed to arouse his suspicions and lead to a police investigation, no autopsy that would show the huge amounts of insulin in Simon's body. How can we find her? She's surely not at home, and she'll never go back to Simon's office."

"I know how Giles's mind works," Barca said. "The puzzle will find her."

36

"T<small>HIS IS A MUCH PRETTIER PUZZLE THAN ANY OF THE</small> first four," Mary said. "My congratulations to Hannibal, Giles."

"It was an easier job," he replied. "Tomorrow is July third."

"Even so," Jane said, "you have two fifteen-letter lights, 17 Across and 56 Across. That's something Kosgrow wasn't able to accomplish."

"Yes," Isabel said. "43 Across, that's a real cute clue for a three-letter word. 3 Down is another good one."

"I like 13 Down," Lydia said, "and 42 Down."

"48 Down is clever," Mary said. "Also 41 Down."

"Don't overlook 54 Down," Kitty said. "But 45 Down is dull."

"Don't knock it," Isabel said. "Remember the conditions under which it was done, and the speed. Giles was practically dead on his feet at the time. Give him the credit he deserves."

"I do," Jane said. "This is so far superior to Kosgrow's work, any amateur could tell that the constructor of this puzzle is far more skilled and talented than the composer of the other four."

"Let's do the message," Lydia said. "You write, Mary. Since it's scheduled for July third, start at 3 and go left, 'LBN.' You shoot down the side of the rectangle to 'N'

213

on the bottom line and, going left, there's 'NWGKRMHBMYSM.' Now to the right side, add 'GD,' and up to the left, 'EVXDRYWTPFX.' Put them all together."

Mary read, "'LBNNWGKRMHBMYSMGDEVXDR-YWTPFX.' Reversed in pairs, that's 'BLNNGWR-KHMMBSYGMEDXVRDWYPTXF.'" Mary studied the message for a moment, then said, "I can't read this one. If you made it too hard, Giles, Mildred Burdock won't be able to read it either. Then what?"

"I didn't think it was too hard," Giles said. "You're so used to grasping things at one glance that—study it awhile, Mary. Try to read it. If you can't, maybe I have wasted all this effort, but I wouldn't underestimate Mildred Burdock a bit; she has to be a very clever woman. And strong and determined, to boot. Try."

"Could 'MBSY' BE 'EMBASSY'?" Kitty asked.

"I'm not going to give hints," Giles said. "I want to see if you can do it on your own."

"'WRKHM' before 'EMBASSY,'" Jane said, "that could make it 'WORK, HOME, EMBASSY.'"

"That's it," Elizabeth said. "'BLNNG' has to be 'BLOWN, NO GOOD.' So it reads, 'BLOWN, NO GOOD'—no, 'NG' must be 'NO GO,' so it becomes 'BLOWN, NO GO WORK, HOME, EMBASSY.' So 'GMED' is 'GO IMMEDIATELY.' But I don't see the rest, Giles. 'XVRDWYPTXF.' What could that be?"

"That's where she's going," Jane said. "It's the address. Latin numerals. 'XV' is 'FIFTEEN.' That makes 'RDWY' either 'ROADWAY' or 'ORDWAY,' and since there's no street in Washington called 'ROADWAY,' the address is 'FIFTEEN ORDWAY.' And 'PTXF' is 'APARTMENT TEN F.' Very good, Giles."

"You had an unfair advantage, Jane," Isabel said. "I didn't know the address of your safe house. Will Mildred Burdock be able to figure it out?"

"She's been working on crosswords for at least five years, eight hours a day, and looking for this code," Giles said. "I'm sure she's not your typical little old lady."

Mary read what she had written. "I've filled in," she said. "'(I AM) BLOWN. (DON'T) GO (TO) WORK, (YOUR) HOME, (ANY) OFFICE, (OR THE) EMBASSY. GO IMMEDIATELY TO 15 ORDWAY, APARTMENT 10 F.'"

"If it's an apartment," Isabel asked, "is there anyone living there? Taking care of it? Don't people get suspicious of an apartment with no occupant? What about the doorman?"

"There is no doorman, and there is no anonymity like being a tenant in a large apartment house," Jane said. "There is someone living there, a young man, a bachelor, who is connected, very distantly, to the people we are connected with. On very short notice he makes his home available to us. I've already called him."

"Will Mildred Burdock go there?" Isabel asked. "Maybe she has another escape route already planned."

"Doubtful," Barca said. "I am sure that to the spymaster Mildred Burdock is as expendable as Kosgrow and Simon were, and more easily replaceable."

"But surely he doesn't want her caught."

"No, my dear, he doesn't. But there are many other ways of accomplishing that."

Isabel was shocked. "You mean? After she gave five years of her life to—that's horrible."

"That's the nature of this business, Isabel. The person in charge must make decisions of life and death coldly; to do what is best for the operation. You really shouldn't waste your pity on Mildred Burdock. She's killed four people that we know of, and, at her age, it's likely that she's killed many more. Actually, she'd be better off if we caught her first; there must be several KGB killers looking for her right now, and they have no reason to keep her alive, as we do."

"Then why should she come to our safe house, Barca?"

"She will be very suspicious, of course, but she can't be sure that they want her dead. She could still be of use to them, so she has some hope. There is a possibility that they want only to get her out of the country. If that could

215

be accomplished, she'd be safe. Even if they had decided to get rid of her, once she was back in Russia, they'd have no reason to kill her, no way then, that she'd endanger Fitzgerald, or the spymaster. On the contrary, they might even give her a medal and a promotion."

"So it's likely she would go to the apartment?"

"It might be her only hope; where else could she go? But she would do it very cautiously, I'm sure."

"It's still not a good plan," Isabel said thoughtfully. "The whole operation of the crossword code was so compartmentalized that no participant knew what any other was doing. What happens if she doesn't know the code, can't read the message?"

"If she doesn't show up at the apartment within twenty-four hours, we'll have to decide whether we want to risk exposing ourselves by telling the FBI everything we know, or to let Mildred Burdock either escape or, more likely, be killed by the KGB. If we decide to risk our own necks— once our existence is suspected, we will be sitting ducks for any organization that wants to eliminate us—we will try to let the FBI and the CIA learn only as much of the story as will encourage them to mount a massive search for her and minimize their finding out about us. At this we may not succeed. We will also hope that they won't find out about Fitzgerald and embarrass the President. That may prove to be impossible. Let us hope she comes to us."

"I thought that the CIA," Isabel said, "couldn't operate in the U.S."

"They're not *allowed* to, Isabel, but that doesn't mean . . . The Group is not quite a legal organization either, but we manage."

Isabel thought for a moment. "All right. We must act as if Mildred Burdock will go to Apartment 10F tomorrow, shortly after the *Gazette* is on the newsstands. What happens when she gets there? How does she get in? How is she captured? In the street? In the apartment house? Do we have a plan? Arrangements? What?"

"This is routine," Barca said. "Obviously, someone has

to be there to open the door. Obviously, there has to be a recognition signal, a password."

"A password? From someone you can't communicate with? That's impossible."

"Giles will think of something, won't you, Giles?" Sullivan nodded.

"Are you kidding, Barca? How will you tell *her* the password? You expect Giles to . . . You're crazy, all of you."

"Giles has never failed us, Isabel. He has accepted the responsibility; therefore he will perform. What else is troubling you?"

"Who will meet her there, Barca? Won't it be dangerous? I mean, if she's expecting the KGB wants to kill her, that the apartment might be a trap, won't she . . ."

"Yes, she will, Isabel. So. You're in charge of the operation. Now. Whom will you send to meet Mildred Burdock?"

"I'd have a dozen FBI men in the street outside. Around the building. Doing normal things. Fixing the street, delivering papers, things like that."

"Amateurish, Isabel. If Burdock saw something like that, which she could see from a block away or crouched low in an apparently empty taxi, she'd disappear in a minute. What if she decided to come at six in the morning, or at midnight? Very few paper deliveries at midnight. You must think of something else, my dear."

"Put them in the apartment house? In the lobby? In the elevator?"

"One man to do all that, Isabel? Ten might stand out. What would you tell the tenants. Exterminators? An infestation of rats? And if there's a gunfight? An innocent tenant wandering by? A dead bystander, or a hostage, would be highly inappropriate, don't you think? Might lead to embarrassing headlines. Remember, if we're discovered, we're dead."

"So it has to be someone in the apartment, doesn't it, Barca?" Isabel sighed.

"I'm afraid so," Barca said. "Who?"

"None of the Ackroyds can be used in Washington," Isabel said more to herself than to the ring of intent eyes.

"I'm sorry, Isabel. Not only are we too well known, but if one of us ended up in a hospital or the morgue, it might lead to exposure of the whole Group."

She drew a deep breath. "I won't send Giles," she said. "I'll go myself."

"I'm afraid that won't do, Miss Isabel," Oliver said from the back of the cluster of chairs. "Miss Burdock spoke with you and Mr. Giles at length this morning at Mr. Simon's house. She'd know you on sight. Nor do you have any combat skills."

"But that leaves..." She gestured helplessly.

"It was obvious from the start," Oliver said. "I was the only one Miss Burdock never met; we all knew that. Barca, I am sure, was merely showing you that it was inevitable. I am grateful for your hesitation, but may I remind you that I am the most highly trained combatant in the Group and that Miss Burdock is a lady of middle age who has led a sedentary life and is somewhat overweight."

"But what if she has a gun, Oliver?"

"I am sure she has, madam, at least one. I will manage."

Barca coughed. "It would be advisable, Oliver, if you carried no weapons. Think how it would look if... Innocence should be the watchword, I should think."

"I wasn't thinking of carrying any conventional weapons, Barca."

"No, no, of course not. But sharpened credit cards, special shoes, a heavy belt and buckle, a piano wire? Miss Burdock is almost certainly a trained KGB killer. She would quickly recognize any of the usual conventional weapons."

"I would not wish to be completely stripped, sir."

"Your usual unarmed skills, Oliver? Not sufficient unto the day?"

"My reflexes are not what they once were, sir. May I suggest a large linen handkerchief, a silk tie, a comb, a nail file, some coins, a roll of new bills, a ring of keys, a thick ball point pen, and a sharpened pencil?"

"The pencil alongside the pen might arouse suspicion, which would add to the danger to you. The nail file, I think that should be eliminated too. A small number of coins, a few keys, a few mixed-age bills, yes, that will be acceptable. No labels on the clothes, please; everything not too expensive and of a kind. Let yourself be inspected by Jane before you leave. Elizabeth, would you rent a car, please? Discreetly, with at least two cutouts, for cash. Oliver, you will leave within an hour; I will have your cover story shortly. Giles, will you have a two-way identification procedure ready by that time?"

"I tug the forelock, sire," Giles said, carefully not looking at Isabel.

"And may I remind you all," Barca said, looking directly at Isabel, "no one is to go near that house. I don't want anyone scaring Mildred Burdock off. It is all in Oliver's hands."

Isabel's eyes were full. "Oliver," she said, "I hope you understand about—when I—in the car—when I said I would get you for this—I was only—"

"I quite understand, madam," Oliver said.

219

37

AT EXACTLY SIX-THIRTY SATURDAY MORNING THE doorbell of Apartment 10F rang. Oliver opened the door a crack, keeping the chain in place. He took one look and opened the door fully, slowly, making sure to show both his hands empty. Directly in front of him, but six feet away, her back against the opposite wall of the corridor, her eyes searching both ends of the hall, stood a well-dressed woman of about forty. She had short brown hair under a small straw hat, brown eyes, and wore little makeup. Her light tan blouse and brown skirt outlined her full figure. Her brown leather shoes looked conservatively expensive. A designer tote bag hung from her left hand and a large leather bag was slung across her right shoulder. Her right hand was in the bag and the bag was pointed at Oliver.

She looked past Oliver into the apartment, then back into his eyes, waiting expectantly. Oliver said slowly and distinctly, "Mill. Bird."

The woman waited for a moment, then said equally clearly and distinctly, "Dread. Dock," completing her names. Oliver relaxed noticeably, but did not move. "Would you like to come in?" he said.

"You first," Mildred Burdock said. "Turn around slowly, and, when you do anything, move very slowly. Nothing sudden. Hands in sight at all times. Are you a professional?" She closed the apartment door behind her with only a slight click, and turned the dead bolt.

Oliver turned his back to her. "In a minor way."

"Then you know what not to do," she said, taking the small automatic from her handbag. "Walk slowly to just before the next room. Don't pass any doors until I say so."

"There is a closet here, madam."

"Open the door very slowly, when I tell you. Keep in mind that it may be small caliber; but it can do a lot of damage at close range. Any trouble, if I get frightened, you die first. Keep your body between me and the opening at all times. Now, open the door."

Oliver slowly opened the closet door. Mildred Burdock took a flashlight from the tote bag with her left hand and shined it onto the floor of the closet, slowly moving it upward. There was no one inside. "Close the door so that the latch snaps fully shut. What other rooms are there?"

"A bathroom next on the right, with a large closet and dressing room combination, and the living quarters, with a complete kitchen in the corner."

"Is there a fire escape or a balcony?"

"Neither."

"Walk to the bathroom door and open it as before." Keeping Oliver as a shield, and with one eye on the door, Mildred Burdock made sure no one was in the dressing room or the shower. "Go out first, slowly, and station yourself between me and the living room."

"May I say, madam," Oliver said calmly, "that you are being unduly cautious? I am here to serve you."

Equally calmly, Mildred replied, "You will speak when I tell you. You will die if you tell me one lie, or if there is anyone else in this apartment. Now go into the living room."

The pair walked slowly into the room, Oliver relaxed; there was no way to attack at this time. Mildred was tense. She looked around the room; there was no place for any-one to hide. "Sit in that chair." She motioned to the big armchair opposite the couch. "Put your open hands on the front of the arms of the chair. Keep your hands open, the fingers spread at all times. If I see your hand closed, even if nothing is in it, I shoot." Oliver sat as directed. "Now, keeping your hands on the arms of the chair, slide forward, forward, until you are sitting on the floor, legs together, straight out in front of you." She relaxed a bit, but the automatic was still pointing at Oliver's midsection.

"I am very uncomfortable, madam," Oliver said. "I am not young and I may not be able to hold this position very long. I do not wish to be shot for fatigue."

Burdock ignored this. "What is your name, your job, your orders?"

"I am Herbert Shanks, a footman at the British Embassy. I am to drive you to Baltimore, where a Polish ship, the *Batory*, is preparing to depart. I am to drop you off at the pier and show my face from the window of the car at precisely twelve-thirty P.M., at which time the first mate, who knows me by sight, will take over."

"What evidence do I have of this?"

"My presence here. Your presence here."

"What identification do you have?"

"None, not even clothing labels. I hope you have none either. The car is rented; a false license in the glove compartment."

"Where is the car, Shanks?"

"One hundred feet down the street, on this side. A black Dodge Aries. The keys are in my right-hand pocket."

"Do you think I cannot kill you and escape?"

"You cannot get on the ship without me; that is certain. What am I to call you, madam?"

"Madam. Is this place bugged?"

"I doubt it. To what end? If it is, or if someone were stationed where he could see the entrance to this building, whoever you are concerned about already knows you are here."

"He was not expecting to see me like this."

"Who is it that you fear, madam? I am here to help you."

"You may think so; possibly they have decided to kill you too."

"I doubt that, madam. It would have been easy to place a radio-controlled bomb in this room before I arrived, or to arrange that the doorbell would send a signal to the people you fear. We are still alive, so your apprehension seems unfounded."

"There is much you don't know, Shanks." She thought for a while. "Undress, Shanks. Slowly. Completely. Place your clothes as far to your left as you can reach without moving suddenly."

"Really, madam. I am not armed, I assure you. I wouldn't know how to—"

"Now, Shanks! I won't waste a bullet on your knee. The first shot is in your heart."

"I can't stand this," Isabel said. "Let's go, Giles."

"Where to, Isabel?"

"Don't play innocent with me, Sullivan; you know exactly where. Oliver, that's where. He's in the hands of that murderer, that double murderer, right now. She's going to kill him; I just know it. And he doesn't have anything to defend himself with."

"He is not quite defenseless, Isabel; he has several weapons and can kill with any of them."

"Handkerchiefs? Combs? Pens?"

"In his hands, yes. Plus his bare hands."

"But she has to have a gun. What good are bare hands if you can't reach—she's a trained killer too. And his reflexes have slowed down, Giles; he said so himself."

"I'm sure that's true, Isabel, but slowed down from what? He's probably still ten percent faster than anyone else I know."

"Faster than a bullet?"

"Isabel, please. Barca said no one was supposed to go near that house."

"He said we shouldn't scare her off. But she has to be

there already. She was there within one hour after the *Gazette* hit the streets."

"That's wishful thinking. We don't even know if the puzzle is in the paper."

"Fair enough; I'm going to drive down to town to get a paper. Coming?"

"Just to keep you out of trouble," Giles said, resigned.

Mildred Burdock pulled some clothes out of her tote bag with her left hand. She took one step toward Oliver, stretched prone on the floor, and dropped the clothes next to him. The gun in her right hand was steady as a rock. "Sit up slowly, Shanks."

"What are these, madam?" Oliver asked.

"Women's clothes," she said. "They used to be mine, when I was older."

"Please give me back my own clothes, madam. This is very embarrassing."

"Now, Shanks. Put them on. Slowly."

Oliver started dressing in Mildred Burdock's former clothes. Slowly.

"See," Isabel said. "The puzzle is in here. Let's go."

"We don't know that she's there, Isabel. It's too early. If she decided to go there at all," he added.

"You're not being logical, Giles," she said. "If our analysis is correct, she didn't go to her home; probably spent the night in a series of diners, bus stations, and the like. Not in a hotel; that's the first place the KGB killers would look. And not in a Y; there are female KGB assassins too, aren't there? So she's tired and suffering from lack of sleep. Where would she go? The longer she stays out, visible, the more likely she is to be gunned down by her own buddies. For the same reason, she can't go to the Russian Embassy or any other Russian organization. What I would do in her place is to see if there is any message from—who else?—the spymaster, the only one who can communicate with her, who might know that she existed.

Her only hope is that there is another message, a message for her; that there was another encoder-constructor in reserve, and a way of getting the coded crossword into the paper."

"But we're not even sure she can read the message. I only took a shot in the dark with the puzzle I constructed, on the off chance that she could."

"We have to continue working on that hope, Giles. If she can't, if no one is in the safe house right now, Oliver is safe, but the KGB will kill her before we can get to her. I think she can read the message. In her place, if I had to make sure a crossword had to be handled a certain way, if I had to make sure that it was published on a certain day, in five years, you can bet your boots that I would have figured out the code. And she may even have been told the code by the spymaster, so she could check that all was going according to plan. If she was, then it wouldn't take a big brain to figure out that if she, as the Watchman, had orders to kill Kosgrow and Simon, to eliminate all possibilities of a lead to the spy, and then to kill the spy, that there was a second Watchman, with orders to kill *her*, after the spy was killed."

"Then why didn't she make arrangements to disappear after she killed Fitzgerald?"

"She did disappear, but how long do you think she could elude the hundreds of KGB people in this country? She's alone, can't you see, completely alone, and can't communicate. A little old lady, deaf and dumb, for all practical purposes. Her only hope is that the spymaster will communicate with her, tell her it's okay to go back to Russia, tell her how to do it without getting caught by the KGB. She had to, absolutely had to, get a copy of the *Gazette*—her only source of reliable information, her only possibility of escape, as soon as she could, and hope there was a message in it for her. So at five this morning, or whenever the paper left the *Gazette* building, she was right there and she got a paper. It took her ten minutes to solve the puzzle, and another two to get the message.

A taxi drops her off two blocks from the apartment house, and she was in the apartment, with a gun in Oliver's back, at six o'clock."

Giles was pale. "If that's true, what can we do about it? If we try to get into the apartment, she'll know it was a trap, and she'll kill Oliver first. She'll probably treat him as a potential KGB agent as it is, and be very suspicious of him. We must leave it all to Oliver; he's very good at situations like that."

"Nobody's good with a gun pointed at his head, especially if the gun is in the hands of an experienced killer. And I didn't say we should break in. All I want to do is wait outside for when she leaves, so if she tries to take Oliver with her as hostage, or to turn him over to someone as a trade for her life, we can do something."

"What, Isabel? This is one time when my sword cane can't work."

"I don't know, Giles. Let's go there now; it's almost seven. She may be gone already. I'll think of something on the way."

"Oliver was supposed to—his story was intended to keep her there until eleven o'clock. That would give him plenty of time to capture her, time for her to relax her attentions. I'm sure Barca had something planned for that time."

"No. You're making a mistake, you and Barca. You think Burdock is the only one who can decode the message. You've forgotten the new decoder, Zulkov's successor. At nine o'clock he will have solved the puzzle. By nine-fifteen, ten KGB agents will be on their way to 15 Ordway, Apartment 10F. When they kill Mildred Burdock, they'll kill Oliver. If Mildred Burdock is half as smart as she must be, she knows it, too, and she'll be out of there before eight."

"Ohmygod," Giles said. "I did forget. In the heat of—"

"Exactly. So let's get moving."

"But if she meets Oliver there—he could only have been sent by the spymaster—won't she believe that they are *not* trying to kill her? Won't she have to go along with

226

the plan to get her out of the country that Oliver presents?"

"With her life at stake she'll never follow anyone else's plan; she'll improvise her own. She's probably still afraid it's a KGB trap. Let's go, Giles; time's a-wasting."

"All right," Giles said reluctantly. "I'll go back and get a gun."

"No, we won't. If we go back, Barca will stop us. Drive."

"At least let me call Barca and tell him that the puzzle is in the paper."

"Certainly not; you're too easy to persuade. What will you do if he orders you not to go?"

"But it's not safe, Isabel; you're not safe. I have my sword cane, but you . . ."

"I'll get a tire iron from the trunk or— Stop at the first hardware store."

"What are you going to get?"

"A knife. Two."

"You? Kill?"

"For Oliver, yes."

"You can wear your own shoes, Shanks," Mildred Burdock said. "But take small ladylike steps, and stay between seven and eight feet from me. Now remain seated on the floor. Close your eyes. I'll be behind you. One twitch and I shoot."

"Do you really think," Oliver said, "that whoever may want to do you harm could possibly mistake a poor old lady for a glamorous young woman like you? There is not the slightest resemblance, as you can see."

"That's my worry, Shanks," she said. "You'll wear this hat and a scarf around your wig. Put the wig on now." She tossed the wig, hat, and scarf into his lap. "Slowly, Shanks, by feel, with your eyes closed."

"I don't resemble you in the slightest, madam. Surely this humiliation is unwarranted. If the first mate sees me like this, he will never recognize me and won't hide you in the ship. May I suggest—"

"Shut up, Shanks; you're beginning to annoy me. You can open your eyes now, but remember, I still have the gun pointed at your heart." She tossed a flash of silver into his lap. "Put these on. Move very slowly, using only one hand at a time."

"Handcuffs? But really, madam—"

"Tightly, Shanks. I want to hear another click from each one. Good. Now one more. I said one more, Shanks. Blue hands or a blue hole in your heart; take your choice."

"Is that the house, Giles? Go past. Slowly. A little more. Park over there. In front of the black car. The Dodge."

"Now what, Isabel? Wait? If she sees us, it's all over for Oliver."

"You stay in the car. Crouch down. Turn the rearview mirror so you can see the entrance of the building."

"What makes you think she'll come out the front entrance?"

"Because the back entrance is too suspicious a way. She has to look as though she's just another tenant on her way to work. That's what she's waiting for, to mingle with the people who are going to work."

"On Saturday, Isabel?"

"All right; an empty street is even better for her, and another reason why she'll be coming out soon, before the shoppers start out. She'll be down in a few minutes; just wait. I know; I'm beginning to think like a spy now myself."

"What do I do if—all right, *when* she comes out."

"I'm going across the street to get above the entrance of the house from you. If she turns your way, keep your head down and your sword cane loose. As soon as she is opposite, jump out of the car and hold the point of the sword at her heart. I'll be running up from behind her and I have something to stop her cold."

"And if she turns toward you?"

"Same thing, only the opposite way around."

"And Oliver?"

"As soon as he sees you, he'll take the opportunity to attack her too. He'll react fast."

"If she has a gun, Isabel?"

"Don't hesitate. Kill her."

"This is ridiculous, madam; you don't look a bit like me. The pants are much too large in the waist and the shoulders of the jacket are far too loose. No one will mistake you for me."

"If you're part of a trap, Shanks, that one second of indecision is all I need. I shoot the killer first as he attacks you, then I shoot you in the back. This is your last chance, Shanks; it's almost eight o'clock. If this is a trap, you die. But if you tell me all about it, I'll leave you here, alive. Is it a trap?"

"There is no trap, madam."

"Okay. Hold yourself bent over and keep the sleeves over the handcuffs. Head down. Walk at an even pace; no sudden moves. Just outside the building door make a slow turn right and keep on until you get to the door of the car. I'll unlock the door and you slide in. Got it? One deviation and I shoot."

"Wait, Isabel. But if she turns your way—You'll go against a trained killer with only a kitchen knife?"

"Nah. I knew that was a bad idea as soon as I got into the hardware store. 'Bye." She slipped out the door and crossed the street.

"Is that the car, Shanks?" Mildred Burdock whispered. "There's another car in front of it."

"It wasn't there when I arrived, madam," Oliver whispered back.

"If this is a trap..." She took the car keys out of her pocket with her left hand, glanced down, and selected the proper key, with her right hand still in her pocket, pointing at Oliver. She bent over slightly, inserted the key into the right-hand door of the black Dodge, turned it, and took

229

out the key. "Open the door slowly," she said, and stepped back a pace. Oliver pulled gently at the door handle until the door was about to open, then he jerked it open fast, partly shielding himself behind the opened door as he put his right foot against the top of the front wheel. Just as Mildred Burdock's bullet splintered the glass of the door's window, the right-hand door of the car in front slammed open. Giles hit the sidewalk running, his long silver blade extended toward the old lady's chest. There was a pounding of feet behind Burdock; she started to turn. *"Not her!"* Isabel screamed. *"Him!"* As Oliver launched himself off the wheel toward Burdock, cuffed hands outstretched, the hat and wig fell off Oliver's head. Giles instinctively slipped the point of the saber up just enough so that it scraped along Oliver's back. Mildred was almost turned toward the new attacker from the rear, her gun shifting to point at Isabel, when the little white bag of carpet tacks exploded in her eyes, the sharp points ripping her eyeballs. She screamed in agony, her hands flew up just as Oliver hit her knees, and, in reflex, her gun fired once.

38

"**M**Y BROTHERS MADE ME PITCH TO THEM ALL THE time," Isabel said. "They never let me hit." She sat up in the bed.

"Drink your cocoa," Barca said. "Fortune works in strange ways. A good hitter would have, uh, struck out in this situation. Why did you decide to get carpet tacks instead of a knife?"

"I realized that another knife—Giles already had his sword cane—against a gun, wouldn't help. So when I saw those little boxes, I bought a batch and emptied them into the chocolate-cookie bag, the empty bag, I had in my pocket. I wasn't sure, either, that I could actually stick a knife into another person when the time came. I think I would, but I wasn't *sure*."

"Those carpet tacks have very long sharp points, Isabel. To throw them into another person's eyes— A knife might have caused less damage."

"Did she? Is she?"

"The shock of those points in her eyes—her hands flew up, a normal reaction—and with Oliver hitting her immediately after— She was going to shoot you, Isabel; the trigger was almost fully pulled. Too bad; I would have liked to question her."

"It was fitting, Father," Elizabeth said. "She made

231

Simon kill himself, and now she's killed herself."

Isabel shivered. "What happened afterward?"

"After you fainted" Lydia said.

"I didn't faint," Isabel protested. "I remember that. I was moving so fast that— Oliver knocked her forward and her head hit mine so hard—the blood all over me—"

"We dragged everybody into our cars," Lydia said. "The whole thing took only five seconds. No one saw a thing. Or heard a thing; those little automatics are very quiet."

"What were you all doing there?" Isabel put her mug of cocoa down on the night table to the right of her bed. "Barca clearly said no one was to go near the building."

"We didn't," Jane said innocently. "We were at the ends of the block; across the avenues, actually. We had hoped to grab her when she came; even if she took a taxi, she would walk the last few blocks."

"Then what was Oliver doing in the apartment?"

"Precaution, my dear," Barca said. "In case we missed her. Fortunate that he was there, but that's what good planning is all about. Your fault, actually, Isabel, for giving us such a poor description."

"She was an old lady when we saw her," Isabel said. "Really. Old and fat."

"I would have expected that of Giles, my dear, he's a man. But you should have observed more carefully."

"When I met her, I wasn't thinking about . . . I had seen three murders in one morning and just walked in on a fourth, what I was sure was a fourth. I was more interested in keeping my breakfast down than in inspecting little old ladies who were crying."

"When you're on assignment, Isabel, you check out everything. You never know what may be important."

"Yeah? Well, we all make mistakes, don't we, Ackroyd? You, for instance, you forgot all about the FBI man, Tom Burke, didn't you? The one who started all this? Doesn't he deserve an explanation, at least?"

"I never forget anything," Barca said smugly. "Tell her, Jane."

"Burke got an anonymous telephone call at his home," Jane reported, "which described, very generally, that thanks to his efforts, a major spy ring was broken and all its members were eliminated."

"He wasn't told about the Group, was he?" Isabel asked. "Even in a general way? I mean, he has the type of mind—he was the only one shrewd enough to be suspicious of Zulkov in the first place."

"It was intimated that a special secret task force, which was disbanded after the spies were caught, took over the project. He was also told to keep his mouth shut; otherwise the goodies would be revoked."

"Goodies? A good guy was rewarded, for once, in Washington?"

"That's how we work," Jane said. "Besides, you never know when you'll need someone like him again, so he was ordered, if anyone ever called him with an odd request accompanied by the signal 'Crossword Code,' to drop everything and do what was asked."

"What goodies did you give him?"

"Aside from being the only non-Groupie in Washington who knows the whole story, Burke got jumped two grades. Then there is a letter of commendation in his file, signed by the President, for 'special services over and beyond the call of duty.' Burke was also assigned directly to the Attorney General's office on what is, in essence, a freelance spy-hunting license. No paperwork, no supervision, and an unlimited expense account. For a man like Burke, heaven on earth."

"So you see, my dear," Barca's voice took on a softer tone, "we do what we can to balance the scales. Now lean back and rest; the doctor said another day in bed for you. You still exhibit some symptoms of concussion."

"I have to go back to Windham on Monday. My vacation—oh, God, I won't have a single day."

"I'll have the—Jane, will you see to it?—the big TV

brought up here, and we'll join you. The fireworks will be spectacular tomorrow, and the President's speech should be, uh, very interesting. You can be proud that you had something to do with whatever he's going to say. Unfortunately," he *tsk*ed falsely, "you'll never be able to tell anyone about it. Lydia, bring Isabel another bag of chocolate chip cookies; the good ones that are cheaper than in a store. Yes, you may have another bag yourself. Save the empty bags; you never know when we'll need to improvise more weapons. Bring a bag for me too. As a reward."

39 ✳✳✳

THE PRESIDENT LOOKED OVER THE BANK OF MICRO-phones at his audience. "My friends," he said, "distinguished guests, members of the Daughters of the American Revolution, and all the citizens who are watching on this beautiful Sunday. My fellow citizens, it is particularly gratifying to me to be addressing you on this Independence Day, the holiday commemorating the birth of our nation.

"The customary procedure, the acceptable speech, would be to give a short review of how this nation came into being, to murmur a few self-congratulatory platitudes, and to let you all return to the pleasures of apple pie, ice cream, hot dogs, and baseball. Some presidents have used this day as an opportunity to make political or policy statements. I don't believe in platitudes, as you well know, and I certainly don't believe in telling the people we are going to horse-trade with exactly what we have in mind. But today I am going to make an exception to my usual ways. With the opening of the Mass Destruction Weapons Disarmament Conference on Tuesday, I am going to take this opportunity to describe, publicly, our position and our policy for one aspect of this conference. I hope the Secretary-General of the Communist Party of the U.S.S.R. will see fit to do the same. If he does, we will give him, I promise, full live coverage, even though I know that my speech is being denied to his people.

"I dislike long speeches, so I will not try to cover all aspects of the coming conference, but I believe my discussion of one aspect of the problems caused by the military buildup of the past decade will serve to guide our actions on all matters our negotiators will be discussing in the coming weeks.

"There has been a great cry for unilateral disarmament in the past months, not just in our country but all over the world. Thousands of people in Europe have been demonstrating against the missiles that were placed there to protect them, by retaliation, against the Soviet missiles placed some years earlier, which missiles are aimed directly at the protestors. The rationale is that the Soviets may become angry and attack these defensive missiles, which will destroy the people living near the missiles. That is a reasonable assumption, and if I lived in Western Europe, I would not want Soviet, or any, missiles fired in my direction. The only trouble is, search as I might, I haven't found one instance of these same demonstrators marching against the Soviet missiles that are aimed directly at them, either when they were first deployed, or now. It is a great puzzlement that they demonstrated only against the missiles aimed *away* from them.

"Can it be these people have a motive other than what they profess? Can it be that they desire not disarmament but *unilateral* disarmament? It certainly looks that way to me. What do you think?

"Is the United States so to be feared? Is the U.S. embarked on world conquest? Think back. Was there not a time when we alone had nuclear weapons? When the other nations of the world were defeated, depleted of manpower and industrial strength, unable to feed their own people? Did we then threaten the world, conquer the world? Or did we open our hearts and our purses, our granaries and our industries, to the world? Did we not help build up these nations to strength again, yea, even the U.S.S.R? Did we not sever all colonial relationships and help other nations do the same?

"Not all nations, agreed. During that time, one nation— I need only recite a list of names: Lithuania, Latvia, Estonia, East Germany, Hungary, Czechoslovakia, Romania, Bulgaria, Poland, Mongolia, Sakhalin, Cuba, Nicaragua, Afghanistan, Angola, South Yemen, Ethiopia, and others. There are some people today who are not aware that on an agreed signal, Hitler's Germany and Stalin's Russia invaded Poland; that Hitler and Stalin were allies for almost two years before; that this was the start of World War Two; that this alliance enabled Hitler to attack Belgium, the Netherlands, France, Norway, Denmark, and England. Only *after* dividing up Poland, when Germany attacked Russia, did the U.S.S.R. fight against Hitler. So which country is imperialist? Which nation should the world fear?

"In spite of this, there has risen in this country a huge clamor for unilateral disarmament. We should lead the way, they cry; we should set the example, be a light for the nations. Now, unilateral disarmament has some strong arguments in its favor. Most important is the horror of nuclear war. Every symposium, every demonstration for unilateral disarmament, starts with a recitation of the effects of nuclear war. It's a *true* horror story, but the repeated recitation is unnecessary, at least in this country. Except for a few suicidal fools, no one wants a nuclear war, or a war of any kind. What should be discussed, what *must* be discussed, is: What is the best way to *avoid* a war? This is where unilateral disarmament comes in, and I have been giving it serious consideration." There was a concerted gasp from the audience.

"Why not? Isn't it my duty, as President, to consider *all* means of avoiding war? The reasoning is that wars are caused by fear. Certainly, some wars might be. So if one side showed its good faith, its confidence, by disarming unilaterally, the other side would no longer fear its opponent, and would begin disarming too. As each side gained

237

confidence, more and more weapons of mass destruction would be themselves destroyed, and in a relatively short time there would be insufficient weapons of mass destruction to destroy the earth and the inhabitants thereof. Then we could all breathe a sigh of relief, and, freed from fear, we could feed the hungry, clothe the naked, house the homeless, and make the earth a Garden of Eden indeed.

"This is a goal, my friends, that no one could quarrel with. Its possibilities are so overwhelmingly good that it is worth some risk. You, my friends, know that I have never been afraid to try the new, provided the benefits are proportional to the risks, and that the possibility of success is good. We have been taught to set examples, to turn the other cheek. We have learned that a soft answer turneth away wrath. Should we not take a chance for peace?

"I have instructed my chief delegate to the Mass Destruction Weapons Disarmament Conference to present a proposal which is not on the agenda, but which is of such importance that I hope it is accepted by the U.S.S.R. I will place this proposal before you, before the world, now, but first let me explain my terms so that there will be no misunderstanding of what I will propose.

"Unilateral total disarmament will be my proposal. Imagine what can be done with all those billions. By *unilateral* I mean the exact dictionary definition of the word: one-sided, regardless of the response or actions of the other side. By *total* I mean all, everything, nothing excluded. By *disarmament* I mean destruction of arms. Not redeployment, not mothballing, but destruction. Here I hedge a bit. I don't mean handguns, hunting weapons, police arms. I mean only weapons of mass destruction. But I consider large armies and massed tanks and artillery, fleets of bombers, as much weapons of mass destruction as nuclear bombs."

The audience was whispering, humming, people looking at each other in shock and amazement.

The President raised his hands for quiet. "I will carry it further. Verification. I would allow any organization, any government, any international agency, to inspect, nay, I would not prevent any concerned citizen of the United States from seeing for himself; it is his life that is at stake. So that's the proposal we will put before the conference; I hope the response will be given in the same spirit as my suggestion."

There was the dead silence of no one breathing. The President took a sip of water and continued. "Yes, my friends, citizens, fellow inhabitants of this planet, the world would be a safer, healthier, happier place if there were unilateral, total, verifiable disarmament." He paused for a moment dramatically, then repeated, "Unilateral, total, verifiable disarmament—by the Communist dictatorships."

There was a moment of absolute silence, shock, then the words sank in. A whisper of embarrassed laughter rippled through the audience, then it grew in strength, building on itself, until the whole auditorium was roaring. The President raised his eyebrows in mock amazement. "Did I say something funny? I wasn't aware that— Did I make a mistake? Surely not. They are Communists, aren't they? Proclaim it over and over. And they are a dictatorship; no one can deny that. Then what—? Oh, I see. You expected me to say that the United States was going to disarm unilaterally. Whatever for? We're not the ones with six million men under arms. We're not the ones with the biggest arsenal in the world, with the most bombs, tanks, planes, submarines, with chemical and biological weapons. We're not the ones who invaded Poland, Hungary, Czechoslovakia, Afghanistan. We're not the ones who support the terrorists. So why be surprised?

"Wherever did you get the idea," he chided, "that if there were to be unilateral disarmament, it should be us? I hope that all of you who have been supporting unilateral disarmament will continue the good fight, and demonstrate to show the U.S.S.R. that you really believe unilateral disarmament is the best road to peace. I hope they heed you; it would be a shame if they decide to scuttle the coming Disarmament Conference because they are not willing to discuss this reasonable proposal, a proposal that they have been advocating for so long through their proxies.

"Thank you, ladies and gentlemen. I leave you with this thought. Let us continue to work for peace and to pray for peace, and to keep our powder dry. Have a happy, peaceful Fourth of July, and do all you can to achieve unilateral disarmament."

"THE OLD FOX," ACKROYD SAID ADMIRINGLY.

"I wish I had voted for him," Isabel said, punching up her pillow. "Maybe I will, next time around. It's hard to be a Democrat in Vermont."

"Do you think it will work?" Jane asked.

"Not a chance," Lydia said. "The Russians disarm totally, unilaterally, and verifiably? Never."

"I don't think that was what the speech was designed to accomplish," Giles said. "The Russians will pull out of the conference, I'm sure. They're not prepared for this turn of events. They were prepared only with a policy and a procedure based on what Fitzgerald transmitted to them. Yesterday the information in the four coded cross-words was in their hands, and everything was orchestrated based on that. They have no leeway; they'll have to go back and rework a response. Meanwhile, they won't be able to respond to the President's proposal. They'll refuse to discuss it, call it frivolous, provocative, and the conference will die. And the world will be shown, once again, if it needs to be shown, what the Russians are."

"They'll try something else," Mary said.

"Of course," Barca said. "And when they do, if we are called in, we will try to stop them."

"I wonder what will happen," Kitty said, "when Zulkov's successor solves today's puzzle."

"It's already happened," Barca said. "I thought of that while you were all worrying about the hardness of Isabel's head. It wasn't *her* blood, you know, anyone could have seen that. If you remember the message, it wasn't addressed to anyone in particular. When Pyotr Kapustin—that's the new decoder's name—read it, he assumed, reasonably, that it was meant for him; who else could it be for? When he went to the apartment, he was greeted by some friends of ours, who showed him what they knew, told him that if he balked, they would turn him over to the dread CIA, and then tell the KGB that he was a double agent. He is now discussing all he knows with them."

"He won't know much," Elizabeth said.

"Every little bit helps," Barca said. "And every spy we remove is one less to plague us. Besides, it is possible that Pyotr will decide to give his masters such information as we decide they should know. After all, no one else in America knows that the spy ring is broken, and we're not going to announce that Professor Fitzgerald is not available for TV panel discussions."

"All's well that ends well," Giles said.

"Thanks for reminding me." Isabel straightened her bed jacket. "Today's the last day of my vacation. Just goes to show you: don't wish; you might get what you want."

"And what did you wish for?" Giles asked.

"To spend my vacation in bed," she said.

TUESDAY, JUNE 29

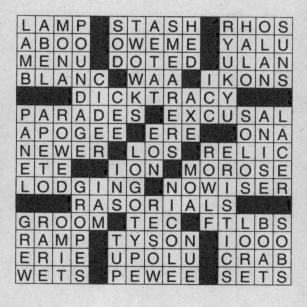

L	A	M	P		S	T	A	S	H		R	H	O	S
A	B	O	O		O	W	E	M	E		Y	A	L	U
M	E	N	U		D	O	T	E	D		U	L	A	N
B	L	A	N	C		W	A	A		I	K	O	N	S
			D	I	C	K	T	R	A	C	Y			
P	A	R	A	D	E	S		E	X	C	U	S	A	L
A	P	O	G	E	E		E	R	E		O	N	A	
N	E	W	E	R		L	O	S		R	E	L	I	C
E	T	E			I	O	N		M	O	R	O	S	E
L	O	D	G	I	N	G		N	O	W	I	S	E	R
			R	A	S	O	R	I	A	L	S			
G	R	O	O	M		T	E	C		F	T	L	B	S
R	A	M	P		T	Y	S	O	N		I	O	O	O
E	R	I	E		U	P	O	L	U		C	R	A	B
W	E	T	S		P	E	W	E	E		S	E	T	S

WEDNESDAY, JUNE 30

B	A	H	,		A	A	R	E			E	S	T	A
E	M	U	S			S	T	U	D	S		U	P	O	N
Y	O	G	A			C	H	I	T	A		R	U	S	T
	K	O	W	L	O	O	N			P	F	O	R	T	E
		N	U	T	S			A	S	A	P				
H	E	R	O	N			M	A	L	A	W	I			
A	L	I	N	E		S	A	I	G	A		O	F	S	
D	O	V	E		F	E	W	T	O		G	N	A	T	
A	P	E		G	A	I	L	Y			C	L	I	P	A
	E	R	S	A	T	Z				H	E	T	T	Y	
		C	R	E	E		G	L	E	N					
C	A	R	U	S	O		C	R	A	Z	E	R	S		
A	X	E	L		F	O	L	O	S		L	O	O	T	
S	L	A	P		A	R	A	F	T		G	O	R	E	
K	E	P	T			A	M	E	S			M	E	X	

THURSDAY, JULY 1

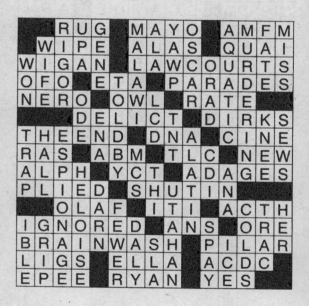

FRIDAY, JULY 2

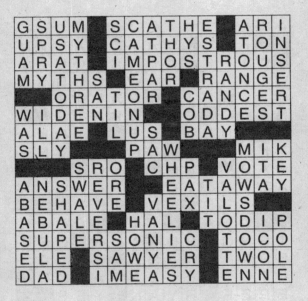

SATURDAY, JULY 3

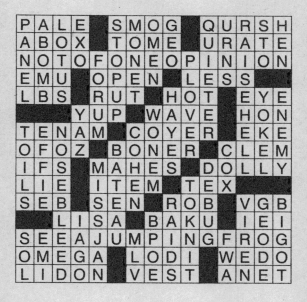

27 million Americans can't read a bedtime story to a child.

It's because 27 million adults in this country simply can't read.

Functional illiteracy has reached one out of five Americans. It robs them of even the simplest of human pleasures, like reading a fairy tale to a child.

You can change all this by joining the fight against illiteracy.

Call the Coalition for Literacy at toll-free **1-800-228-8813** and volunteer.

**Volunteer
Against Illiteracy.
The only degree you need
is a degree of caring.**

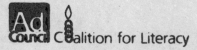

Ad Council   Coalition for Literacy

LV-3